REVIVAL

I0728566

Other titles by S. Usher Evans

THE RAZIA SERIES
Double Life
Alliances
Conviction
Fusion

Empath

THE MADION WAR TRILOGY
The Island
The Chasm
The Union

THE LEXIE CARRIGAN CHRONICLES
Spells and Sorcery
Magic and Mayhem
Dawn and Devilry
Illusion and Indemnity

REVIVAL

DEMON SPRING TRILOGY
Book Two

S. USHER EVANS

Sun's Golden Ray
Publishing
Pensacola, FL

DEMON SPRING TRILOGY

Resurgence
Revival
Redemption

DEMON FALL TRILOGY

Reawakening
Resurrection
Reclamation

Copyright © 2018 S. Usher Evans
ISBN: 1945438126
ISBN-13: 978-1945438127

All rights reserved. No portion of this publication may be reproduced, stored
in a retrieval system, or transmitted by any means—electronic, mechanical,
photocopying, recording, or any other—except for brief quotations in printed
reviews, without the prior written permission of the publisher.

Demon Art by Ashley Gonzales, Zeefa Studio
Line Editing by Danielle Fine, By Definition Editing

Sun's Golden Ray Publishing
Pensacola, FL
www.sgr-pub.com

For ordering information, please visit
www.sgr-pub.com/orders

DEDICATION

To Neveah

My little bookworm

(You can't read this for another decade)

CONTENTS

Demonology 9
Chapter One 17
Chapter Two 26
Chapter Three 35
Chapter Four 43
Chapter Five 53
Chapter Six 66
Chapter Seven 79
Chapter Eight 87
Chapter Nine 98
Chapter Ten 110
Chapter Eleven 122
Chapter Twelve 128
Chapter Thirteen 137
Chapter Fourteen 148
Chapter Fifteen 162
Chapter Sixteen 171
Chapter Seventeen 182
Chapter Eighteen 194
Chapter Nineteen 205
Chapter Twenty 212
Chapter Twenty-One 222
Chapter Twenty-Two 236
Chapter Twenty-Three 249
Chapter Twenty-Four 254
Chapter Twenty-Five 265
Chapter Twenty-Six 274
Chapter Twenty-Seven 286
Chapter Twenty-Eight 293
Chapter Twenty-Nine 302
Chapter Thirty 313
Chapter Thirty-One 322
Chapter Thirty-Two 333
Chapter Thirty-Three 346
Chapter Thirty-Four 358

DEMONOLOGY

The following is a brief introduction to the five kinds of demons found in the human world. The International Coalition for Demon Management (ICDM) is charged with protecting humans from unwanted demonic transformation, but we can't do it alone.

Learn the signs of demonic coercion and don't become a victim.

ATHTAR

First Seen: 1500 BC, Syria
Magical Element: Void
Original Sin: Pride
Original Demon: Bael

The oldest and rarest demons, Athtars live in the Underworld and appear during Demon Spring. They have the ability to manipulate time and space. If you encounter an athtar demon, seek shelter as quickly as possible, and alert your local US Division office.

ELOKO

First Seen: 400 AD, Democratic Republic of the Congo
Magical Element: Earth
Original Sin: Envy
Original Demon: Biloko

Eloko demons use the sound of a bell to hypnotize their victims into a false sense of security. If you think an eloko is trying to coerce you, stomp your feet or clap your hands to disrupt the magic, then run away.

KAPPA

First Seen: 600 BC, Japan
Magical Element: Water
Original Sin: Greed
Original Demon: Mizuchi

Kappas mostly live near water, and will create an illusion of a house or structure. When the victim enters the illusion, it will break and the human will be drawn underwater, given the option to transform or drown. When near bodies of water, familiarize yourself with existing structures, and watch for others coming in and out.

LILIN

First Seen: 200 AD, Germany
Magical Element: Air
Original Sin: Lust
Original Demon: Freyja

Lilins use a mixture of pheromones and glamour (illusion) to lure humans into sexual intercourse, then transformation. If you think a lilin is trying to coerce you, pinch yourself or think of something unsettling, then run away.

NOX

First Seen: 1400 AD, Mexico
Magical Element: Fire
Original Sin: Anger
Original Demon: Mot and Xo

Nox demons use the human's innate fear of demons to construct terrifying nightmares, and the human agrees to transform to cease them. To combat a nox demon, take a deep breath and remind yourself it's only a vision.

PROTECT YOURSELF

If you encounter any demon or supposed demon, contact your local US Division of the International Coalition for Demon Management right away to report the incident.

UNITED STATES DIVISION
INTERNATIONAL COALITION
FOR DEMON MANAGEMENT

#demonspring

CHAPTER ONE

"Have you lost your fucking mind?"

Jack Grenard glanced at the startled Waffle House waitress nearby. Based on the size of her eyes, she'd heard the expletive-laced fuming coming from Jack's former partner Camilla Macarro. Jack, a handsome, fair-skinned, late-twenty-something from Charleston, flashed the waitress a smile and winked before turning back to the borrowed restaurant phone.

"Calm down, Cam—"

"Calm down? *Calm down?* Jack, you ditched me in the middle of a battle to run after La Colibrí. *Again.* And now you're telling me you're joining her on a half-cocked plan to find some hypothetical witch who maybe cursed her?"

Jack lost whatever Cam said next as it descended into rapid-fire Spanish. He smiled again at the waitress, who was eyeing him while she served a hot stack of pancakes to a trucker.

"Are you done or are you reloading?" Jack asked when there was a long pause.

"Jack, your mother is terrified for you. I didn't even get a chance to properly yell at you for disappearing into the Underworld. We thought you were *dead*. Did something happen down there? Is that why you've gone crazy?"

"No, nothing happened to me." Jack sighed, too tired to explain it all, and knowing his time was running short. "Look, I'll check in when I can. Care to expedite things and tell me more about the Aztec talismans?"

The line was silent, and Jack could almost see Cam warring between wanting to showcase her ample intellect and not wanting to help him on his crazy scheme.

"Come home, Jack," she pleaded. "I promise, your grandfather can smooth everything over. We'll say you were a hostage."

Jack glanced at the clock; he'd been on the line for about one minute. Any longer and they'd be able to trace the call.

"Love you, Cam."

"Wait, Jack—"

A piece of Jack's already shattered heart broke off as he hung up. He stared at the receiver for a moment, tossed down a twenty-dollar bill for the waitress, then slipped from the diner without making eye contact with anyone else.

He wasn't even sure what this town was called, or how far they were from Atlanta. His accomplice had used her athtar magic, the type of demonic energy that could slow time and cross distance in the blink of an eye, to carry them out of Atlanta as the US Division of the International Coalition for Demon Management closed in. But whatever powers she had were limited, and she'd collapsed in the middle of a field. Jack had carried her small body a few miles into the nearest town, where he'd paid for a night at the hotel, then set out to find a phone.

It had taken some charming on Jack's part to convince the front desk receptionist that he wasn't doing anything unseemly with the unconscious woman. Even now, as he walked by her with a friendly wave, her eyes narrowed suspiciously.

"How's your wife?" she asked.

"Gonna check on her now," he said with what he hoped was a genuine smile.

He padded down the short hallway and stopped at the room, pressing his ear to the door and listening. It honestly wouldn't have surprised him if his new partner was gone. When he cracked open the door, she was where he'd left her, although her eyes were open.

Anya was a wisp of a person, barely a hundred pounds if Jack had any measure from carrying her. Although she'd briefly grown healthier on the magic of Ath-kur, the land of athtars in the demon underworld, it had disappeared, leaving her curly black hair frizzy and her bronze skin sallow again. Deep purple bags hung from her eyes, even though she'd been resting.

"Where'd you go?" she asked, sleep in her voice.

"Wanted to let Cam know I wasn't dead," he replied, sitting down on the bed. "How are you feeling?"

She pushed herself to sit and rubbed her face. "Shitty. But that's to be expected."

Jack swallowed his questions about athtar magic in favor of fetching her a glass of water from the bathroom. She took it without a word, but nodded her thanks.

So there they were. Jack and Anya, or Anat, as she was known to all demonkind. The right hand to the King of the Underworld, she'd been responsible for the slaughter of over ten thousand humans. Then, supposedly, she was cursed to repent for every life she'd taken. Even when Bael had removed the small charm from her neck, she hadn't lost the haunted look nor the guilt.

"So where to first?" Jack asked.

She put down the glass and wiped her upper lip. "You should return to Atlanta."

Jack sat on the bed across from her. "Does that mean you're going back to Bael?"

She jumped, as if the very mention of the King of the Demons would summon him to this dingy hotel room.

"I don't know what I'm going to do," she murmured, placing a hand against her neck where her curse had rested for over a century. "But I can't drag you down into this. I don't want to. I don't even know what *this* is."

"Why don't we start at the beginning?" Jack said.

She took another long drink of water. "I guess the beginning is with that Demon Spring in 1886. Bael hadn't been topside since before the American War of Independence. He liked to show up about once a century, just to rattle cages and remind the lords who was in charge. He chose Charleston because he was curious about America, and what it had turned into while he'd been away. Obviously, the South was still rebuilding from the Civil War. So he told me to just..." She trailed off, flexing her thin fingers. "I'd made it down to New Orleans and was having fun...doing what I do..." She made a small gesture of slashing. "I was...well, I got cocky. Bael told me I could... He let me do what I wanted. Anything I wanted. So, I found myself a few bedfellows. One of them brought some friends. Witches, if I had to guess."

"Witches exist?" Jack asked.

She quirked a brow. "What do you call what your friend did to me?"

Jack lifted his right hand, where a set of five coins hung from a leather bracelet. He showed her his anti-athtar talisman. "Is this the same symbol that hung around your neck?"

She squinted, keeping a healthy distance from it. "No. It's not." She swiped a pen and paper pad from the bedside table and drew a small symbol with dots and squiggles. "This is...well, this is close enough to it. I got pretty familiar with it over the years."

"If it was just a necklace, why didn't you just take it off?" Jack said.

"I couldn't." She rubbed her face. "It felt like every time I reached for it, my entire body seized up. Like the souls I'd taken were sitting on my chest." She rubbed her neck. "I still feel like they're there."

"Did the witches say anything in particular when you were cursed?"

"Nothing more than I was cursed," she said. "If I wanted to get rid of it, I had to save one life for every one I'd taken."

"What did you do then?"

"At first, I thought maybe I could save ten thousand lives in a month. Demon Spring was still happening, so there were plenty of humans in need of saving. I killed more demons than I probably should have. But once the schism closed again and Bael was…was gone, I counted up the number of humans I'd saved and it was maybe two hundred." She sighed heavily. "Then I knew it would take longer than I'd thought."

"How do you know when you've saved a human?"

"If a human is in trouble, and I save them, it counts as one."

"How do you know for sure?" That certainly didn't seem to be very scientific.

She licked her lips. "I don't. But when I save someone, it feels…better."

That could've been for a number of reasons, but Jack didn't want to derail the conversation. "When Bael removed the curse, did you feel any different?"

"No," she said with a swift shake of her head. "It wasn't like the bullet your friend shot at me. I knew when that thing came out. Maybe my curse had just been on too long. Maybe it takes a while to fade away."

"Is it possible…it was all in your head?" Jack offered quietly.

Her eyes snapped up, a bit of fire in them. "Are you saying I relentlessly tortured myself, starved of the very magic that keeps me alive, and stayed away from the man I love, because I *thought* I had to?"

"Maybe not," Jack said, holding up his hands in surrender. Duly noted; that was a sensitive topic. "So maybe we start in New Orleans?"

The anger faded from her face. "You should go home."

"There is no home for me," Jack said. "You saw my place in Atlanta. I'd barely unpacked. I can't go back to D.C. either. Too many memories. Same for Charleston." He stood and walked to the window, glancing out the blinds at the highway beyond. "Ever since Sara died, I haven't known what to do with myself. But helping you? Figuring this out? For some reason it gives me purpose."

"I told you, I'm not your charity case."

"No, I'm yours," Jack said, turning back around. "You still have to save lives, so save this one. Let's help each other."

She didn't immediately respond. After a moment, she stood and joined him at the window, folding her arms across her chest. "I haven't been back to New Orleans since they cursed me. To be honest, I'm…well, I'm a little afraid."

"You? The bringer-of-destruction? The Lady of the Mountain—"

"Shut it," she snapped with a glare. "From this moment on, I'm Anya, got it? Bael has spies everywhere. Even humans can't be trusted. You never know who has a kappa sister or an eloko father. All it takes is one person, one slip-up, and he's here.

Neither of us want that."

Jack had seen first-hand how athtar magic worked. "Bael can get here in a moment, right? Will he pass out after such a long journey, too?"

She worked her jaw for a moment. "No. The bullet wound took a lot out of me. I'm still recovering." With a single finger, she opened the window blinds to stare at the interstate beyond. "We may have to steal a car."

Jack quirked a brow. "Really?"

"Unless you're going to pull one out of your ass, yes." She opened the blinds fully and scanned the parking lot. "I'll make sure to wire payment to the owner. I can find a job in New Orleans that will more than cover it."

"What kind?"

She nodded. "There's a big underground market in every city. A lot of humans don't like to rely on the Division to fix their problems. They feel, rightfully so, that the government is more inclined to keep the peace than seek justice. So they go around the system. The demons involved don't like advertising that they're offing each other, and they don't want the Division on their tails. Nobody asks what you are or why you're doing it. They just want results."

Jack had heard of these markets, but the Division didn't have the resources to investigate fully. Or they were looking the other way.

"It may take me a day or two to find an in, but I'll find it." She swallowed. "And maybe pay off some people who might know something about this curse."

"I'll see what I can find without bribery," Jack said, pulling out his wallet. "I've got some cash, but we'll need to hit an ATM before we go. That should cover hotel and food."

She spun on her heel and caught his gaze, her green eyes showing sparks of life. "Jack…listen. If we're going to do this, it means we're going to have to keep moving. Bael not only knows I'm alive, but I've run from him. Twice. He's not going to let me walk away unscathed. And anyone who helps me…will also suffer that same fate."

He nodded, all too familiar with what Bael could do. "I understand."

"But that also means…" She chewed her lip. "That means you're going to have to be cut off from everyone. You can't contact your partner anymore. You can't use your bank card or ATM card or anything that might let anyone know where you are. Are you *sure* you want to do this?"

Jack could have walked—probably should have, actually. There was nothing tethering him to this demon woman, and he would be risking his career, his family, and his life for her. But it had felt right to help her escape Atlanta the day before, and it felt right to stay.

"Yeah," Jack said with a grin. "I've always wanted to commit grand theft auto."

CHAPTER TWO

Stealing a car was actually quite easy with an athtar demon doing the heavy lifting. They waited at the roadside gas station near their hotel for about half an hour before a twenty-something guy in a white car rolled up and ran inside while he was still filling up. Anya disappeared and reappeared in a blur, the man's keys jangling from her pocket. She'd also lifted his license.

"So I can return the car to him," she said with a shrug.

The car smelled of pot and old food, but the tank was full. Having lost his cell phone sometime during the battle in Atlanta, Jack was flying blind on the back roads in the small town. Keeping the afternoon sun in the forefront, he eventually found a sign for I-65 and followed it onto the interstate.

Beside him, Anya slept. Back at the hotel, Jack had caught a glimpse of the Cam-inflicted wound at her shoulder—still a violent shade of red, although no longer an open wound. Demons, as a whole, healed quickly, which was why decapitation was the only way to kill them. The bullet had been in her body for less than an hour; perhaps there *was* something to the curse's effects remaining after it had been removed.

As they drove through Montgomery, the Division offices loomed where he and Cam—well, mostly Cam—had run a cease-fire operation with an eloko lord named Parras. At the time, Parras been a low-level menace, someone that they thought was getting "too big for his britches." Cam had had a hunch something more was going on, and, as usual, she'd been right. During the first few minutes of Demon Spring, Bael had killed Nunzia, the lilin lord of Atlanta, and ordered the death of the Dallas lord, effectively putting Parras in charge.

After that, Bael had asked Anya to return with him, and she'd agreed. But Jack couldn't shake the feeling she was making a mistake and got involved—earning him a trip to the Underworld. There, Jack had seen Bael and Anya's relationship for what it really was. And why she feared him.

Even with her face covered in tears and bruises, she still swore she loved him. Yet when she was given the chance to escape, she took it and there they were. Anya and Bael's was a relationship Jack couldn't understand. And it really wasn't his place to, either. He was simply a sounding board, a safe haven until she figured out what she was doing. Maybe, selfishly, he was hoping that by helping Anya, he might figure out what he was doing, too.

He reached for the radio, turning the dial until he found something he could stomach—a talk radio station.

"The demon invasion of Atlanta has ebbed. No new demons have come out of the schism, although it remains open. ICDM is still asking all Atlanta residents to shelter-in-place, if possible. The Georgia National Guard is going door-to-door to evacuate residents remaining in the city. ICDM is not saying when the breach to the demon world will close, although they continue to maintain a perimeter around it. Stay tuned to WXFS for more on this developing story..."

"Tell me about what your partner shot me with," Anya said from the other side of the car. "If it's not the curse."

"I don't know much about it," Jack said. "When we were at the Academy together, Cam brought it up as some old superstition that had been in her family for generations. Kind of like an old wives' tale. The day I graduated, her mom gifted me with a set and said it would keep me safe."

"Did it?"

"As far as I could tell, yeah," Jack said, feeling the coins around his wrist. "Nothing concrete. Even Cam didn't have a lot of info, except what she could glean from the older members of her family. But her great-aunt—she's on the council like my grandfather—didn't really believe in them." He paused. "Guess she does now."

"Seems to have worked," Anya said, rolling the shoulder that had been shot. "It burned. My curse never burned like that."

"It was supposed to be an anti-athtar talisman," Jack replied. "There are different kinds for each demon. Maybe the thing around your neck was related to something else."

"Maybe." She chewed on her nail. "So what's the deal with you and your partner? Are you in love with her?"

"If I had a nickel for every time we got that," Jack said with a genuine laugh. "No. I mean, I love her, and she loves me. But it's not that kind of love."

She stared at the road. "So you've never slept with her?"

Jack glared at her out the corner of his eye. "Why so interested?"

"Because I know you did."

He blinked, casting a sideways glance at her. "How?"

"You two act like a pair of friends who've made some bad decisions." She kicked her feet to the top of the dashboard and leaned back. "I've been around a long time."

Three thousand years. Jack hesitated. His presence was a mere blip in the long span of her life.

"Once," he said quietly. "At the Academy. We got drunk, and one thing led to another. I was so scared that Cam was in love with me and I'd have to break her heart. Imagine my surprise when she woke up and said the same thing to me." He chuckled at the memory. "It changed our relationship, though. Strangely made us closer."

"So why didn't you just tell me?" Her voice took on an acidic edge. "If you're lying to me about something small, what's to say—"

"Because I never told my wife," he admitted quietly. "Or anyone else. Cam made me swear on my life that I wouldn't, and made me swear again when I started dating her sister."

"Why?"

"I think she was embarrassed that she'd made such a colossal mistake," Jack said, moving his hand along the wheel. "She tried so hard to be perfect all the time. It was a catastrophe if she ever earned less than an A on papers. I only graduated with honors because she kept my ass in the library most weekends." He slid his hands down the wheel, frowning. "And I guess she always felt like she was in my shadow."

"How's that?"

"I mean, she and I came from the same kind of family. Demon hunters for centuries, leadership roles in our respective countries. But I think Cam felt I got a leg up since my name was recognizable and hers wasn't. If anyone found out we'd slept together—even as a mistake—she was afraid she'd be forever branded as my fuck buddy or something."

"Is that how you see her?"

"Cam? God, no." Jack blanched. "Cam is… I mean, she's Cam. She's the strongest person I know. I don't know how she managed to take care of me after Sara died and still keep herself together."

"She didn't want you to see her fall apart," Anya said. "But she did, on her own. That's how it happens with strong women. We get so used to keeping the world on our shoulders that we're afraid to put it down."

Jack glanced over once then back at the road. "Yeah, something like that."

"If you love her so much, why aren't you with her right now? Why give all that up for me? I'm a stranger."

"Because you need help. That's why I decided to work in the field. To help people. And I haven't helped a single person since I got to Atlanta."

He couldn't read her expression, but she didn't argue with him, so he hoped he'd passed the test.

They drove in relative silence for the next few hours, with Anya dozing before jerking awake with a fearful expression. She'd ask where they were, then settle back against the seat and fall quiet for another hour or so.

Finally, as the mile markers ticked down to zero, she stayed awake.

"Pull over here," she said, pointing to a small rest area.

"Why? We're good on gas."

"We're ditching the car," she replied.

"W-why?"

"Because I assume the considerable forces of ICDM are focused on trying to find you by now. A stolen car in a small podunk Alabama town outside Montgomery? Definitely a red flag. So, they've already put out an APB for the tag number."

Jack hadn't even considered that. "Sure."

"If we stop here, they'll lose our trail. Did we go toward New Orleans? Florida? It'll split up their resources and help us hide better."

"How are we planning to get to New Orleans, then?"

"I'll get us there," she said with a grunt.

"Is that wise?" Jack said, as he pulled the car into the gas station. "You keep falling asleep."

She clenched and unclenched her jaw a few times. "I am well enough to get us to New Orleans."

"But—"

"I know my strength," she snapped, dialing a number on her phone.

"What are you doing?"

"Calling in the car. Yes, hi. I just saw two guys jump out of this car at a gas station on exit one on I-65 and make a break for it." A pause. "Two men. I didn't get a good look. On the taller side." Another pause. "No, I don't want to leave my name and number. Thanks."

"You're the most conscientious car thief I've ever met," Jack said, a little awestruck.

"I'll remind you I'm trying to *repent* for my sins, not add more to my list." She reached for the necklace that wasn't there, this time stopping herself mid-movement. "And until we know whether I'm still cursed or not, I'd like to keep my conscience clear."

Anya left the license on the floor of the vehicle, as if it had just fallen out of the pocket of the original owner. Then she hoisted both of their black duffel bags over her shoulder and marched toward the back of the rest area.

"And what if you aren't cursed? Are you going back to Bael?"

Again, she flinched. "Please stop saying his name."

"He's not Beetlejuice. You can't summon him by saying his name three times." Jack paused. "Can you?"

"No, but people—demons—don't go around saying his name casually," Anya said. "And any demon within earshot will be interested to know why a human is referring to the King of the Underworld."

Jack looked around the empty gas station. "There's nobody here."

Anya glared at him and pointed at the crows sitting in a nearby field. "They're here."

"You're paranoid."

"Paranoia is how I evaded capture for a hundred and thirty years, so maybe you should pay attention, hm?" With a steadying breath, she took Jack's arm.

It was as if time itself had stopped. The cars along the interstate slowed to a crawl, the wind in the trees disappeared, and the flapping of a nearby crow was a low boom. Jack's own movements remained unchanged, as did Anya's, whose eyes had glowed an eerie black. She inhaled deeply, and the world around them shifted, as if they were being flung through an invisible tunnel.

Exhale. They stood in the center of the interstate, with an eighteen-wheeler careening toward them.

Inhale. The tunnel dropped them in a cotton field.

Exhale. Anya pressed her forehead against his chest as they paused on the banks of a lake.

"Anya—"

Inhale, exhale. Anya collapsed in Jack's arms. He hoisted her up, glancing around and nearly collapsing in relief himself as he saw a telltale sign for the Saints football team on a nearby billboard. They were somewhere in the city of New Orleans, or relatively close to it.

"Anya?" Jack asked, shaking the woman in his arms. Yet again, she was unreachable. "We're going to have a conversation about why you keep passing out…"

CHAPTER THREE

Two years ago, Cam had arrived in Atlanta with a plan. This was a stepping stone, an in-between place in her grand scheme to becoming a major player in ICDM. She'd had the credentials and the experience; all she needed was to get a few big deals under her belt to wow the bureaucrats.

She'd managed to charm Director Anne Navarro with her brashness and intellect, and told her that she was a two-for-one deal.

"Eventually, my partner Jackson Grenard is going to join me here," she'd said. Which had netted her this swanky office with two desks.

Getting her partner five hundred miles south had been another story. Jack had been a shell, sounding dead and lifeless when she called to check in every night. So Cam had taken control. She'd filled out the transfer paperwork. She'd found him an apartment and helped him unpack it, hoping that settling in would bring him back to life.

Now, of course, the desk across from hers was empty yet again. His week-old coffee cup from the shop across the street still sat on his desk. Cam should've knocked it into the trashcan. It would smell soon.

Cam couldn't bring herself to do it, just as she couldn't bring herself to get out of this chair and continue working. A far cry from the fever pitch of the previous week.

After Jack had been taken by Bael to the Underworld, Cam hadn't allowed herself to hope he might come back. Instead, she'd funneled her anger into making new anti-demonic weapons, ready for when the demons made their next appearance.

But Jack had come back. Then left again.

"Cam, she's dying—and you don't know the whole story, either."

Damn Jack and his hero complex. Cam should've known when he started following that bitch around like a lost puppy. She'd plucked all his wounded male strings, and he'd toppled like a domino.

She wasn't pissed that he'd taken off after La Colibrí, the hummingbird. What pissed her off was that he'd left her to deal with the aftermath. Again.

Although, with her trusty talisman launchers, the demons were a little less eager to start killing and had high-tailed it back into their little demon underworld. That, at least, was a blessing.

From the last report that had crossed her inbox, the demonic schism was still on open, but secure. Another influx of Division resources from Los Angeles had given the Atlanta team a brief respite. Cam could return to this empty office and wonder where the hell her partner was.

She hadn't heard from him since that damned call where he'd sounded so...so much like Jack. Trying to weasel information out of her about the talismans. He'd sounded in control of his faculties—as if running around with a demon woman wasn't the definition of insane. Before Demon Spring, he'd admitted that his interest in the mystery woman hadn't been wholly driven by career reasons. After the way Jack had tortured himself after Sara's death, her wayward partner undoubtably saw saving La Colibrí as some kind of penance.

Except that his wife had been killed by demons and Anya *was* a demon.

And not just any demon, but the girlfriend/lover/whatever of Bael, the king of them all.

Cam rested her head on her hands for just a moment then stood up. She needed to keep moving, or the full force of her emotions would come crashing down on her. When she'd lost Sara, she'd had to stay together for Jack and her family. But with Jack gone, there was nothing keeping her from falling apart except to keep pushing to get him back.

Jack must've known that they were tracing his call, which was why he'd cut it off as quickly as he had. But she'd gotten a location: a small Alabama town outside Montgomery called

Wetumpka. She'd called in a favor to the Montgomery office, and they'd sniffed around. The Waffle House waitress had been a little help, but the hotel said a man fitting Jack's description had brought in an unconscious woman, calling her his wife and saying she was a heavy sleeper.

But Anya must've woken up sometime after that, because there was a report of a man and woman stealing a car at a nearby gas station.

Now Cam was *really* hoping Jack would give her some indication that he was being coerced. Otherwise, he was looking at grand theft auto charges—something even his grandfather might not be able to get him out of.

A soft knock at the door broke her half-awake musings. The very man she'd been thinking about stood in the doorframe. Frank Grenard was the US representative on the Council of Fifteen, the international governing body for ICDM. Thanks to his grandson's antics, Cam wasn't sure how much longer he'd hold onto that position, but the old man didn't seem too worried.

Cam had always liked Frank. He was like her fifth grandparent, and she was starting to get the feeling that Frank was beginning to consider her more of a protégé than his own grandchild. All the Grenard men shared the same features, sharp cheekbones, larger ears, and a clear adoration of Cam.

"How are you doing?" Frank asked, taking Jack's empty chair. "Heard from Jack?"

She shook her head. "Not since that phone call. I hear

they…stole a car."

Frank chuckled, as if this wasn't new information to him. "What's our boy got himself wrapped up in now?"

"I don't know. I was so happy to have him back, and now he does this." Cam shrugged weakly.

"Jackie doesn't do anything without probable cause. There's got to be some reason he feels compelled to help this woman."

"Lust?"

Frank shook his head. "Jack's a little smarter than that."

"I don't know, Bael said they slept together," Cam said, her filter disappearing with her lack of sleep. "Maybe he's fallen head over heels for this demon woman, and he'll never come back. Maybe I've just been reading this all wrong."

"Maybe you should go home and get some sleep," Frank said, gently. "I've had Jack's mother *and yours* calling me to make sure I keep an eye on you."

"Mama called you?" Cam had been hoping to take a quick trip back to El Paso to see her family after Demon Spring. She couldn't even remember the last time she'd called home.

"You have a lot of people worried about you, Cam," he said.

"I'm kind of worried about Jack," she said. "Then I'll worry about myself."

Frank opened his mouth, but there was a rap at the door. Director Navarro, an older, pale woman with short blond hair and a penchant for professionalism, walked into the room. She nodded once to Frank, then turned to Cam, exhaustion evident on her face.

"We found the car in Mobile," she said. "The gas station owner says a couple matching their description appeared, but then vanished into thin air."

"Athtar magic," Frank said. "That certainly makes this tricky."

"Are you sending a team to Mobile?" Cam asked.

"We've got one on the way, but I doubt we'll find anything that we don't already know," Navarro said. "What we need to know is where they went."

"New Orleans," Cam said, leaning back in her chair.

"You sure?" Frank asked.

She shrugged. "There were a few leads when we were searching for this demon curse thing. I figure that's where Jack would want to start."

"Then we'll send a team—

"No," Cam said, standing slowly. "I'll go. I have a better chance of getting through to him."

"You should be accompanied by a team," Frank said. "And you should get some rest, too."

Rest she couldn't argue with. "I'll head out tomorrow."

The street lamps cast an eerie glow on the empty streets, still vacant from Demon Spring. At this hour, Cam should've been fighting hundreds of other cars to get home. She was grateful for the lack of traffic; she was in no mood to deal with people.

What she wanted was to talk with her sister. That deep-seated desire hadn't yet come to terms with reality.

She pulled to a stop at a light and grabbed her phone, finding the stash of photos of the two of them. Cam looked more like their mother, strong and stocky, whereas Sara resembled the willowy, tall woman on their father's side—a natural beauty. They'd always been mismatched, but inseparable. Even when Cam had left for the Academy in Denver, she and Sara never went longer than a day without speaking. And when the three of them had moved to D.C., Cam couldn't believe she had her two best friends right there with her. Days with Jack hunting demons and causing trouble, weekends spent with Sara exploring their new home and drinking too much wine on their couch.

Things were perfect. And Cam just knew any day, Sara would sit her down and tell her she and Jack would be adding a fourth to their trio.

Instead, she got the worst news of her life.

She jammed her key into the lock and walked into her dark house.

Back in D.C., Cam had never taken the time to fix up her house. But when she'd moved to Atlanta, she was determined to build herself a life. She'd taken a few weekends to browse some farmers markets for local paintings and bought some statues from her cousin in Oaxaca. The furniture was bright, and so were the throw pillows and blankets. All in the pursuit of building a new life out of the rubble.

Now it was all a mockery.

She went to the kitchen and uncorked the half-empty bottle

of wine. She began pouring, intending on a full cup, then stopped herself. She had a long drive in the morning, and red wine gave her a headache. At least the cheap shit she'd picked up at the corner grocery did.

That was Cam. Always responsible.

Sometimes, she wished to be the irresponsible one. Maybe she would've found someone to share this empty apartment with if she hadn't been so focused on being the best at everything. She'd been seeing a guy for a few weeks in D.C. when Sara died, and that relationship had fizzled in the blink of an eye. He hadn't been able to handle it. Then again, he couldn't handle a lot of things—namely that Cam was smarter than he was.

Par for the course with most people.

Except Jack. He didn't care that Cam was smarter than he was—he was grateful for it. They excelled in different areas—Jack could see the forest while Cam counted each tree to check his math. More than that, Jack was the devil on her shoulder. He used to make sure she had fun, that she didn't work so hard. They were a perfect team.

Were.

Already nursing a headache, Cam poured the wine down the drain and headed for the bedroom, wishing she was just a little more irresponsible.

CHAPTER FOUR

"What's wrong with your lady?"

Jack had carried Anya through a neighborhood of one story houses and palm trees. After walking for a good half-hour, and getting some directions from a few folks waiting at a bus station, Jack found a hotel that seemed clean, but was seedy enough that they might not ask too many questions about the unconscious woman with him.

As predicted, the hotel manager was concerned, but didn't immediately reach for the phone.

"Yeah, she started partying a little too early," Jack said, the first thing that came to mind. "We need to stay a night so she'll sleep it off. My cousin's getting married in the city, and my mom would have a fit if she saw her like this."

Jack prayed that the manager would buy his lie, but he looked unconvinced.

"Yeah," came Anya's quiet voice as she stirred to life. "I'm so wasted. Good thing my boyfriend takes such good care of me. Don't you, Honey?" She grabbed his chin and puckered his lips, pecking him once. Then she slumped backward, her head lolling against Jack's arm.

"I'd say I hadn't seen it before but..." He shook his head. "Here's your key. Take care she aims for the toilet when she vomits."

Jack nodded and hoisted her into his arms, carrying her up the stairs. He laid her down in the queen bed and adjusted the pillows under her head.

"Nice one," Jack said, pulling the bedspread out from under her. "I thought they were going to call the cops on me."

"Still might," she said, tucking her feet under and curling up against the pillow. "Though you have one of those innocent faces. Wouldn't hurt a fly."

Jack took exception to that comment, but she'd already fallen back asleep.

While she slept, he plotted out their next moves on paper based on what he could remember of his investigations and what Anya had told him about her curse. Most of what he had was nothing—some nebulous references to curses that came from New Orleans. In the pre-ICDM days of Europe, some would've called the act of demonic transformation a curse, which muddied the water a little.

Without a laptop or internet connectivity (she had a laptop, but he didn't have her log-in information), there was little he could do from his hotel room. So he left her a note telling her he'd be back soon, and set out to make himself useful.

He wandered down the side of I-10 until he came across a large shopping center with a bus stop out front. A quick review of the map told him this bus would take him right into the center of the city, so he waited in the sweltering humidity, wondering if he shouldn't head into that superstore and buy some new cotton t-shirts on his way back. After all, he hadn't had time to grab any clothes, and his were getting a bit funky, after being washed in the hotel laundromat. He wasn't sure if Anya had any clothes, but he might get her a few extra shirts as well. Least he could do.

An hour later, Jack hopped off the bus at Canal Street, taking in the sights, sounds, and smells of the French Quarter. Although the tourists wouldn't know much about local demonic activity, the locals who worked there might. And they might know something about curses, too.

A loud gurgling in the pit of his stomach stopped him in his tracks. First, he needed a square meal. The last one he'd had was...probably at Bael's castle in the Underworld, and it hadn't set well then. Besides that, Jack could never say no to a good bowl of gumbo, either.

Drawn by the smell of good Cajun food, he walked into a small restaurant and took an empty table, ordering a beer and the gumbo, and helping himself to some saltines to tide him over. The television was showing the news, scenes from Atlanta, and Jack's stomach turned sour, especially when he saw the legions of Division agents patrolling the city. Was Cam amongst them? Or was she on her way to China?

Right before hell broke loose, Cam had been offered a fellowship to the prestigious International Weapons Institute in Shanghai. She was going to take the weaponized talisman idea she'd come up with and make it into something the entire demon management community could use.

But now, she was probably on the road looking for him. It was her worst trait, her need to make sure everyone else was set before she saw to herself. For once, he wished she'd be selfish.

After he finished his meal, he continued with his original plan to seek out tourist shops. It was a Tuesday (or Wednesday —he was starting to lose track of the days), but the French Quarter was always partying. Mardi Gras had been the month before, yet the shops were filled with green, yellow, and purple beads. He purchased a nondescript hat and sunglasses using the last of his cash. He thought Anya was a little paranoid about the whole ATM thing, but left his bank cards in his wallet.

After an hour of seeing the same shops over and over again, Jack finally stumbled on something unique: an old bookstore. If any place had information about demons and curses, it would be this one, which boasted old mahogany shelves bursting with books.

The young man at the counter was decidedly human. And a young brunette who scampered down the back stairs seemed almost a little too skittish as she ran out the back door, but was also human.

"What can I help you with?" asked the young man.

"I need some books on magic," he said. "Human magic. Talismans, that kind of thing. I've heard there's some activity in the city."

"Hm... as in non-fiction?" He scratched his chin. "I don't know anything about that. Maybe try the library?"

Jack got directions and hoofed it a mile north, earning himself another sweaty t-shirt and a firm decision that he needed to buy some toiletries. The library was well air-conditioned, but busy, which was good. Hopefully none of the librarians would remember his face. He opted for an older woman and approached her with a genuine smile.

"Can I help you, sugar?" she asked, with that thick Louisiana drawl.

"Yeah, I'm looking for information on human magic or curses?"

She chuckled, as if she were about to bless his heart. "You might want to check the tourist shops—"

Jack smiled, resisting the urge to pull his Division badge, which he no longer carried anyway. "I'm working on a research project. Looking for anything you have on credible reports of witchcraft—especially as it relates to defense against demons."

"Oh, I see," she said with a knowing nod. "Because of what the Division are doing in Atlanta, right? I've had a few folks come in asking about it, but to be honest, we don't know much more than what's reported in the media."

"Do you have any books about it?"

"Not that I know of, but you can use the public computers to check the card catalog." She gestured behind him. "If you need any help finding the books, let me know."

Jack thanked her and wrote down the books she suggested on New Orleans legends and lore. He spent about an hour thumbing through books on some of the quirkier residents of the city's ancient past. With the exception of a few notable lilins, he didn't find much on demons.

However, he was at a computer with internet access. He could set up a burner email address, one that would expire five minutes after he created it. Cam was practically married to her phone, so she'd see the email immediately and they could have a few moments of conversation.

Cam,

I know you're looking for me. It's probably useless to ask you to stop, and you know it's useless to tell me to. So let's help each other. I need information about Anya's curse and your talismans. If you have any idea where to start, I'm all ears.

He sent the email and waited. As predicted...

Jackass,

Fuck you and your email.

Jack snorted, and checked his watch. Cam would glare

daggers at the wall, fuming at his audacity and the sheer professionalism of his email. Then, she'd take a deep breath and type out an email with her lips pursed in superiority.

A new email arrived.

Jackson,

I have thoughts. How are you going to help me?

Jack stretched his fingers as he contemplated, then responded.

Cam,

The sooner I get Anya un-cursed, the sooner I come home so you can yell at me in person. How does that work?

He waited.

If I were looking for information about old curses, I might start with a demon who's been around for a while. There's a kappa demon in the swamps of New Orleans who's a few thousand years old. Name's Wani.

I've got ten pages of an ass-chewing written, one for each day you've been gone.

Come home soon.

"What the hell is *wrong* with you?"

Jack knew Anya would be upset, but that she'd be more upset if he lied to her. She was a ticking time bomb, ready to bolt at the first sign of trouble. She hadn't even bothered to thank him for the bag of white t-shirts he'd bought her at the grocery store.

"I didn't offer anything, just asked for some help," Jack said, tossing the rest of the toiletries on the bed. "And she gave us help —"

"How convenient that she offered Wani up, since *she didn't know you were in New Orleans.*"

Jack hadn't even considered that, and a small blush warmed on his face. "Oh."

"Yeah, *oh.*" Anya stopped and pressed her hands against the cheap dresser. "I'm surprised you didn't give her the address of the hotel."

"I'm not that stupid," Jack said. "And it makes sense Cam knew we were going here. She was helping me with the investigation."

"And I'm sure she'll bring her entire contingent of Division friends to come find you, too." She made a frustrated sound as she grabbed the white shirts and threw them in a small bag with the rest of her things.

"Hang on," Jack said, sitting up. "You can't leave—"

"*We're* leaving, idiot," she snapped.

"Because of Cam?"

"Because I don't like staying in a hotel for more than one night. People remember your face."

Jack sighed. "Fine. Fair enough. But I don't have any money."

"I do," she said. "I did a job while you were out giving away our location."

Jack was speechless. She still appeared pale and sickly to him. "Are you sure that was…advisable?"

"Simple human recovery, no big deal. I have another one tonight." She popped her shoulders. "You're coming, too."

"Why? Need my help?"

"No. You're obviously too stupid to be left alone," she said, tossing her bag over her shoulder.

He glared at her back as she stormed out of the room, then grabbed his few belongings and followed her.

"You can't seriously be that angry about the email," Jack said, keeping his voice low as they left the hotel. "Cam is too pissed at me to tell anyone. She wants to be the one to find me and be the first to lecture me." Anya didn't look amused, so he continued, "And besides that, why would she tell me about Wani if not to help us?"

"To lay a trap."

"Sure, but she wouldn't do that."

She adjusted the bag against her shoulder. "Bael might."

"I thought he went back down to the Underworld?" Jack said. "I heard it on the news—nobody's seen him in a while."

"Yes, but the schism remains open," she whispered, casting

nervous glances around to the empty street. "Presumably, until I return to him."

Jack didn't ask whether that was her end goal once they figured out whether she was still cursed; he didn't want to know. He just hoped he could get her to see reason before that time came.

"What does that have to do with Cam, though?" Jack said. "Unless you think Cam's email has been hacked by demons?"

She quirked a brow.

"Oh, come on," he said with something of a nervous laugh. "You're paranoid."

"I'm not paranoid, I'm *smart*."

"Well, why didn't you mention Wani as someone we should talk to, then?" Jack asked.

For a brief moment, she looked stumped, as if she had no good retort, but the dark cloud returned to her face as quickly as it had disappeared. "I will take the idea under advisement, but only after I've made sure your Cam hasn't screwed us."

Jack smiled.

"But first, we need to complete this job and find a new place to sleep."

CHAPTER FIVE

Anonymity apparently didn't mean skimping on the finery, or Anya was simply a woman with better tastes, because their next lodgings were square in the center of the French Quarter. She was either still pissed about Cam, or not feeling chatty, so Jack took a long shower, thankful he had clean clothes to change into and a sharp razor.

But when he walked out of the bathroom, the woman on the bed wasn't Anya.

"Oh, shit." He blinked once, twice...squinting at the new woman. "Wait...is that you?"

"Good," Anya's voice came from the stranger. Her hair was now a sandy blond, nearly matching the color of her tan skin. There were other differences too—her nose was a little bigger, her chin a tad longer. She might've been taller, too.

"What happened to you?" Jack asked.

"Lilin magic," she said, holding a white sparkly vial between her fingers. "I keep a bottle of it for when people are getting too close."

Jack wondered about her phrasing, but didn't mention it. "It's not permanent, is it?"

"Fades after a few hours." She popped the cap off. "Come sit on the bed. You're recognizable too."

Lilins, the lust demons, used a blend of glamour and pheromones to ensnare humans. Jack was sure it was highly illegal to use demonic magic this way, but sat on the bed anyway. She poured no more than a drop into her hands, rubbed them together, then slid her palms over his face. The sensation sent jolts of pleasure from her fingertips down his spine and right into his groin.

Almost immediately, memories of the one night they'd slept together resurfaced. It had been a spur of the moment mistake for both of them—she looking to convince him to drop the investigation, he to prove to himself he could still be reckless.

Her lips, now pursed in concentration, had been so feather light against his manhood, her fingers so soft as they danced across his skin. His groin swelled, and he struggled to adjust himself before she saw, but there wasn't any hiding it with his boxers. And the more her fingers slid across his face, the more he wanted her to see it. The more he wanted her to *act* on it.

"Are you all right?" The timbre of her voice sent shivers down his spine. He could take no more.

He closed the distance between them, but the kiss only

exacerbated his need for her. He gripped her face, pulling her closer and ravaging her mouth. But she didn't kiss him back, and some small voice in the back of his mind told him to stop.

"Do you want this to continue?" she asked, her voice even and without any of the lusty undertones he wanted. She slid her hand around his wrist, lifting it toward her and drawing her fingers along his wrist with a delicate touch.

She hissed and retracted her hand. "Son of a bitch."

"Careful," he murmured, bringing her finger to his lips and kissing it gently. "The talisman will—"

Something cold pressed into his palm, and the erotic need fell away, leaving him with her finger against his lips and an erection pressing at his boxers.

"I'm sorry," he said, dropping her hand as if it were on fire. "I'm not sure what came over me."

"It's the magic," she said. "It's not made for humans. But if you'd like a roll in the sack to get rid of it—"

"Another pity-fuck? No thank you."

It had come out meaner than he'd intended, but fucking of any kind seemed more appealing than he wanted to admit. She paused, only momentarily, then continued her work. When she finished, Jack went to look at himself in the mirror. She'd turned his reddish-brown hair darker and his brown eyes blue. Much like her own disguise, there were small differences in the size and shape of his features.

"Do you think this will work?" he asked, still amazed at how effective it was.

"Just keep that talisman handy so you don't hump everything in sight."

Even with the glamour, Jack still felt odd walking in the twilight with Anya by his side. He had questions about it—did it work on demons, for one? Based on the way Anya kept her head down and avoided the main streets, he guessed it wasn't as effective. Or maybe that was just habit for her.

Jack's groin had subsided, but his embarrassment was still fresh. He'd been training in defensive maneuvers since his first semester at the Academy. Lilin magic was one of the easiest to detect and deflect—just think of something unsexy. Even though the magic had been directly on his skin, that didn't really excuse it in his mind. He needed to be better. Anya was counting on him to be.

Their destination was an old building, probably from the mid-nineteenth century or earlier. A small etching on the brick near the door looked like a gang sign or some other kind of graffiti. The hair on Jack's arms stood up as the door opened.

"You didn't mention it's a nox bar."

"Didn't think it was important." She put her hand on her hips. "Problem?"

It had been three years since Jack had felt nox miasma. The memories it triggered were bad enough, but the magic itself was a torturous evil, forcing the human to relive and remember. Remembering his failure to ward off the lilin magic, Jack reminded himself it was just magic—there was nothing to be afraid of.

"I don't like noxes," Jack said, hating that his heart was throbbing. Did lilin glamour hide flushed faces?

She smirked. "The death and destruction demons get under the big, bad Division agent's—"

"A nox killed my wife."

She quieted immediately and her hand twitched, as if reaching for her talisman. "I'm sorry."

"It's fine," Jack said, running a hand through his goopy hair. He glanced at his hand, seeing nothing. "I just…"

Anya closed the distance between them and placed her fingers in his hair, stroking gently. The movement, while unexpected and awkward, was also weirdly soothing.

"Thanks."

"No, you wiped away the glamour on your hair," Anya said, her face a mask of indifference. "Don't touch yourself."

"Roger that."

"Look," she said after a moment, "I'm not the biggest fan of noxes either. But they're the only demons who aren't actively allied with Bael. This bar also does a heavy dealing in freelance bounties, so they won't alert the Division either." She put her hand on the door and pointed to the graffiti, an inverted shield-looking symbol. "See that? That's our little symbol that this is a vigilante bar."

Jack nodded. "I'm fine. I just need a bit more warning next time."

"Here's a warning for you: we will be dealing with all kinds of demons, so get your head on straight or go the hell home," she growled, fire flashing in her eyes. "And don't come in until ten minutes after I do."

Jack wasn't sure which annoyed him more: that Anya treated him like a child, or that his performance warranted it. Still, he did as he was told, taking a walk around the block to clear his mind and try to keep the lilin glamour from messing with his head further. He wasn't sure if it had been ten minutes, but when he came back to the bar entrance, he walked inside.

The nox miasma was thick, sending chills up Jack's spine. The strength of the nox demon's magic was the difference between a cold sweat and a pissing-yourself-in-the-corner sobfest. He held his nox talisman firmly against his skin as he slid onto a barstool, even though the miasma was light. He didn't want to take any chances.

"What d'ya want?" the bartender asked.

"Whiskey," Jack croaked, his pulse quickening at the nearness of the demon. "Neat."

The bartender poured the amber liquid, and Jack took a sip, nodding his thanks. He released a breath when the nox was farther away and scanned the bar for Anya. She was seated alone, nursing a drink and looking miserable.

His ears perked up when he heard the name *Anat*. Straining, he struggled to catch wisps of the conversation. He made a show of cracking his back, finding the source: two men engaged in conversation three seats down.

"I'm not gonna even go there," said the one on the right, a

Chinese man hunched over his drink. "I've heard the stories. She's athtar. They can slice your head off before you can even think to strike them."

"Yeah, but I hear she's weak. Been too long out of the miasma," said the one on the left, a tanned man with long black hair tied in a ponytail. "And King Bael says he'll make a lord outta any demon who finds 'em."

Jack was suddenly very grateful for the lilin glamour.

"You'd best throw your lot in with Parras," Rightie replied. "You hear he's now the lord of Atlanta to Dallas. I'm one of the lucky ones—my maker swore allegiance to Bael when the athtars were out killing Xerxes and his folk. But my girlfriend, she's back to human." He chuckled. "I told her I'd turn her back, but she's hoping to get in with Parras. Says it would make things weird between us if I did it."

"I'm in that boat," Leftie said. "Woke up the other day without any magic. Human as human can get. But I hadn't been demon for more than five years. So I'm hoping one of Parras' seconds will take me. Got an appointment with the man tomorrow."

Rightie chuckled. "I'll take you."

His friend gave him a once-over then shook his head. "I may be human, but I know a weak demon when I see one."

"Who you calling weak?" Rightie said, his face growing red.

Jack felt the slightest brush against his hand, then glanced at Anya. She was back on the barstool, but caught his eye for a moment and gave the slightest of head tilts toward the back.

Then she downed the rest of her drink and slid away from the bar.

With the argument growing louder, Jack used the distraction to leave as well, tossing a ten-dollar bill onto the bar and heading toward the back. Anya was waiting by the bathrooms, a bored look on her face.

"What are they bitching about?" she asked.

"Demon bullshit," Jack said with a shrug. "More importantly, did you know we had a bounty on our head?"

Anya actually looked surprised. "What kind of bounty?"

"I heard them talking about it," Jack said, nodding to the two who were now in each other's faces. "Bael's promised a lordship to whoever brings us to him."

"'Bring us to him' is a strong phrase," Anya said, a haunted look in her eyes. "It would be enough to keep me in place long enough for Bael to arrive. He just needs to know where I am."

The sound of bells clanging reached both of their ears. Rightie's eyes had turned red, and Leftie's angry expression had melted into one of complacence. A decade of Division training kicked in, and Jack started forward to prevent the impending demonic transformation.

Anya clamped down on his wrist—hard. "Are you *crazy*?" she hissed at him. "Don't get involved."

"But..." Jack said, helplessly watching as the eloko grabbed the human by the cheeks and covered his mouth, blowing into it. A gust of wind brushed by, bringing with it an earthy scent and louder bells. Then the eloko, his eyes still an eerie red, dropped his new spawn to the floor, wiping his mouth.

"What a rush!" he cried, flexing his hands.

"Oi!" The nox bartender cried. "Read the damned sign!"

He pointed to a sign above the bar that read, *No transformations. No exceptions.*

"Take your trash and go!" the bartender said.

"Oh yeah?" the eloko barked, his eyes still vaguely glowing. "Why don't you come out here and make me?"

"Amateur," Anya muttered, leaning against the wall.

The nox bartender vaulted over the bar and into the room, facing the eloko with an axe in his hands. The nervous feeling Jack had been nursing in the back of his mind came roaring to the front, filling him with the sort of dread he hadn't felt since the night he'd discovered Sara's body…

But then, just as quickly as it had arrived, it was beaten back by the clanging of bells, reminding him of the bars he and Cam used to frequent after work, the laughing, and—

Back to anxious dread. But in the brief interlude between the competing feelings, he found himself long enough to press the eloko and nox talismans into his palm.

The sound and anxiety disappeared immediately, leaving only annoyance. The fight in the center was…over. Or about to be.

The eloko was cowering in the corner, his eyes wide. His new spawn hadn't given him enough power to fight the nox's magic, and he was as susceptible as any human. But unlike a human, the nox had other plans for the eloko.

Jack looked away just in time, but the sound of an axe slicing through flesh was unmistakable.

"W…what?" On the floor was Leftie, newly re-reverted to human. He took one look at the scene around him, the nox with the bloody axe, the decapitated eloko, then scrambled to his feet and ran out of the bar as fast as he could.

"Well, that was entertaining," Anya drawled.

"That was…something," Jack said, rubbing his head.

"C'mon, we don't have all night."

She opened a door to what Jack had thought was the bathroom, but turned out to be a smallish meeting room. Two humans sat inside, both looking as out of place as a baby in a bar. The WASPs had done their best to hide their status, but they'd chosen Lacoste black sweaters and the woman still wore nice gold stud earrings and flashy diamond rings on her hand. Except for their pale, gaunt faces, filled with terror, they would've fit in at any of the country clubs Jack had grown up in.

He joined Anya sitting across from them, and offered them a kind smile to let them know that he was, in fact, human, even if his partner was not.

"S-so you're the one who answered the ad?" the man asked, his voice a pleasing baritone with a Louisiana drawl.

"I'm here, aren't I?" Anya replied.

"Yes, we are," Jack intervened. "I'm J—"

"We're nobody," she snapped. "What's the job?"

"It's…it's our son, Johnny," the woman whispered. Up close, her eyes were bloodshot and her rouged cheeks bore tear stains. "He told us he was a…a…"

"Demon?" Jack said.

"*Homosexual.*"

Jack's eyebrows shot up in surprise. "Excuse me?"

"He came home one day and told us he was," she leaned in to whisper, "*gay*, and he had a boyfriend and…" She dabbed at her eyes with a tissue. "Lord help us."

Jack sat back, shaking his head in disbelief. On occasion, he'd heard of cases of extremely conservative parents bringing cases to the Division, claiming their children had been possessed when they'd just been honest about who they were. He'd never witnessed one in person, and based on Anya's expression, neither had she.

"You realize that demons don't turn people gay, right?" she deadpanned.

"Of course," Mr. WASP bristled.

"After he told us that, we'd….well, John signed him up for a camp—"

"A camp?" Jack said, squeezing the bridge of his nose. "A conversion camp?"

"What's that?" Anya asked.

"You don't want to know," Jack said to Anya, before leaning across the table to the parents. He was suddenly less inclined to be so kind. "So let me guess: Johnny decided he'd rather take his chances as a demon than at that camp?"

They nodded.

"You realize this means he thought a *demon* was a better

parent than either of you, right?" Jack drawled.

"I th-thought you were here to h-help us," she said, dabbing at her eyes again.

"Sounds like he might be in a better position," Anya said with a furious glare at the father. "Speaking as one, demons tend to be a bit less caring about who you decide to roll around with."

"We know we made a mistake, but we love our son," John Sr. replied with a bit of a nervous look at the demon. "We'll do anything to get him back. Pay anything. Please!"

"Anya, sidebar," Jack said, standing up.

"The hell is a sidebar?" she snapped at him, but followed him to the other side of the room. "What?"

"I think we should help them," Jack said.

Anya glared furiously at the parents. "Why? They don't deserve it. Their son is probably better off."

"Is he, though?" Jack said. "There are ways to get away from your parents other than turning into a demon."

"Oh yeah, like what?" Anya said, her glare still on the parents.

"Like moving out, getting your own job. There are resources out there for kids in Johnny's situation," Jack said. "Besides that, you won't get your money if you don't help them."

Her scowl lessened, but only a bit. "I don't like parents that throw their kids out," she said, with another hefty glare at the father. "And I still think that kid's better off as a demon."

Because that had been the path for her. But Anya hadn't found much salvation with Bael, and Jack was pretty sure

Johnny wouldn't find being a demon to be so wonderful.

"I think we need to bring him home," Jack said after a moment. "Not for his parents, but for him. Imagine living a thousand years and never getting to reconcile with your parents. It could eat a person up inside."

She turned to him, a dangerous glint in her eye. "And what, precisely, is *that* supposed to mean?"

Jack shrugged, remaining steadfast under her withering glare.

After a long staring contest, she sniffed loudly and said, "Fine. We will retrieve him. But if his parents don't shape up, I'm charging them an extra two grand and giving it to him."

CHAPTER SIX

The parents provided Anya with a photo and some basic information about his friends, as well as the teen's computer, although Anya was fairly sure she'd find nothing on it, since most kids his age lived and died on their mobile devices.

"Which makes it easy for us," she said, opening her laptop back in their hotel room. "As those things are incredibly insecure."

"So why not go to the police?" Jack asked. "If it's so easy?"

"The police don't deal in demonic transformations. They'd kick it over to your friends at the Division. Who'd then feed the parents some bullshit line about how 'they can't revert the boy because he was turned by a too-powerful demon' and they'd be back to me anyway." She returned to the computer. "I get results."

"That you do," Jack mumbled, going to the window and

staring outside. As a Division agent, Jack had said those exact words to grieving parents more times than he could remember. Even back then, he'd thought it was a bum rap. The Division *could* have arrested the demons, but in order to keep the political peace, they almost always let it slide. Now, seeing how easily Anya moved in the world outside politics and bureaucracy, his previous adherence to the rules made him sick.

"Ah, see? Moron," Anya replied. "He just posted a photo of himself and his new demonic boyfriend."

"R-really?" Jack wasn't sure what surprised him more: that the boy had been so flagrant or that Anya was able to find him so quickly.

But there he was, grinning happily with a bleached-blond surfer dude. Had Jack not known there was a demon involved, he would've thought it any normal photograph.

"Let's see if we can't find out where he took this photo," Anya said, peering into her computer.

"I seriously can't believe you're a technology genius, along with all the other stuff you do," Jack said, sitting down on the bed.

Her cheeks grew a little pink. "I'm not...well, I'm not actually doing the heavy lifting here. I have a guy."

"A guy?" Jack said, amazed she'd told him anything at all. "What's his name?"

"His name is none of your business."

Jack should've expected that. Two steps forward, one back. "So, this guy, does he do all your hacking stuff? Is he the one who broke into my phone? The Division headquarters? Where'd you find him? How—"

"If you ask one more question, I will throw you out the window."

He wouldn't put it past her, so he clammed up.

She typed on the keyboard for a moment and then grinned. "See, this is why I like human recovery cases. Once we get a signature on the phone he used to take the photo, I can find him, as long as he doesn't lose his phone. Simple. Easy. Over in an hour."

Jack nodded, still wary of her threat.

"Fine. *Obviously*, I'm not capable of handling this new technology. I'd be spending all my time learning every new thing that pops up. So, every couple years, I do a job for someone computer savvy. Instead of cash, they pay me in services. I use them a few times then ghost."

Again, he nodded without a word.

"Oh, for fuck's sake, I'm not going to throw you out the window," she snarled.

"Can't be too sure with you," Jack said. "Thanks for telling me. So, where's he at?"

She closed her laptop. "Last photo was taken about an hour ago at a bar in Algiers, and from what I can tell, he's still there. Let's go."

"Are we taking your car or the bus?" Jack asked with a smile.

"My c... You mean, my magic?" Anya asked, then glowered at him. "No, we're not taking my magic. I'll use it when I damned well want to, understand?"

"Yes, ma'am."

Anya was starting to give Jack whiplash. Perhaps asking her to use magic was offensive. He wouldn't make that mistake again.

Instead, he busied himself digging in the weapons bag for his knives and holster. There, he found Anya's bejeweled sword, the one Bael had given her in Atlanta, along with an assortment of other items. Then, in the bottom of the bag, his holster and weapons.

He was amazed he still had them, actually. He'd been wearing them when Bael took him to the Underworld, and since they all considered him a weak human, they'd allowed him to keep his weapons. For that, he was grateful. The knives had been a gift from Frank on his graduation from the Academy for Demon Management, and were old friends—

I love watching you wear your knives, Jackie.

As Sara's voice echoed in his mind, so did the memories. A familiar chill enveloped him as darkness descended over his mood. That old sadness, the one that had lodged in his mind in the days following Sara's death, was back in full force. He hadn't even noticed it had been gone. But now, it was so very inconvenient, appearing just when he needed to be on his game. Between the nox magic and the lilin magic, not to mention this feeling of being ten steps behind Anya at all times, Jack was already struggling to keep pace.

"You okay?" Anya's voice cut through the spiral, and Jack

met her gaze in the mirror.

"Yeah, just thinking," he replied softly. "Ready to go?"

Early on after Sara died, Jack had learned that there was no fighting grief. The sadness would always be waiting in the background, ready to pounce at a moment's notice. Now, as the taxi drew closer to their destination, Jack wished he'd tried a little harder to move past it.

Johnny's phone was currently at a bar teeming with lilin miasma. Anya led the way inside, unaffected, and Jack followed her a little slower, easing himself into it. Once inside, he didn't find it too bothersome. Perhaps it was the potent glamour he still wore, or maybe the lingering grief, but his head remained clear.

Everyone else, on the other hand, seemed drunk on it. Partners and groups of three and four people slowly moved together, kissing and licking and sucking on whatever they could get their lips on. Gasps of pleasure echoed through the room— clearly no one was taking notice of the heavily armed woman standing in the center.

"I don't see him," Jack began, but Anya must have, because she strode forward. Using strength he wasn't sure how she possessed, she pried apart two men and a woman, grabbing the second man and dragging him to the door. He was probably a good foot taller than she was, but she didn't stop until they were out into the empty streets.

"Where's your maker?" Anya snarled.

"W-who the fuck are you?" he said, taking a moment to snap

out of his reverie. "Let me go! I'm a demon—"

"So am I, kid. And trust me, I'm worse than whatever pissant lilin made you."

Either he was gullible, or she was putting out some demonic magic that Jack couldn't sense, because the boy slumped.

"H-his name is Gerry. He's out right now—"

"Then I suppose you'd better find him, huh?" Anya said, throwing him to the ground. "And don't take too long, I don't have all night."

"I don't understand," Johnny said, rubbing his cheek where it had hit the ground. "Why do you want Gerry?"

She sighed, looking almost pained. "Your parents hired me."

He went from wide-eyed shock to jaded disgust in an instant. "Fuck off, then. You can kill me, or whatever, but I'm not letting you turn me back into a human."

"You little—" Anya started, but Jack stopped her with a gentle hand on her shoulder.

"Let me handle this," Jack said, then turned to the kid. It had been a while since he'd done the official Division school visits, but he remembered the gist of what he was supposed to say. "Look, I know you're furious at your parents. And you have every right to be—"

"Do you *know* where they wanted to send me?" he said, disgusted.

"Yes," Jack said. "Your parents are garbage. There's no debating that. But that doesn't mean you have to become a demon to escape them."

"What am I supposed to do with myself then? Dad said if I didn't go, he'd kick me out. Forget about college." He looked at the ground. "Gerry said I could still go. He said he'd pay for me." The boy's eyes filled with loving tears. "He's the first person I've ever met who really got me. Says I'm the last human he'll ever turn. That we'll be together forever."

Anya snorted, and even Jack had a hard time keeping the pity off his face. This kid had needed a savior, and gotten a predator instead. "I understand how you feel, but being a demon isn't your only option. We'll change you back to human and get you help."

"I don't want your help," he said with a scowl. "I want to stay with Gerry."

"This conversation is boring me," Anya announced. "What will it matter? I'm killing his master anyway."

"Ignore her," Jack said, helping the kid to his feet.

"What do you mean kill my master?" Johnny said. "You can't kill Gerry! I love him!"

"I am sure you do. The question is, does he love you back?" Anya nodded toward a group of people approaching, hiding in the shadows between the street lights.

"What's going on here?" one of them called.

"Gerry!" Johnny cried, but Jack grabbed him before he could scamper away.

The aforementioned Gerry appeared in the light, with two young girls by his side. The lilin, a surfer dude with bronzed skin and bleached blonde hair, seemed quite close to his new friends, who didn't look older than sixteen. They, a pair of young black girls, were oblivious to anyone except the demon.

"Who's this?" Johnny asked, pushing Jack away. "I thought you said I was going to be your last?"

"Did I say that?" Gerry said with a casual sort of sneer. "I don't recall."

Anya snorted, glancing at the boy who looked like his world had been shattered. "Lilins. They'll say anything to get you in bed."

Jack had seen this before. Demons promising the moon, then leaving their new spawn to fend for themselves once they got what they wanted.

"He's only interested in growing more powerful," Jack said to Johnny. "Every time he spawns, he gets stronger."

"And who might you be?" Gerry asked Anya, letting the two girls go, but keeping an eagle-eye on them until they were safely inside the bar. "You smell like lilins, but you…aren't."

That must've been why no one in the bar had said anything about her. Jack had had no idea demons could smell each other, but he was grateful she had masked her athtar scent. It would've been a dead giveaway.

"I'm here on business," Anya said, pulling her swords off her back. "And you're my business. You're that boy's master, right?" She glanced over her shoulder at Johnny. "He's your master, right? The one who transformed you?"

Johnny stared at the ground, tears welling in his eyes. "I got nowhere else to go. Maybe I should just stay here with Gerry."

"For what it's worth," Jack said, placing his hands on his knives, "your parents are worried sick about you."

The teenager kicked the ground, a frown on his face. "Worried enough to kick me out."

"Worried enough to hire demon hunters like us to get you home," Jack said. "Do you have an aunt or uncle nearby? Someplace to crash?"

"I got an aunt," he mumbled.

"Good enough for me," Anya said, turning to the lilin.

Jack caught a whiff of flowers and sex, and Johnny's eyes grew lovesick and glassy.

"Show me what you got," Gerry snarled, and the flower smell got stronger. "Or are you afraid to go toe-to-toe with New Orleans' new demon lord?"

"I think you've got a few people vying for that title," Anya said, her movements fluid and controlled. "And you're nothing but a neophyte compared to them."

She lunged at the lilin, swords bared, but the demon jumped away, a rare miss for Anya. She wasn't using her athtar magic at all. Was this intentional, or did she feel he wasn't worthy of using magic?

It seemed it was the latter when she re-sheathed her swords and landed a hard blow to Gerry's stomach with her fist. He fell backward, coughing and clutching his midsection as she pulled her sword back out, readying the killing blow. But before she could, the door swung open and two large men ambled out of the bar.

"What is it with you lilins and your muscle men?" Anya asked with a shake of her head.

"My heroes," Gerry said, getting up slowly.

"You're up," Anya said to Jack, licking her lips. "I'll kill this one."

"Stay back, kid," Jack said to Johnny, who was still in his sickly-sweet daze. Jack just hoped he didn't make a run for it; then they might never find him. "If you stick around, we'll make sure you get to your aunt's house tonight."

He nodded hesitantly, but flattened himself against the wall. Jack turned to the two henchmen, pulling his knives from his holster. They still felt odd in his hands, and the old calluses on his palms hadn't formed back yet. Perhaps he should've taken the Division trainer's advice and practiced a little bit more.

Hoping to buy Anya some time, he stepped in front of the other men. He wasn't short or scrawny, but he sure felt that way facing these monsters. The little defeating voice in the back of his mind hummed, but he stood his ground. One guy lifted his sword and swung it down, Jack blocked with his knives in front of him, struggling under the weight of the sword and the man holding it. His knees shook, his arms felt like jelly, and the tip of the sword dipped closer to his forehead.

Out the corner of his eye, he saw the second man raise his sword. Jack would have to choose—let one sword slice him lengthwise or the other sideways.

"Do I have to do *everything* myself?" came Anya's exasperated voice.

Just as he was sure he could hold out no longer, the weight of the sword disappeared, as did the heads of both demons. They rolled down the street, looks of glee frozen in place.

"W-w-w-" Gerry began, then gasped in horror. "You're *Anat!*"

She flinched, but recovered quickly. Soon Gerry's head followed down the street to join his bodyguards'.

The street illuminated with a bright white light that faded as quickly as it had come. Jack slumped on the ground, thankful it was over.

"And see *that* is why I didn't want to use my magic," Anya said, kicking Gerry's body. "Now anyone who was listening will know I was here."

Jack looked right, then left, but saw no one living except the two of them and Johnny, who was passed out. "I don't think anyone heard you."

"They *could* have," she said, wiping her sword on Gerry's shirt. "Aren't you supposed to be a Division agent? You're pretty pisspoor in the fighting department."

"I haven't been out in the field in a while," Jack said, managing an icy glare. He didn't feel like sharing the rest of his issues related to his wife. He was already feeling shitty, and he didn't want to add Anya's commentary to the one already happening in his head.

Since Anya didn't move to grab the now-human teenager, Jack did the honors, tossing the small frame over his shoulder. "Is he gonna be okay?"

"Tomorrow, he'll wake up with a wicked hangover, but he won't be any worse for the wear," she said. "C'mon, let's get a cab and get him back to his parents."

Johnny was muttering incoherently when they arrived at the swanky house near Magazine Street. His mother screamed when she opened the door, falling to her knees in hysteria while John, Sr. took his son into his arms as if he were a toddler.

"Where's the money?" Anya barked as they put their son on the couch and fussed over him.

"F-five thousand, right?" John Sr. said, going to his briefcase and pulling out two stacks of hundred-dollar bills.

"Depends," Anya said, leveling her gaze at him. "Are you gonna send your son back to that camp? Or are you gonna accept him as he is, and treat him better?"

John stared back at them, wordless, but his wife lifted her chin. "We promise. John, no." She shook her head at her husband as he started to protest. "I don't care what he is as long as I have him."

"He wanted to move in with his aunt," Jack said. "I think it might be best if he stayed there while you three can work out your differences."

Johnny's mother nodded, looking stricken for a moment. "I'll give you the address."

While she did that, Anya kept her steely gaze on John Sr. In a blur, she was at his throat with her sword.

"I'm not saving your son a second time. So if you fail to do what I asked—and I *will* find out—I'll come back and take your life as payment. Understood?"

He nodded, the movement causing a small tear at the skin of his neck. Anya sheathed her sword and swiped the bills off the desk.

"H-here it is," Johnny's mother said, wiping a tear from her eyes. "P-please tell him…tell him I love him?"

Jack nodded, and turned to find Anya, but she'd disappeared. Which left him the odious task of taking a comatose boy across town and having to explain the particulars of his very eventful night to his bewildered aunt.

CHAPTER SEVEN

Cam wasn't really sure what she was doing in New Orleans. Everyone was happy or drunk (or both), and their revelry fell flat on her sour mood. She'd slept fitfully in the hotel bed, memories of Bael snatching Jack and carrying him down to the Underworld plaguing her nightmares. Each time, she'd wake, knowing, for sure, that he was dead. Then she'd relive the moment he came back alive, but chose the demon woman over her, and anger would surge. It was an exhausting roller coaster, and Cam wanted off.

She had nothing substantial to report to Navarro or Frank, so she'd resorted to sending brief update emails about the conversations she was having with local demons. Whether they were kappa, eloko, nox, or lilin, the answer was always the same: no one had seen a demon woman and a human man who matched their descriptions.

Cam didn't think they were lying. From what she could scrounge up from Jack's research on Anya, the woman was fearsome, cunning, and bloodthirsty. She'd also been under the radar for so long that everyone assumed she was dead. This same woman had hacked into the Division resources to wipe Jack's measly research and broke into an encrypted phone. She clearly took great pains to hide herself.

She checked her phone for the billionth time, hoping to find another email from a burner email account.

It was still hard to believe he'd just popped up in her inbox, asking for help again. But that was Jack. That was her frustrating partner.

It was tempting to travel to Wani's place and wait for him. In her quiet moments, she envisioned herself hog-tying Jack and dragging him kicking and screaming back to Atlanta (La Colibrí was facedown in the mud with a sword in her back). But even if she managed to get her hands on Jack, he'd just wriggle his way back out. No, he needed to complete whatever idiotic mission he was on before he'd come willingly.

Which begged the question: Why was Cam in New Orleans at all?

Maybe she just needed to see the man. Maybe she just wanted to look into those big brown eyes of his and know for herself that he wasn't being held against his will. Maybe she just wanted a chance to punch him in the face. Most likely, she wanted to feel like she was being useful after being so powerless against everything happening around her.

At the end of another long, fruitless day, she sidled up to the hotel bar and ordered a glass of wine—the good stuff. It was bitter and pungent on her tongue, and tasted of dark cherries. Cam thought she might order herself a fancy, overpriced meat-and-cheese plate as well. After all, she was on per diem, and she'd barely eaten since she'd arrived.

But as with all good things, before she got too far into her delicious glass of wine, her phone buzzed. Hope flitted through her, disappearing as soon as she saw the name.

"Macarro," she said, wearily.

"We've gotten reports of a group of lilins who were killed last night—beheaded." Patti Kim's voice was gruff on the other end of the line. She was the Deputy Director in Atlanta, and a thorn in Cam's side. "Want you to look into it and see if there's any evidence of Grenard."

Cam pinched the bridge of her nose. "Will do."

"I also got a report from them saying you were requesting information on a demon named Wani," Kim said. "Care to share anything with the class?"

Cam didn't like her tone, but she was already skating on thin ice where Kim was concerned. "Got a tip from a barfly who said he might be a good contact. Knows a lot about demon activity in New Orleans."

She held her breath, hoping Kim would buy it. The last thing Cam needed was to be pulled off the case.

"So, explain those emails you got from Grenard."

Shit. "He contacted me from a burner account—"

"You aided and abetted a fugitive. We're looking at some serious disciplinary action."

"I'm sure," Cam snapped. She'd already been on the receiving end of Kim's threats—even been fired briefly until Director Navarro overruled Kim. And once Demon Spring had started, Kim had been begging her to come back.

"Anything else you're keeping from us? Maybe why they were so interested in Wani?"

Cam swallowed, praying she hadn't sent anything too incriminating. There was always a risk, using her professional email, that her communications were being monitored. But this was a particularly low blow from Kim.

"I assume it's something to do with this curse thing," Cam said, finally. "Wani's an older demon. He probably knows a bit about it."

"And what do you know about it?"

"Nothing, other than his name."

"Then I suggest you pay him a visit and find out what they wanted from him. But after you check out that lilin place. I want a report by noon tomorrow."

Click.

Cam flung her smartphone onto the bar and buried her head in her hands. Perfect. She'd had a good laugh imagining Jack wading through swamps, getting eaten alive by mosquitos the size of rats. She supposed this was karma.

Of course, she could say she went and lie to Kim. After all, it was probably a good bet Wani wouldn't speak to her unless she had something to offer (that was the kappa way), and Cam didn't have the kind of money to appease a two-thousand-year-old demon.

And on top of that, she had to go on a wild goose chase to a lilin bar that probably had nothing to do with Jack or La Colibrí. Why would Jack even be at a lilin bar? They were after Wani. It made no sense.

Cam laid her head down on the bar and sighed heavily.

"You look like you've had a rough day."

The man who sat down next to Cam was gorgeous, the kind of man who graced the covers of magazines, and made her forget all about whatever had been bothering her a few moments before. He leaned on the bar with an easy smile, gazing into Cam's eyes and making her heart flutter.

"I'm sorry, what?" Cam said.

"I asked if you needed a refill," he said, nodding to her empty wine glass.

"I..." she said after staring at him a moment. "No, I think I'm going to head on home." Why she didn't mention she was going to her room upstairs, she didn't know. Why she didn't *invite* this gorgeous man up to her room, she didn't know.

"Come on, let me buy you one," he said, nodding to the bartender and holding up two fingers. "I've had a day myself and I need a drinking partner."

Cam had been about to leave, but something about this man made her stay. Whether it was the promise of another glass of that amazing red wine, or even just the smell of the man's cologne, Cam's annoyance faded.

And as it did, an itch started in the back of her mind. Something wasn't right. Slowly, she slid a hand into her pocket and grasped her talismans. The veil lifted from her mind and she kicked herself for nearly getting taken.

The lilin, while pretty, wasn't nearly as attractive as he'd been a minute before. He smiled with a confidence that said he thought Cam still under his control. Cam decided to play along, hoping she could find out who this demon was and why he'd chosen Cam as a target.

"You're Division, right?" the man asked, sipping his wine.

"Yeah," Cam said, covertly glancing down at her shirt and phone. Nothing about her said Division, although she supposed he could've overheard her talking.

"What do you hear about the athtar and the Division agent?" he asked.

He must think I'm suckered, Cam thought, amazed. "Not much. You?"

"Oh." His face fell. "I'd heard the Division was getting close to finding them. They obviously have a unit here in New Orleans looking."

Unit? Cam forced a shrug. "Haven't seen anyone out of the ordinary here."

"Maybe that's because they aren't telling you something," the demon said, leaning in closer. "Why don't you tell me what *you* know, Cam, and—"

"I'll tell you what I know," Cam said, holding up her

talismans. That he knew her name sent up giant red flags and forced her to end the charade. "Your magic isn't working here, lilin. Tell your boss I'm not sharing a thing."

He smiled, sliding his hand onto the bar and tapping his fingers. "We work for the same person, you know. There's a reason Bael calls himself the king of the five realms. Ath-kur, Liley, Elonsi, Kappanchi, and, of course, this world."

"Spies would indicate I am not in command of all I survey in the Underworld and here in the human realm. And that, human, is most assuredly not the case."

A shudder ran through her body. Sure, the Division kissed a lot of demon ass, but Cam was fairly sure the humans were still in charge. Even so, Bael had his fingers in everything. Whatever they knew, he presumably did, too.

"You're better off going back home and letting the demons catch them. Bael has promised a major city to any demon who can bring her back."

Cam narrowed her eyes. "She's an athtar. I doubt someone like you could even get a word out in her presence."

He shrugged, sipping his wine. "As a favor, I'll save you a trip: It was Anat who killed those lilins at the bar. He was an acquaintance of mine—a fifth cousin twice removed, if you will."

She had no reason to doubt the lilin, as the Division agents were already combing the crime scene. But much as she'd said to Kim, it made no sense.

"And why were they there?"

"Oh, who knows?" he said with a casual shrug. "Maybe they'd run afoul of someone, or maybe they were just looking for someone to kill. Stories of Anat's bloodlust are legendary, you know."

Anya might've been ruthless, but Jack was not. And she wasn't convinced Anya would expose herself needlessly. That, at least, she knew about La Colibrí.

"And what did you want in return for this information?" she asked.

"I'd offer to join you upstairs in your room, but since you're being so cold, I'll save myself the disappointment." He stood. "So, you may pay for all our drinks, and we'll call it even."

Cam flung two twenty-dollar bills on the bar, knowing it was probably twice what the drinks costs, but not wanting to wait around long enough for change. She turned on her heel and strode out of the bar, forcing herself to look confident until she stepped onto the elevator.

There, she slumped against the wall and buried her head in her hands. That had been weird—and Cam had seen her share of weird over the past three weeks. She sure hoped Jack had vacated the city before he was caught up in any more of it.

CHAPTER EIGHT

When Jack returned from dropping Johnny at his aunt's house, it was almost dawn. Anya was already asleep in her bed, so he climbed into the second one and passed out. When he woke, the blinds were closed, but there was a little light streaming in, reflecting off Anya's face as she typed away at the computer.

Jack sat up and stretched. "Good—"

"I've contacted Wani's people."

"—morning," he finished with a yawn. "What made you change your mind?"

"There was nothing to change. It was a good idea." She glanced up at him. "Your partner is in New Orleans."

"I had a feeling she'd be here," Jack said with a grimace. "How do you know?"

"She came alone," Anya said, apparently not interested in

answering his questions. "That tells me she's not working wholly within the lines of your investigation. She looks like shit, which tells me she's more interested in *your* wellbeing than bringing either of us in." Anya paused. "You're lucky to have someone who cares so much about you."

"And so, because of all that, you're willing to meet with Wani?" Jack asked, ignoring the pang of guilt.

"I'm willing to believe she won't have an elaborate trap waiting for us."

"Well, progress is progress," Jack said. "And by the way, thanks for leaving me holding the bag with Johnny last night."

"It's only fair, since you nearly got us both killed," she said.

"I think you handled it fine."

She pursed her lips. "I told you—one slip-up and Bael is here."

Jack really couldn't argue that point, so he changed the subject. "So, why haven't I heard of this Wani guy before?"

"Wani is old. He's been here for a few hundred years, but he's not interested in lordship." She folded her arms across her chest. "That's why I didn't think of him. He keeps to himself."

"A demon who doesn't want to be in charge," Jack said with a chuckle. "Never heard of such a phenomenon."

She glared at him. "We're just as different as you. Some people want power. Others just want to be left alone."

"So I'm finding."

They lifted yet another car to get out of the city, with Anya also pulling the license to return the car once they'd finished with it. They hopped back on I-10, rolling over Lake Pontchartrain and into Slidell, just east of the city. There was nothing but swamp trees and a few random palms as they pulled over on the side of the road.

"How far away are we?"

"Two miles, maybe," Anya said, putting her phone into her pocket and retrieving her swords from the back of the car.

"Are you sure we need to walk into his house wearing weapons?" Jack asked.

"What does it matter? You can't wield them anyway," she said with a smirk.

Ow. Jack glared at the back of her head and snatched his knives from the trunk. He *could* wield them; he was just out of practice. But he doubted she'd be willing to help him practice— or that he'd want to go a few rounds with her. It might result in more verbal lashes than physical ones.

She finished strapping on her weapons and turned to him, oblivious of the shittiness of her comment. "Well?"

"Waiting on you," he said with a scowl.

She positioned herself in front of him, and her eyes grew black. The world slowed once more, and he could now hear the movement of critters and creatures in the swamp around them. She inhaled sharply and the world lurched, then sped up to normal again.

"You okay?" Jack asked.

"Fine," she said, shrugging casually, though she'd grown a

shade paler—not that Jack was going to mention it. "So, this goes without saying, but this is an old kappa we're dealing with. One of the first humans transitioned by Mizuchi."

"Yep," Jack said with a nod.

"Try not to gawk at him or say anything stupid while we're in there," she said. "Wani spent a long time in the Underworld before settling up here."

Jack slowed his gait. "So, you're saying he looks like Mizuchi?"

"I'm saying the miasma changed him, yes," Anya said.

"So why didn't it change you or Bael?" Jack asked, picking up the pace behind her. "You two look human to me."

"It is said by some that an athtar's ugliness lies inside," she replied softly. "Those who repeat that in front of Bael don't live very long after."

"Got it," Jack said with a firm nod. "So have you met Wani before?"

"No," she said with a shake of her head. "I know of him because some of the servants at Bael's castle spoke about him. Besides that, he's pretty well known amongst the topside kappas."

"Are you safe talking to him? Shouldn't he be close with the belu?"

She cast a glance over her shoulder. "Mizuchi's direct spawn number in the tens of thousands by now. I doubt he'd recognize Wani if he came right up and introduced himself. That's what happens when you spread yourself too thin. I wouldn't be going if I didn't think it was safe."

"How many spawn does Bael have?"

Anya frowned, looking almost offended. "We aren't *spawn*. That's what lesser demons are called. We're simply athtar."

"So how many athtar are there?"

"Four hundred and sixty-two," she said, without missing a beat.

"And they're all seconds to Bael, right?" Jack asked.

She nodded. "Stop talking about him."

Jack stuffed his hands into his pockets. "Okay, alternate question: what happened to the noxes after the belus were killed?"

"Their son kept the line going," she replied with an even tone.

"Yeah, and how does *that* work?" Jack asked. "Since when can demons have children?"

"When they're belus and they want to."

Jack watched her retreating back, curious about the almost wistful note in her voice. But a pair of lights turned on in the distance, and Jack jogged after her into the clearing.

The shack was exactly that—a shack. It resembled every stereotypical swamp house Jack had ever seen in any movie. The doors were hanging off the hinges, the windows cloudy with green mildew. And Jack could see clear to the other side—there was no one in the house.

"Use that talisman," Anya said, her voice cracking through his mind like a whip.

"What?"

"You're looking at an illusion," she said. "It's how kappas entrap you. They put an illusion over water, then drag you under."

"I know how kappas trick people," Jack said, although he pressed the green-coated medallion to his palm.

The shack faded away, revealing a murky swamp with more than a few alligators ready to chow down on a Jack-sized meal. Anya kept walking along the banks of the shore until she came upon a nicer house. This one had two women out front in rocking chairs, each holding shotguns. They made no move to stop Anya or Jack from walking up the stairs, but Jack didn't make eye contact either.

Inside, there was a distinct breeze from the air conditioner. The walls were paper thin, the floors shiny wood, and there was even a small water feature burbling happily in the front entrance.

"Take your shoes off," Anya snapped, doing the same.

"What?"

"Take off your shoes," she hissed. "We're in Wani's house. We have to show deference."

Jack slid off his shoes and followed Anya. A man and a woman stood on either side of the door, sliding a panel back with almost fluid motion.

"Come in, come in!" came the gurgled voice from the other side of the room.

Jack could scarcely believe his eyes—the man seated at the table looked more frog than human. And it had nothing to do with the effects of the latent miasma; this man was solid kappa. He even had an indentation on top of his head, surrounded by a black circle of hair. There were hints of Japanese in his features, but the kappa magic had disfigured him completely. His eyes bulged from their sockets, his lips, a greenish-pink, split his pale green skin, revealing a tongue of the same color. His limbs were spindly, curled under him in a kneeling position.

Anya approached the frog-man passively, pulled her swords off her back, knelt before him, and laid her weapons in front of her. Jack was surprised, but followed suit.

"Lord Wani," she said, lifting her head after a moment.

"Lady Anat the Destroyer, Lady of the Mountain, Slayer of the Belu Noxes." Wani smiled, his lips stretching seemingly from one ear to the other. He bowed, but only slightly, so as not to spill the precious water atop his head. "It is my honor to have you in my home."

"How do you know who I am?" she asked.

"My dear, we may be in the swamps, but I have cable," he said with a chuckle. "Besides, we've met in passing. I may not have made an impression, but you made an impression on me."

Anya's lips twitched, but she said nothing. "If you tell anyone I've come to see you—"

"Don't fret, my lady. It is not in my nature to spill secrets without just cause." His frogish smile widened, and Jack caught the double meaning.

"We want information on curses," Anya said.

"Like the one that hung from your neck?" he asked, tapping

one long finger against his chin. "I seem to recall something about such a thing."

"Is it something worth the trouble of doing you a favor?" she asked with a growl.

"It is worth the trouble I'll ask in return, yes," he said enigmatically. He pushed himself to stand, revealing a rotund belly that sat on his stick legs like an orange on two toothpicks.

"These past few weeks have been quite exciting, no?" he said, walking over to a tapestry that hung behind him. The artistry was Japanese, but that was all Jack could make out, as age and time had faded the ink. "Poor Nunzia met her fate, as did, I hear, Lord Xerxes in Dallas. Two lords of considerable stature killed within minutes of each other. Their empires decimated just like that."

Anya's hand twitched, but her face remained impassive. Jack wished he could read her mind.

"And the new lord of Dallas to Atlanta, Lord Parras? He's an interesting fellow. A pup, barely two hundred years old. Now ruler of the Deep South." Wani chuckled. "Now, I've seen my share of leaders rise and fall, but never so close together and never one handed an empire thusly. It seems to me such a situation would be ripe for a power vacuum."

"You realize that Parras has Bael's special attention," Anya said, her voice clear and dripping with sarcasm. "If you were to make a move, Bael would take revenge. It would make Nunzia and Xerxes' deaths look like child's play."

The frog-man bellowed with laughter, and nervous smiles

appeared on his spawn around him. Jack didn't share in their amusement, not after seeing Bael decapitate Nunzia with one swing.

"No, my lady. I want you to grant me an audience with Lord Parras. Lords Nunzia and Xerxes understood the nature of my arrangement here in the swamps. I don't want it to change. But sadly, Lord Parras hasn't accepted my invitation to chat. I fear he thinks I'm some backwater hick." He chuckled. "But if you were to persuade him—"

"No." Anya stood. "I'm not going to speak with him. I said he's in with Bael, and Bael is looking for me."

"To misquote a movie, don't you have ways of making people talk, or in this case, not talk?" He returned to his seat and rang a small bell. His manservant came into the room, carrying a tea tray. "You were a fearsome creature in the Underworld. I daresay if you swing your sword around, Parras might think twice about crossing it."

"If it's a choice between my sword and Bael's—"

"Bael has returned to the Underworld, licking his wounds," Wani said. "The humans have become quite adept at defense, suddenly, and he's not willing to suffer another embarrassment in public."

Anya crossed her arms across her chest, staring down the kappa so harshly Jack was sure the frog would explode.

"Parras is in Montgomery, or Dallas, or even Atlanta. I can't travel that far. I'm sure you understand."

"Indeed I do, which is why I'm pleased to inform you that

he's taken up residence in a hotel in the French Quarter. Celebrating his newfound glory with some of his closest associates, and I guess some new friends."

Anya clicked her tongue. "How convenient."

"He is," Jack said with a nod. "I heard those two elokos talking about it in the bar the other..." His words died under the icy glare Anya sent him.

"It's a mere fifteen miles from here to his hotel, as the crow flies," Wani replied. "A simple trick for a powerful athtar such as yourself."

She retrieved her swords from the ground and placed them on her back. There was still no trace of emotion on her face. As far as Jack could tell, she would sooner agree to Wani as slice his head off.

"If I bring Parras to you for a short conversation, you'll answer my questions?" she asked after securing her weapons.

The kappa nodded, and a bit of water splashed on the floor.

"Fine," she said. "Let's go."

Jack hopped to his feet, only just remembering to grab his knives before running out after her.

"So you're taking him at his word?" Jack asked as she slipped her shoes back on at the door.

"For being a Division agent, you don't know a lot about kappas," she said, leaving him while he laced up his shoes. He quickly tied them off and followed her.

"I know plenty about the topside demons, but give me some credit here." Jack looked back at the house once more. "We don't get a lot of demons like that."

"A fully transformed kappa must keep water atop their head," Anya said, hopping over a root. "Spilling water means they won't go back on their word."

Bael had explained something like that in the Underworld, when Mizuchi had spilled all his water, and Bael refilled it.

"So…Parras," Jack said, as Anya stopped in the middle of the swamp.

"We'll not discuss it here," she said, taking Jack by the arm. The world tunneled again, and they were back in their hotel room, their mud-soaked shoes now out of place on the lush carpet. Anya released him, swaying a bit on her feet as she stumbled to the bathroom.

"You okay?" Jack called.

"Fuck off," she said, right before the door slammed shut.

CHAPTER NINE

"Is it normal for you to be this tired all the time?" Jack asked with a quirked brow. "Or are you still healing from the talisman bullet?"

Anya looked even closer to death than usual. Her skin was pale, the purple bags under her eyes more prevalent than ever. And even though her lids drooped, she didn't sleep.

"Don't concern yourself with me," she said. "We need to find Parras."

"He should be fairly easy to locate," Jack said. "I'll call around, say I'm a Division agent looking to find a room but I don't want to stay where the lord is."

"Does that work?" Anya asked, opening one eye.

"You'd be surprised how stupid people are," Jack said. He glanced at the laptop on the bed. "Can I use your computer?"

"I don't know. Can you?"

"I don't know. Can you tell me the password?" Jack shot back, tired of her attitude. "Because I'm not psychic."

A faint blush added some color to her face, and she swiped the computer off the bed. She typed in the credentials, then handed the machine to him.

"Thank you," Jack said. "You know, things could be a lot easier if you'd lay off the shitty remarks."

"I am sorry."

He nearly dropped the computer. "What?"

"I said… I'm sorry. I have a splitting headache, I'm exhausted, and I don't like how long we've stayed in this city." She exhaled loudly. "But you're right, I shouldn't take it out on you."

"Do you want me to get some pain reliever?" he asked, then chuckled. "Does that even work on demons? I thought you had super healing?"

"Jack, please…no more questions," Anya said, pinching the bridge of her nose. "I don't have the energy to be nice right now."

"Then why don't you get some rest?" Jack said, nodding to the bed. "It may take me a while to find Parras anyway."

He felt her gaze on him, but didn't meet it, jotting down the phone number for a few popular hotels in the French Quarter. After a moment, she pushed herself off the bed and stood in front of him. In one fluid movement, she pulled her shirt off, followed by her bra, pants and underwear. There she remained, her hands on her hips and a smirk on her lips.

Jack was incredibly confused. Was she trying to seduce him again? Or was she just fucking with him?

"Um. Can I help you?"

"Are you uncomfortable with nudity?" she asked. "Or are you looking for that pity-fuck?"

"Neither," Jack said, although his cheeks grew warm. "Just wasn't expecting you to undress."

Not wanting to get caught looking, Jack met her gaze with a steely expression.

"Fine, I'll go shower," she replied after a moment. Jack might've misread the situation, but she looked almost defeated as she returned to their open bag and pulled out the shower things. "I don't like this crap, by the way. Smells like shit."

"So sorry," Jack said, leaning back in the chair. "If you tell me what kind you like, I'll pick some up next time I'm out."

Her eyes narrowed again, and she marched inside the bathroom with the shitty-smelling soap. A few moments later, he heard water running in the bathroom.

"Crazy demon," he muttered to himself, reaching for the phone.

It didn't take long for Jack to find out which hotel Parras was staying in—it was the only one in the city fully booked. They all seemed to be elokos at different levels in the larger eloko hierarchy, all trying to get the ear of their new demon lord. After all, Bael's proclamation had given Parras purview over nearly a thousand miles of the southern United States.

The hoarde of elokos had spread out into the city as well, filling bars and restaurants with the clanging of bells everywhere they went. The noise was distracting, but with so many competing sounds, annoyance was a bigger danger than hypnotism. This time, Jack and Anya forewent their lilin glamour, opting instead for hats and sunglasses to blend in with the crowds. The city was busier than it had been, and it was easy to fall in line with the moving mass of humanity.

As usual, Anya took little notice of the demonic activity—either she didn't hear it, or just didn't care. She barely showed any trace of emotion until they reached Parras' hotel, and her grim expression grew more sour. They found an empty couch and hid behind a pair of magazines while they scanned the room.

"Do you see him?" Jack asked.

"No, but I see a lot of elokos here, so your lead was probably correct," she said. "We'll need to figure out how to get him alone."

"Are there any athtars around?" Jack asked. "I mean, Bael did say he was the new lord. Maybe he left a few behind for security."

She shook her head. "No. Bael believes his word travels far and carries a lot of weight. If he said Parras is the new lord, then he expects the demons to adhere to it."

Jack had doubts that would be the case. "Why don't we just grab him from his room? Why all this sneaking around?"

"If Parras suddenly disappears into thin air, they'll suspect something. And I don't want to run the risk they'll suspect *us*."

She chewed her nail as a pair of elokos walked out of the elevator. "I'd rather keep the number of people who know where I am to as low as possible."

"But Parras will know. Won't he say something?"

"He will. *After* we leave the city," Anya said. If I kill him, well, that'll just raise even more suspicion. Not to mention cause even more of a ruckus."

"We could also try something else," Jack said, cocking his head to the side. "This is a lot of risk, you know."

"You mean…without getting information from Wani?" Anya asked, nearly dropping the magazine. "Then we'd be back to square one."

Jack flipped the page. "Just wanted to remind you that was an option." He felt her gaze on him, and raised his brow at her. "What?"

She didn't answer, narrowing her eyes as if trying to read him. Then, with a slight pout, she returned to the magazine and disappeared behind it for a moment longer. "We're already here. Might as well keep going. If we need to leave in a hurry, we can."

Jack hid his smile behind the magazine. He was starting to get the measure of her—she tried very hard to keep herself distant and aloof, keeping her distance from risky situations. But there was a side to her that *did* want to risk a little.

"There he is," Anya said, pulling her magazine up higher. "Walking out of the elevator with two women."

Jack glanced up for a split second, recognizing the eloko

demon instantly. "That's him."

Parras looked much more relaxed than the last time Jack had seen him. The new lord of the deep south was looking high on the hog, wearing a seersucker linen jacket and crisp white shirt. The eloko demon didn't need to use his demonic tricks now—everyone within his circle was already fawning over him.

"I think I see how I can get him alone, too," she said, pulling the small vial of glamour out of her pocket. "I just need to get one of those humans out of the way."

As casually as possible, they left the lobby and followed Parras out into the night. It wasn't hard to blend in—half the eloko-filled lobby left with them, too.

"Won't he be able to tell you aren't an eloko?" Jack asked under his breath.

"Hm?"

"At the lilin bar, that Gerry guy said you smelled like a lilin. Won't Parras be able to tell you aren't an eloko?"

"Do they not teach you *anything* in that academy?" Anya sighed. "Tell me they at least teach you the elements."

"Meaning… which element applies to which demon?" Jack said after a few moments. "I mean, I think I remember, but it usually doesn't come up in the field."

"Lilins are air demons," she said. "Therefore, their sense of smell is heightened."

"…Ah."

"Elokos are…"

"Earth demons," he said, knowing that much. "So what,

they have a good sense of gravity?"

"Sound."

"They definitely don't teach us that," Jack said with a shrug. "Then again, it really never comes up. It doesn't matter if a demon can smell or hear or whatever. What matters is how we can get them not to turn humans into more demons."

She chuckled, although it was less sardonic than usual. "I suppose."

"So what are athtars then?"

"Void," she said. "We have a thing called Sight, where we can see places farther away. It helps us move from place to place." She frowned. "I haven't been able to See very well in a long time."

"How do you jump from place to place then?"

"It's more like skipping and hoping I don't end up in the middle of the ocean," she said with something of a wry smile.

Parras finally chose a restaurant—an older place, presumably on all the top restaurant lists in New Orleans. The windows were open to the street, but Parras was seated in the center of the dining room, his twenty-person entourage taking the seats around him. The two women sat on either side, fluttering their eyes and absorbing every word he said. But what interested Jack was the waitstaff, and how Parras barely acknowledged them.

"Forget the glamour," Jack said. "The way we used to do these ops at the Division was to infiltrate the staff. Wait for him to hit the head then grab him."

"I doubt I could get him to Wani's and back in the time it

takes for him to have a piss break," she said, pulling the glamour out of her pocket. "I still say my way is better."

"What way? Take the place of one of the women, then tell him you want to give him a blow job in the back?"

She shrugged, heading toward the restaurant. "Usually how it works."

"Well, what do you want me to do, then?" Jack asked.

"I don't know, whatever you normally do when you are useless."

"That's just hurtful," Jack said with a glare. "I can help—"

"I can stop time, remember?" she said. "Parras looks away for one moment, I knock the bitch out, throw her in a closet, then take her clothes and reappear."

He scowled. "So you really don't need me at all, then?"

"Only to ask obnoxious questions," she said. "Which you've done. Admirably. Now wait here until I come back for you. Or not. I don't care."

She slipped through the door, leaving Jack alone in the alley. He spun on his heel and walked out to observe. At least then he could jump in if something went wrong. That's what he told himself anyway. Anything to keep from agreeing that he was, in fact, "useless."

He crossed the street to one of the gift shops that lined the city and kept an eye on the restaurant. He had no idea which woman Anya was going to impersonate, or even if she was already there.

Until he saw the one on the right lean in and whisper in

Parras' ear. His eyes lit up, and he casually threw his napkin down on the table and stood up. Then he softly caressed the hand of the woman, and they walked toward the back of the restaurant together.

"I guess it is that easy," Jack said.

The music pumping through the speakers dropped to a low hum, and the laughing, drunk passers-by slowed down. The woman—Anya in glamour—appeared beside him with Parras still puckering up for a kiss. She took Jack's hand and exhaled once more. The ritzy, twinkling lights of the French Quarter melted into the thick, humid air of the backwater swamps. One more breath, and the swamp became the inside of Wani's house, and the world resumed normal speed.

"What the actual fuck just happened?" Parras gasped, as Anya-as-the-other-woman released him. Still drunk, he spun around three times, before finally settling on the kappa demon, who was waiting in much the same position he'd been in the day before.

Then Parras exploded.

"How *dare* you!" he bellowed, the stench of alcohol thick on his breath. "I am the *demon lord*. You—"

"Generally, if you have to announce your position, you haven't earned it," Jack replied, casually.

Parras swayed as he looked over his shoulder, burping as he squinted at Jack. "Oh, 's you! The Division dude. Ben or whatever."

"Wani, my patience is running thin," Anya announced, her

voice even sounding a few notes higher than usual. "Speak with the man and be done with it."

"And who the fuck are you, tits?" Parras asked. "How'd I get here? Are you…" His eyes widened and the drunkeness seemed to melt away from his face. "It's you…An…An…."

"She is merely an athtar that is helping me with a little task," Wani said with a grin showcasing every one of his teeth. "With the schism open, I find many of my old, dear friends come to visit. This particular athtar was willing to do me a small favor."

That explanation seemed incredibly far-fetched, but Parras wasn't really in a deep-thinking mood. "So what'dya want, frog-face? I'm busy celebrating."

Jack thought that was a rather risky move considering the age and standing of the kappa demon, but Wani didn't seem to mind the drunken ramblings of the eloko.

"We have business to discuss, demon-to-demon." He glanced at Anya and bowed his head slightly, but not enough to spill water. "If you'll grant us a bit of privacy."

"You have exactly two minutes," Anya barked, grabbing Jack by the shoulder and dragging him outside.

"You don't have to manhandle me, you know," Jack said, pulling his shirt out of her grasp. "I'm pretty good at reading signs."

"Then read a clock and tell me when two minutes are up."

"Any particular reason you're more of a bitch than usual tonight?" Jack asked, glancing at his watch and marking the time.

"Bitch would be to carve new markings in your stomach," Anya said, pressing her hand over her eyes. "I have another headache."

"From the curse?" Jack said. "I told you we could do something else—"

"When I want your opinion, I'll ask for it," she said, squeezing the bridge of her nose.

"Lady," came a soft voice from the door. "Lord Wani has concluded his business. You may return Lord Parras."

"Yeah, but he's going to answer my questions now," Anya said, walking back inside. "I don't want to have to take another trip out here."

She didn't bother kicking off her shoes this time, walking right into Wani's den and past Parras, who looked a little dazed and confused…and wet. Jack supposed the old kappa had overpowered the eloko quite easily.

"You've got what you wanted, now it's my turn," Anya said. "And it had better be good. Curses. What do you know?"

Wani's chuckles came out more like watery gurgles. He crossed his fingers over his belly and sat back. "Humans have been trying to fight demons since they existed together, but the magical humans are a special breed."

"Magical…humans?" Jack quirked a brow.

"Well, not magic in the sense of demonic magic. Magic of this world. Some humans are attuned to it and can harness it. It's an old art, lost to many civilizations. Some humans think it's too close to demonic magic to put any stock in."

"So who still practices it?" Anya asked.

"Oh, that'll cost you a bit more—"

Anya roared and pulled her sword, sticking the tip between the kappa's eyes. But her display of frustration was short-lived, and she put her sword away, storming out in grand fashion.

Jack, however, remained. "Give us the name of the magic, or at least somewhere to look."

His frog-like expression widened. "I would begin with eloko lore. The very first magical humans, I've heard, were the selfsame ones who met Biloko on his initial entry into the world."

CHAPTER TEN

Anya and Jack arrived with a mumbling and wet Parras back on the same French Quarter street from which they'd kidnapped him. Jack presumed Anya would throw the eloko into an alley, threaten with his life, all that, but she collapsed into Jack's arms the moment they arrived and was unresponsive. Jack hoisted her onto his back and carried her back to the hotel. She remained in bed for the rest of the night and half the next day.

When she finally woke, she seemed groggy and sick, but brushed off Jack's concerns.

"I'll be sick until we undo this curse," she said. "Tell me what Wani said."

"He said that the magical humans met Biloko during his first Demon Spring," Jack said. "And we should look into eloko-human lore."

"So he gave us nothing," Anya said, lying back in bed.

"He didn't give us nothing," Jack said. "I mean, he didn't give us much, but it's more than we had before. We just need to do some research on the first eloko breach."

"I was there."

He paused, sitting up. "R-really?"

She nodded. "I mean, I didn't go with Biloko, but I remember him going the first time."

"That's incredible," Jack said with a bit of an awed smile. "I can't believe you remember events in history I learned about in school."

She turned to look at him, again showing the gauntness of her face. "You're so odd."

"Fine, why don't we start from the beginning, hm?" Jack said. "Tell me about when the first demons were made. Maybe there's something there."

"Obviously, I wasn't around *then*."

"When were you around?" Jack asked. "Bael said you were the first athtar ever made—the first demon ever made, right?"

She nodded, then stopped, looking unsure. "Bael never really told me how or why the six original demons were banished."

"Six?"

"Six. Athtar, kappa, eloko, lilin, and two noxes—Mot and Xo."

Jack straightened. "So there were *two* original noxes?"

"Yes, and from what I can tell from the other demons, it drove Bael crazy," Anya said. "Freyja said it was what made him create the first schism, his rage at not having a partner."

"So he made the schism and found you?"

She nodded. "I was the first human to be made from Bael. When he brought me to the Underworld, it looked nothing like what you saw. There were animals, but the only speaking creatures there were the belus."

"Then what happened?"

"Bael realized he could use humans to garner favors with the other belus," Anya said. "Every four years, he and I would venture into the human world alone and deliver the humans. The belus who got on his good side got more, those who didn't…" She shrugged. "The noxes wanted nothing to do with it, of course. They hated Bael."

"Of course."

"After a few centuries, the belus got a bit braver and asked Bael if *they* could go to the human world, so they could see their homelands once more. The first one he allowed was the kappa. About four centuries later, he let the lilin go and finally the eloko."

"But not the noxes?"

She shook her head. "They'd picked up a few humans here and there. But their numbers were small compared to the rest. Until, of course, they created their own schism."

Jack's brows shot up. "Really?"

"Yeah," she said with a shudder. "Bael was livid."

"Is that why he made you kill them?"

Her eyes flashed with rage, the abrupt transition taking Jack by surprise. "Bael made me do *nothing*. The belu noxes deserved to die. They deserved to die a thousand times."

"For creating a schism?" Jack asked.

"No, for…for something else," she said. "I never cared about their power. I told Bael he shouldn't be bothered with them. He was far more fearsome. But he never listened. He was obsessed with keeping himself head and shoulders above everyone else. After Mot and Xo were out of the way, their son took over, and they've laid low ever since."

Jack had more questions—how did demons have children, what could have caused her to seek revenge against the two original noxes—but it was more important to stay focused on the eloko lore. Besides, based on Anya's reaction, he wasn't sure he wanted to talk about the noxes for a while.

"Biloko's schism happened in the Congo, right?" Jack asked then chuckled. "Man, would be nice if Cam could mail me one of our old history books. I could've sworn I learned about all this stuff at the Academy."

"From what I've seen, the ICDM's version of events is a bit far from the truth," Anya said. "Biloko was the last demon to go, as back then, he was on Bael's shitlist. He'd originally been allied with the noxes. As punishment, Bael sent him into the middle of nowhere. Freyja returned with a thousand humans the first time, as did Mizuchi. Poor Biloko could only rustle up fifty."

"But now he and Bael are best friends?"

"No. Bael is friends with nobody. Biloko bows to him and Bael lets him stay in his shadow." Anya chewed on her thumb. "I don't remember him saying anything about running into some magical humans."

"Maybe that's why he could only bring back fifty new demons? Maybe the talismans prevented him from finding more?"

She shrugged. "I would assume he would've said something. But then again, it was fifteen hundred years ago, and I can't remember every little conversation I had with everyone."

"So our best lead is to seek out one of Biloko's first spawn and see if they know anything about the talismans," Jack said, jotting the thought down on the hotel pad. "Any ideas on where to start there?"

"Just one problem with that idea," Anya said. "Any eloko that old would be close to their master. They'd give us up in a heartbeat."

"Wani didn't," Jack replied.

"That's because he's a kappa. They're greedy bastards and bribable. Bael dislikes them because he doesn't have absolute control. But the lilins and elokos are under his thumb because he knows how to work them. Bael will roll with Freyja about once a century, and he makes Biloko feel special. They'll do anything for him."

"Really?" Jack asked. Bael had treated the lilin demon pretty harshly. "You don't mind if Bael sleeps with someone else?"

Anya half-smiled. "Mind? He'd let me join in. Sex with a lilin is indescribable." She hesitated, as if she might've said something she hadn't meant to. Her voice was quieter, "I mean, Bael obviously was the best."

"Obviously," Jack said, resisting the urge to roll his eyes. Every half-hearted justification she gave for Bael just made him seem like more of a creep. "So back to this eloko problem. Maybe we could find a second to the old eloko? Someone who could get us in the door. Or maybe you could find an eloko in need of a favor."

"Still feels risky," she said. "Why don't we see what your ICDM has on the original eloko? Don't you have an archive in Charleston?"

Jack's eyebrows shot up. "Going to find an eloko is too risky, but breaking into Charleston is fine?"

"You don't think so?"

Jack swallowed. "Considering the whole damned agency is out looking for us?"

"Exactly. They won't think to look in their backyard. And you've got familiarity with the city. You know the places to hide."

"Sure, and we'll call my mom and get some low country boil going, too," Jack said sarcastically.

"I'm less concerned about your mother talking to Bael," Anya said.

"Are you? Weren't you the one who said Bael has spies in the Division? If we go to ICDM headquarters, it'll be hard for us to hide from him."

They stared at each other, Jack not wanting to back down and Anya seemingly feeling the same way. Finally, she averted her gaze and rose from the bed, walking to the window.

Jack grabbed Anya's laptop and logged in. He'd had his share of disagreements with Cam, but she was always swayed to his side when he presented her facts and reason. He felt Anya's gaze as he typed, searching the internet for talk about the original eloko demon.

And he struck gold.

"Hey, come look at this."

She clicked her tongue and crossed the room, looking over his shoulder.

"The Royal Museum for Central Africa is in Belgium, and it's reopening," he said, pointing to the news article about it. "They've got a few exhibits about early human-demon interactions. Maybe we'll find something about your talisman there?"

She pointed at the name of one of the sponsors. "He's a demon."

"How do you know?"

"I know. He's been around for centuries. Eloko."

"So…?"

She sniffed and folded her arms over her chest. "Do you want a cookie or something?"

"Acknowledgement that I'm not completely useless."

She opened her mouth, but a look of fear crossed her face. "We have to leave."

"What?"

"There's an athtar nearby. We have to go—*now*!"

Before Jack could even blink, two bags were in his hands,

and his body had been moved from the hotel room across the city. Anya slumped against him, her heart pounding so fast he could feel it against his skin.

"Um. What just happened?"

"If I felt him, he felt me." Her fear melted into rage. "And why the hell didn't we leave New Orleans after we dropped Parras off? Didn't I tell you—"

"Perhaps because you were dead to the world... *again*," Jack said. "Care to share what's going on with that?"

"How about I share this: when we make contact with a demon like Parras, it's generally a good idea to *get the hell out of the city.*"

"Duly noted," Jack said. "I'll just—"

She swooned, and he caught her before she hit the ground. Yet again, she'd overdone it. And yet again, Jack was left carrying a comatose woman and their bags down an interstate until he found a dinky hotel that wouldn't think twice about him doing so.

This time, Anya slept for two whole days, but Jack used the time to get more information about the museum exhibit, though he didn't find anything on Biloko's emergence other than the year and location where it happened. Charleston was an option, of course, but Jack's feelings on the city weren't the most reasonable. Hence why he decided not to share them with Anya.

On the third morning, Jack woke to the sound of typing on the keyboard.

"We need to get a car and get to Dallas," she said.

"Typically, people say 'good morning' when they've been asleep for two days," he said. "And also 'thank you for not leaving me in a ditch.'"

"You're welcome for not letting an athtar sever your head."

"Fair point," Jack said. "Do you think that was a coincidence or…"

"I think we stayed too fucking long in New Orleans," she said with a glare. "I told you. One slip-up."

Jack nodded. That had been close. "You said you felt him. What does that mean?"

"Athtars have a pretty potent miasma," she said. "When one's in range—a few hundred feet—it's easy to pick up. And once he knew I was there, he could get word back to Bael, and then…" She twisted her hand in the air. "You know."

"Yeah, I know," Jack said, standing and stretching. "Why are we going to Dallas?"

"So we can pick up our fake passports and plane tickets to Europe," she said softly. "Checking out your lead in Brussels. I read the rest of what you found, too."

"Glad you found it helpful." His stomach grumbled. "There's a Waffle House next door if you're hungry. I can bring something back for you."

She paused. "Eggs and hash browns. And…coffee, I guess. And toast. And maybe some sausage." Another brief pause. "Three eggs. Large coffee."

He nodded, hoping he could remember all that, and went

for the door. It wasn't until he was halfway across the street that he realized it was the first time she'd actually given him an answer when he asked if she was hungry.

To get to Dallas, they stole another car. Their passports and tickets were waiting in a lockbox at a bank, and Jack was given a new name—Richard Gibbs. Anya was his wife, Emily. They were from Houston. The photo of Jack was the same as from his Division ID badge. Whoever her hackers were, they were good at their jobs.

With little fuss, they boarded the plane. Anya fidgeted as they sat on the tarmac. Finally, about an hour into the flight, she stood and walked to the back of the plane. Jack twisted in his seat, watching her look at every person on the plane before returning to her seat.

"No demons on board," she whispered to Jack.

"Except you."

She actually cracked a half-smile. "I wouldn't call myself a demon anymore."

Jack begged to differ, but, perhaps, she really was a sliver of the athtar she used to be. "Were you really concerned about that?"

"Concerned enough," she said, glancing behind her. "I don't like flying if I can help it."

"Why? Afraid of heights?"

"Limited escape routes." She sank back into her cushion and yawned. "Look, I'm...sorry for being short with you lately. I do appreciate you looking out for me while I'm not well."

"And is this a common occurrence, the passing out?" Jack asked. "I've noticed it happens after you use your magic."

"It's the curse."

"Mm-hm." Jack wasn't convinced of that. If it were just the curse, then she would've been dead in a ditch a long time ago, running by herself. "It's a long flight. At least you can get some rest."

Anya did just that, settling in and finally losing that crease between her brows. Her head drooped toward him and he allowed it to rest lightly on his shoulder, especially as she adjusted herself to curl next to him. She'd probably wake up and bark at him, with some snooty remark about him trying to cop a feel. But for now, it was nice to know that she trusted him subconsciously.

"Folks, this is your captain speaking. We're about to hit a rough patch of air in the skies near Atlanta, so please fasten your seatbelts."

Jack searched the skyline for anything familiar and saw it immediately. Not so much the black hole separating this world and the demon one, but the aura turning the sky a bloody shade of red.

He felt a pang of...something. Not homesickness or nostalgia, but something unpleasant. That city had been a disastrous start of a new life—one that he was now sure he was abandoning. He'd tried so hard to be the man he used to be, but he wasn't that man anymore. He was someone new, someone who stole cars and used fake passports to fly to Belgium.

Someone who helped an athtar save gay teens' lives in exchange for money to hide from her ex-boyfriend. Someone who was strangely fine with giving up his career for the wild unknown.

Anya jerked and was wide-eyed awake. "Where…?"

"On the plane," Jack said, patting her hand. "Go back to sleep."

She wiped her face, probably finding the drool on her lips, and nodded, turning to the window and resting her head there.

Well, it was good while it lasted, Jack thought.

CHAPTER ELEVEN

As she wiped another bug off her face, Cam decided she was just about done with Louisiana.

She was a passenger on an airboat, gliding over the swamps of Louisiana on her way to a two-thousand-year-old kappa who didn't have the courtesy to live anywhere she could drive to. Her pilot, a Cajun who spoke with a thick accent, came highly recommended by the New Orleans office. She wasn't convinced they weren't playing a trick on her, but he seemed to know where he was going.

Which was more than Cam could say for herself. She'd already packed her bags and as soon as she washed the mosquitos and flies off her face, she was heading back to Atlanta.

As per Kim's direction, Cam had gone out to the lilin bar where several demons had been beheaded. And not just any demons—big demons with heads the size of tree trunks. Sort of like the other lilin demons La Colibrí had decapitated when they'd all first met.

The lilins hadn't talked—not to Cam and not to the New Orleans office. Nobody else had been around to give a deposition either. The local office had determined it was a pure intrademonic dispute, probably between warring factions of lilins, and all but closed the case.

Another fat bug smacked into her forehead, and she wiped it off with a grimace. There was a really good chance she would end up with nothing except a new collection of mosquito-borne diseases.

So why, she asked herself for the millionth time, was she so determined to find someone who didn't want to be found?

Because Sara, the voice that sounded an awful lot like her mother's replied.

Cam had seen Jack in the hours after he'd found Sara's body, and had known he was in for a long recovery. So, kneeling in front of her closed casket, Cam had promised to take care of him.

Cam had thought a lot about that promise in the past few days. Sara might've agreed that Jack had lost his mind, and that Cam should let him go. But that felt harder than letting go of her sister. She lay awake at night and asked herself why, hoping if she found the answer, she'd find the solution.

Maybe some of the incessant need to find Jack was about this new, terrifying idea that he might've found love again. As much as Cam had pushed him to move on, maybe she wasn't ready to lose her partner to another woman.

Especially one who wasn't entirely human.

But she'd also asked herself if her jealousy was rooted in romantic love. It was a question she often pondered, usually when she was fresh off a break-up and second-guessing every romantic decision she'd ever made. Eventually, she always came back to the same conclusion. She and Jack had a unique friendship that was somehow deeper than a romantic love, but when it came to romance itself, there was nothing there.

Which brought Cam back to the question of why she was pursuing him like a woman in love.

It wasn't as if she didn't have other things to worry about. She could've been halfway around the world in Shanghai, taking advantage of a fellowship at the Weapons Institute. She could've been back at work, helping to mitigate the issues from the ongoing Demon Spring. She could've even been back in Charleston with Frank.

As the airboat slowed, Cam decided her pursuit of Jack was merely her inability to let anything go. And that would be the explanation until she decided otherwise.

Cam thanked the man, asked him to hang around with a twenty-dollar bill, and climbed off the airboat. Prepared as she was in thick rubber boots and doused in bug spray, Cam was still miserably uncomfortable as she trudged through muck and slime to get to the lights ahead. She kept her kappa talisman against her palm, just in case, but with the smell of DDT and the press of humidity against her skin, she was pretty sure annoyance would keep the kappa magic at bay.

Although it was a little strange that she didn't feel even a *hint* of magic. Especially from an old demon like Wani, the air should've been thick with it.

One step inside his house told her why.

Wani was dead. Decapitated.

As was every other demon in his house.

Cam wasn't a stranger to carnage, but two things struck her as odd. First: Wani would've presumably been the first to snuff it, thus rendering all his spawn (and Cam assumed these others were his spawn) as human. So why go to the trouble of killing them?

The second was more ominous than odd: These kills were clean and quick, like the third of Nunzia's Colibrí had killed without blinking an eye—or like Bael killing Nunzia herself.

Cam reached for her phone and dialed Kim.

"What?"

"Wani's dead," Cam said. "Along with everyone in his little den here."

The silence stretched out for a while, and Cam was almost afraid they'd been disconnected. Finally, Kim spoke again. "Was it her?"

Cam turned away from the scene, unable to look at it anymore. "I have no idea. But the lilin den…it was also decapitation. I think only an athtar could do that."

"So she's back to killing, then? So much for the curse."

"No," Cam said with a shake of her head. "Jack wouldn't

have let her do this—curse or no. Wani had no enemies. He's lived here in the swamps since the Louisiana Purchase and not one demon lord has anything bad to say about him. So why now?"

"Because there's an athtar named Anat wandering around who's decapitating demons," Kim drawled.

"I told you, Jack wouldn't let her do this."

"Jack's not thinking clearly, obviously."

"He's thinking clearly enough," Cam said, with a bit more confidence.

"Then perhaps you should accept the fact that he might not be with her willingly." Kim sighed loudly. "I was going to wait until you came back, but I might as well tell you now. We're putting out an official ICDM-wide bulletin on them. It's clear they don't want to be found, and when we're fighting an athtar, we have to use every tool available. The only way we can get eyes on this is if we get the public involved."

"The public and every demon lord on the planet," Cam said. "Bael's already got a bounty on their heads. Whoever brings them to him gets a city."

"Then we'd better hope the Division gets to them before he does."

"Well, holy shit, Kim. If we find him, are we arresting him, too?" Cam asked, staring at the sky for some sort of guidance.

The pause on the other end didn't give Cam a warm fuzzy. "Let's find him first, and then make that determination. I assume his grandfather will pull some strings to give him a level of immunity. And, of course, I'm sure he was traumatized from the Underworld trip. There are ways we can lessen the heat on him, depending on what trouble he gets into."

She could scarcely believe what Kim was saying. "You're talking like you've already built a case against him."

"The case has built itself, Cam. Between the lilin bar fiasco, and now Wani, grand theft auto—"

"Hey, that car was returned."

"Not to mention aiding and abetting a wanted demon—"

"Wanted by whom?" Cam said. "The Division has no issue with Colibrí."

"Like I said, let's just focus on finding him. Then we'll talk about…whatever case we may or may not have against him."

Cam pinched the bridge of her nose, unable to come up with a biting retort that would convince Kim (and herself) that Kim was wrong. Instead, she just sighed deeply. "Do you want to inform the New Orleans office about Wani, or should I?"

"I'll do it. Get back to Atlanta. It's clear Anat is back to her old tricks. If I were you, I'd stay out of the line of fire so you don't end up like Wani."

CHAPTER TWELVE

When the plane touched down at Heathrow Airport, Jack felt like a zombie. He'd caught minutes of sleep here and there, but hadn't really been able to rest. Anya, on the other hand, looked wide awake and ready to get off the plane.

Jack had hoped they could stop and get food, but Anya was already five steps ahead—bypassing the food court entirely and heading straight for the exits.

"Where are you going?" Jack asked, looking at his tickets—then blinked. "Why do these say we're going to Zurich?"

She didn't stop or answer him, so he supposed the answer was no. "So you bought plane tickets to the wrong place. We had fake IDs. What's the big deal?"

"What if my tech guy has been compromised?" Anya said with a glare over her shoulder. "Bael could be waiting for us."

Jack stopped, considered what she'd said, then followed. "So you don't even trust your tech guy?"

"I trust no one."

Including Jack, who decided just to follow instead of asking where she was leading him. He had a feeling, especially when they took the tube from Heathrow to St. Pancras, that she wouldn't tell him anyway. Once there, she headed toward the Eurostar lines, and Jack went in search of food. If she left without him, well, so be it. He was hungry.

He bought a large coffee and a few pieces of fruit to tide him over on the train ride he supposed they were about to take. The front page of the international newspapers all depicted the scenes in Atlanta, including a very striking photo of Bael staring him down. They'd cut it close in New Orleans with that athtar, but how many of those close calls were they going to get?

Perhaps he should stop criticizing her paranoid tendencies.

"*There* you are," came the object of his thoughts. "You're dawdling. We're going to miss our train."

"Okay then," Jack said, tearing off a large bite of an apple and following Anya. She remained unsettled and nervous, even when they found their seats in a mostly empty car.

Jack ignored her fidgeting and sipped his coffee. "Where's this train going to?"

"Can we leave already?" she said, glancing over her shoulder.

"Did you see something back there?" he asked. "Or were you just afraid to tell the ticket kiosk where we're going?"

"I'm wondering if I should throw you off this train," Anya snapped. "Do you think this is a game? Do you think—"

"Calm down," Jack said, holding his hands up in surrender. "I was just giving you a hard time."

"My time is hard enough."

"Here," Jack said, reaching into the bag and handing her one of his apples. "Peace offering. You haven't eaten in a while. You need to keep your strength up."

She took the fruit but didn't eat it.

"I get why you're paranoid," he said. "Did you see something back there that spooked you?"

"No," she said softly, running her fingernails along the edge of the skin. "But...doesn't mean I won't. It'll be better when we're moving."

Move they did, although it took another fifteen minutes to get there. She finally settled once the train was up to speed, although the dark cloud remained on her face. It was a few minutes more before she finally began to eat.

After a moment, the crease in her brow softened. "Thank you for the food, and...I'm sorry for snapping."

"It's really all right," Jack said, leaning back in the chair.

"You can't blame me for being a little cautious."

Jack tilted his head. "Cautious is one thing. Have you really lived your whole life fleeing from city to city?"

"No, not really. Before, I was fairly sure Bael thought I was dead," Anya said. "And so it was important to fly under the radar so nobody learned otherwise. But now? Well, you heard them. The demons are hunting for me so Bael will give them an entire city. Flying under the radar isn't enough anymore." She shivered. "And now that the athtars are wandering around, it makes it more dangerous than ever. They can move a lot faster."

"Would any of them be our allies?" Jack asked.

She barked a laugh. "Not a chance. To my face, I was revered. Idolized. I had scores of young athtars who worshipped the ground I walked on. But Bael likes to pit his seconds against each other—not hard to do considering they're all ambitious little weasels. So if they have a chance to take me out, they will."

"You were considered a second?" Jack asked.

"To them, I was," she said, looking out the window. "To Bael, I was his lady. That's why I'm a bigger target." She quieted, staring out the window in pensive thought.

"So what's it like?" Jack asked.

"What?"

"Living for thousands of years."

Anya tore her gaze away from the apple and looked perplexed. "I don't really understand the question. What's it like living every day for you?"

"I mean, for me, I have some idea that I'm going to die in fifty, sixty years. Seventy if I'm lucky. Since I was a kid, the world's gone through major technological advancements. Internet, computers, all of that came in my lifetime. But you… Man. You've seen civilizations rise and fall."

"I spent most of my time in the Underworld," she said. "When Bael would let me loose up here, things had changed. But we usually arrived in a different city, and I didn't care what the humans were doing."

"What about since you've been up here?"

"Why are you so interested?" she snapped.

"Because I think it's fascinating," he said, sitting back.

"The days run together," she said. "Centuries pass in seconds, but...big moments stand out." Sadness crept into her voice, piquing Jack's curiosity. But she said no more, and that was the end of it.

Their arrival in Paris only lasted as long as it took them to transfer from one train to another. Then they were back zooming through the French countryside. When the conductor stopped by to check their tickets, Anya spoke in what seemed to be perfect French, which begged another question.

"Were the demons speaking English for my benefit?" Jack asked.

"What?"

"When I was in the Underworld, how did I understand them?"

"I suppose we sort of slip into different human languages without knowing," Anya said with a frown. "Or maybe they took their cue from Bael. I don't...I guess I don't notice when I start speaking another language."

"How many do you speak?"

"All of them," she said. "I mean, I've been around a long time. The new demons that flooded the Underworld after every Demon Spring would always come with different languages. One of the, well...benefits of creating more demons is you pick up some of their knowledge."

More information Jack's Academy education hadn't given him. "So, in the Underworld, when Bael was talking to the belus in English?"

"Probably just putting on a show for your benefit," Anya replied. "He likes to do that, you know. Show off to new demons. He'd throw a huge party at the end of Demon Spring, inviting all the neophytes to his castle. It would last for weeks—months sometimes."

"All in pursuit of making them love him," Jack noted quietly.

"Yeah." She looked out the window, seemingly eager to change the subject. "You know, the world really has changed."

"Hm?"

"I guess I never really stopped to think about it before you asked. I came to Paris once, in maybe the mid-fifteenth century." They passed by a solar farm and the corners of her mouth quirked up. "Hygiene was a wonderful invention. Or re-invention."

"What was the best city you've visited?" he asked.

Her smile disappeared, replaced by a look of guilt. "My definition of best was twisted for a long time."

Jack sat back, a little disappointed. "Fine, maybe not best. But there has to be something non-violent that stuck with you."

She was quiet for a long time. Then she turned to him with a light in her eyes. "Shanghai."

"Shanghai?" Jack said, almost falling off his seat. "As in,

Shanghai where demons killed thousands of people?"

"Yes, but not… not because of that. Well, partially." She squinted out the window, as they passed by a quaint village. "The humans had crafted these weapons, beautiful things that were beyond anything I'd seen in the Underworld."

"That's amazing," Jack said. "That battle—those weapons, we learned about them in the Academy. A whole semester dedicated to Chinese weaponry and history. And you were *there*."

"I mean…" She looked at her hands. "I was responsible for a lot of the slaughter. But it was…I suppose it was nice to see a bit of fight from the humans."

"We're scrappy things when we want to be," Jack said with a laugh. "You know, if we ever get out of this mess, you'll have to tell Cam you were there."

Guilt gnawed at him. Cam should've been on her way to Shanghai on a weapons fellowship. Instead she was probably… who knew where.

"What?" Anya asked. "Do you miss your partner?"

"Yes, but…it's more that she's putting aside her own life—again—to clean up my fuckups."

"You think this is a fuckup?" For a split second, Jack thought he saw a flash of hurt on her face, but it was gone before he could be sure.

"No, but I'm sure Cam does," he replied, after a moment. "She never really liked you."

"I'm sorry you can't communicate with her," she said,

picking at the seat cushion. "I know it's hard."

"I think the longest we've ever gone without speaking is two weeks," Jack said. "And that's when Sara and I had our first fight." He chuckled. "Sara and I made up after four hours."

"So why was Cam still mad with you?"

"She was trying to show solidarity for her sister," Jack said. "Blood being thicker and all that. Made working together incredibly difficult. I've still got all Cam's passive aggressive notes saved on my computer."

She nodded, staring out the window. "And you think she thinks you're making a mistake."

Jack honestly didn't know the answer to that question. "Cam's always been a big believer in gut feelings. She used to tell me that if I thought something was right, it usually was."

Anya stared at him a long time, then said quietly, "Your partner was being targeted by a lilin when I saw her."

He jumped. "I'm sorry, what?"

"Back in New Orleans, when I saw her. A lilin came by to try to get information out of her," Anya said, wrenching her gaze downward. "I was…well, I thought about stepping in to help. After all, it was clear her defenses were down. She was tired. But she handled it."

He smiled, but it was tempered by the knowledge that Cam was killing herself on his behalf. "She does that. Thanks for checking up on her."

She abruptly stood and retrieved her laptop from the bag, sitting back down and logging in. Perhaps the conversation was getting a little too personal for her comfort.

"What should I do tomorrow?"

She paused, her eyes growing wide and then narrowing. "Stay out of sight."

"Why?"

She flipped her laptop around, showing Jack a photo of himself on a US Division bulletin. He was now a person of interest, and anyone with information on his whereabouts was directed to contact their local Division office.

"Son of a bitch," Jack said, pulling the laptop to himself to look at it. "What the hell am I wanted for?"

"Aiding a fugitive, grand theft auto, and wanted for questioning in several Division cases," she said with a shake of her head. "It appears your partner has lost control of the investigation, if they're putting out an alert for you. We'll just need to be careful. My hope is we'll be in and out of there before anyone even knows we're here. It's a good thing nobody's seen us already."

But Jack stared at the photo, unwilling to believe that this was actually happening. Sure, he'd left the Division. Sure, he was AWOL. Sure, he'd done a few extrajudicial things. But to see his face on a wanted poster, to see the list of crimes listed like he was a common criminal, was like waking up from one nightmare into a worse one.

"Do you still think this is the right thing?" she asked softly. "In your gut?"

He handed the computer back to her. "Yeah. I do."

CHAPTER THIRTEEN

They'd arrived after midnight in Brussels. Jack barely remembered lumbering to their hostel and falling asleep. The next morning, Anya had left a plate of bread and cheese, as well as a carafe of coffee. Jack helped himself to all of it, finding no note from his partner, but sensing the breakfast was message enough.

Almost as soon as he'd finished the spread, she appeared in the middle of the room, sounding winded.

"We have a lot to talk about."

"Good morning," Jack said emphatically. One day she *would* say it. "Thanks for the breakfast."

"I tried to wake you, but you were unresponsive," she said sharply. Maybe the breakfast was a fluke.

"Yeah, I suppose time changes aren't much of a problem to athtar demons," Jack said, taking another bite of the bread.

"What'd you find?"

"The Royal Museum for Central Africa is about twelve miles as the crow flies, but the city is already teeming with elokos. They're all here with their demon lord, Adelbert. He was a wealthy man when he was turned and now he's had a few hundred years to let his riches accumulate. He may not be powerful in the demonic sense, but that money makes up for it. He donated all the artifacts."

"And that doesn't strike you as odd? Why did a demon keep artifacts from the first eloko emergence?"

"I'm sure as a trophy," Anya said. "Some demons like to collect trinkets of their lineage."

"But why give them to the humans at all?"

"Adelbert probably got a tax break or something from the local government." Anya paused. "Or something more illegal."

"Is he allied with Bael?" Jack asked.

"His maker was killed in a Demon Spring a few hundred years ago, though, obviously, Adelbert was strong enough to soldier on without him," Anya said. "Those without a direct link to Biloko tend to be a bit more independent, but I still don't want to take any chances. The city's already on edge. Brussels is a lilin city, and they don't like having all of the elokos here."

"Yeah, that seems like a horrible idea," Jack said, sitting up. "A bunch of elokos in a lilin town? Surprised they haven't burned the place to the ground."

"I'm sure Bael has a lot to do with it. No one wants a repeat of what happened in Atlanta, with demon lords getting beheaded."

"What does that mean for us?"

"It means we'll have to be careful." Anya stood and handed him a flyer from her back pocket. "The museum opens in two days, and they're throwing a grand reception gala. I think that's the best time to get a close look at the artifacts."

"Couldn't we go in at night?" Jack asked. "Or can't you use your magic to—"

"No," she said with a shake of her head. "I don't want to use magic unless absolutely necessary." She rubbed her face. "I know you think it's this panacea that can fix all our problems—"

"I don't," Jack said, gently. "I'm just trying to mitigate our risk."

"And I'm telling you *this* is the lowest risk," she said. "The gala will be invite only to patrons of the museum. Security will be low, and there will be plenty of rich humans amongst the demons. The most I'll have to do is find a pair of invites and we can use glamour for the rest."

"Oh."

"This may surprise you, but this isn't my first time doing this sort of thing," Anya said with a haughty look. "And considering your track record thus far, I would suggest spending a little less time second-guessing my plans and a little more time making sure you're ready in case things *do* go wrong."

Chastened, Jack simply nodded. "What can I do to help?"

"We'll need formal clothes. I don't want to waste lilin glamour on clothes. It's a formal event, so make sure you don't buy something cheap." She tossed a wad of bills on the bed. "Use that."

"Oh, uh…" Jack picked it up and counted, as his face grew warm. "Shouldn't you go get your own dress?"

Anya stopped and turned to him, a dangerous look on her face. "Why? Because I'm a woman?"

"No, because you speak French," Jack said with a wince. "And I don't know your measurements. And trust me, I know not to guess about sizes. One time, I was out shopping with Sara, and she grabbed a dress that was mislabeled two sizes smaller. She was so upset and—"

The words died on his throat as Anya crossed the room. Bending at the waist, she lowered her head until it was mere inches from his. Was she going to toss him out the window this time?

"I will fit into the smallest dress," she said quietly. "And my ego is not as fragile as your late wife's. No offense intended." She paused and straightened. "I need you to get the outfits because I have to find invitations to steal."

"F-fine," Jack said, sliding out from beneath her gaze. "I'll be back in a bit."

He was halfway to the door when he slowed, realizing the mention of Sara hadn't come with an accompanying twist of the knife in his chest. It was a small victory, although it had presumably only happened because Anya was laying into him.

"What is it now?" Anya drawled.

"Nothing," Jack said, closing the door behind him.

It took him most of the day, but Jack was able to find outfits for the two of them. Most of the difficulty was him not speaking the language, but he also took his time returning. His patience with Anya's attitude was running thin. Sure, she was under a lot of stress, but that didn't mean she could be an asshole to him all day. And the small flashes of progress weren't coming quickly enough to endear her to him.

Beyond that, it was painfully obvious Jack wasn't offering anything useful on this journey, except to make sure she wasn't dead after she used magic. But she'd been taking care of herself for over a hundred and thirty years without him.

Neither of them spoke when Jack returned with the outfits. Anya snatched hers and disappeared into the bathroom, and Jack laid his out on the bed, untying and unbuttoning each of the pieces.

The monotony drew him back to the last time he'd worn such an outfit, at his wedding. He wasn't a fan of suits in general —too confining. Since Sara had nixed a beach wedding with flip-flops and Florida shirts, and his mother had insisted on a formal event (even though it was held in his own backyard), tuxedo it was.

Cam and Sara, of course, had reminded him that Spanx were far more constricting than a tuxedo, and said he should shut his trap before they strangled him with theirs.

This memory, unlike the one earlier in the day, came with that familiar squeezing in his chest. It was almost a relief, a reminder that Sara remained firmly in the back of his mind even as Anya took up most of the front. And at the same time, it was disappointing that he hadn't made as much progress as he'd thought.

Anya emerged from the bathroom, dressed in the gold gown Jack had found. Her now bottle-blond hair hung against her alabaster skin. The only recognizable feature was her scowl and the way she barked orders.

"Are you daydreaming?" Anya asked, motioning to her open hands. "Come here and let me put this on you. I don't have much left, and Freyja doesn't exactly make house calls."

"Wish she did," Jack said, dully. "I've had so much lilin magic on my body, I should just sleep with one and get it over with."

"Be careful what you ask for. Most humans who sleep with powerful lilins get so obsessed with them, they either turn into a demon themselves or waste away. Sleeping with the belu?" She tutted. "You might be ruined for any other woman."

"I might be ruined anyway," he said without thinking.

"What does that mean?"

"Means…" He sighed. "Means that I've pretty much given up on finding someone else. Sara was my true love. You don't get two of those."

"There's no such thing as true love," Anya said. "Love is attachment, that's it. You've formed a bond with someone, they form the same bond with you, and that's that. Bonds break and are reformed with someone else."

"That's how you feel about Bael?" Jack asked.

She flinched. "It's different between demon and maker."

"But you've almost surpassed demon and maker, haven't you?" Jack asked. "I mean, you're nearly as old as he is."

"He's got a few thousand years on me."

Silence stretched out between them as they fell into their respective minds. Anya smeared the glamour over his face, but this time, the stirrings of lust seemed out of place—muted almost.

"Huh," Anya said, stepping back from him. "You aren't trying to kiss me. What's wrong?"

"Just don't feel like it," Jack said with a half-hearted shrug. "We should get going. The gala's going to start soon."

If he was feeling better, he might've found victory in the look on her face. But he just couldn't bring himself to it.

Jack wasn't exactly sure what to expect from a demon-funded museum gala, but the first thing he noticed was the extreme *lack* of demonic miasma. Even without his talismans, he didn't feel the tingling across his skin or hear any bells clanging. The museum was lit up, revealing turrets and stone columns graced with large banners showcasing the most valuable of its artifacts.

"Are there any demons in there?" Jack asked under his breath.

"What do you mean?"

"I don't feel any miasma. Where are the demons?"

She half-smiled. "Demons can rein it in if they want to. In this case, I'd wager the humans who own the museum have made a deal with the eloko lord. No miasma, no coercion. That's not to say it won't happen after hours."

"Why would a demon agree to that?"

"Because this demon runs on money, and that's something the humans can promise," she replied, linking her arm with his. "Quit asking stupid questions and let's find these artifacts. I don't want to be here longer than we have to."

Anya had been right about one thing: the security was incredibly lax. Attendees could walk right up to the artifacts and touch them if they pleased, with security guards posted at the front doors only. Presumably, those in attendance had effectively paid for the artifacts in donations, so there was little to worry about.

He and Anya made a show of smiling and nodding to others, while Anya kept an eye on the pieces they passed. On occasion, she'd pause and point out something, and they'd make a show of discussing the origins while Anya bent down for a closer look. When another group was nearby, Jack would engage with them, keeping conversations light and introductions nonexistent.

"Oh yes, we're big fans of history," he said to a couple from Brazil who'd stopped to chat. "My wife is taking a sabbatical to research some of the old kappa documents in Japan. We're on our way back to visit the parents and just *had* to stop in."

They nodded and walked away, and Anya tugged at his arm. "They think you're full of shit."

"So little you know about rich Academy kids," Jack said with a bit of a chuckle. "Those who graduate and don't actually want to work take their little trips to study obscure topics on their parents' dimes. That story about kappas? Friend of mine is doing just that."

Anya relinquished his sleeve. "Humans are ridiculous."

"Rich ones are, anyway," Jack said.

A nearby group of patrons turned. Among them was an older Mexican woman wearing a conservative black dress, her black hair streaked with gray balled at the base of her neck. A flash of recognition crossed Jack's mind—followed by panic.

"Holy shit," Jack said, quickly turning Anya the other way.

"What?" she said, glancing behind her.

"That's Cam's *great aunt*," Jack said, his heart hammering in his chest as he snuck another look to make sure he hadn't been seen. "Councilwoman García. And she's with the councilman from Europe."

"You're unrecognizable," Anya deadpanned.

That was true, but it didn't lesson the shock of seeing her. "Why's she here?"

"It's a museum opening about demons," Anya replied, as if none of this were surprising to her. "I'd be more surprised if there *weren't* members of ICDM here."

Members of ICDM were one thing, but the Council of Fifteen was quite another matter. Frank was invited to thousands of events all over the United States and Canada—his jurisdiction —but it was rare for him to actually show up. Rarer still for him to go somewhere outside of his purview. María was the Councilwoman from Mexico and Central America, so what was she doing in Brussels?

"She won't recognize you," Anya repeated, tugging at his arm. "Unless she has one of those talismans."

"N-no," Jack said with a small shake of his head. "She's very anti-anything not found in official ICDM protocols."

"I can certainly get that from her attire," Anya said, giving her a once-over. "I doubt her presence is anything to be concerned about. Let's not get distracted."

It was hard to walk around the room with María in plain view, but Anya was right—with his blond hair and green eyes, there was no way she'd recognize him.

"There," Anya said, pointing to a case titled 'early weaponry.' "We might find something there."

As casually as they could, Jack and Anya maneuvered to the exhibit, pretending to be interested in a piece on early pottery before moving on. This section of the exhibit hall was mostly empty, so while there was no one to talk to, there was also no one to observe them, save one security guard, who'd wandered in to watch them.

"Make it quick," Jack said, feeling like the eyes of the guard were on them, and not liking that at all.

"Oh, you know how I get with early weaponry," Anya said with an uncharacteristic giggle. She grabbed his shirt collar and pulled him close. "If you're a good boy, maybe I'll give you a present in the taxi home."

That turned off the security guard, who pressed his finger to his ear and turned away.

"Nice work," Jack whispered.

Anya didn't acknowledge the compliment, using the time given by the guard's inattention to scan each of the artifacts. Jack followed, albeit more slowly while watching for the guard to come back.

"There's nothing here," Anya said after a moment. "Nothing about talismans, nothing about magical humans. Nothing. The humans don't even have *weapons* in these drawings."

As much as he didn't want to admit it, Anya was right. Save a consistent pattern of humans with upside-down shields approaching what was clearly Biloko, there was nothing of interest on any of the vases.

"Well, look there," Jack said, pointing to an empty spot in the back. "It says those pieces are on loan to ICDM World Headquarters for refurbishment."

"I thought you were diametrically opposed to going to ICDM headquarters," Anya drawled with a hand on her hip.

"Geneva is different than Charleston."

"How so?"

The air changed, and the hair on Jack's neck stood up as he felt a presence behind them. Anya licked her lips as she stared over his shoulder. Jack spun to see the security guard with a sharply-dressed eloko wearing a curious smile.

"Excuse me, Lord Adelbert has asked for a private audience."

CHAPTER FOURTEEN

Conscious that they both still wore lilin glamour, and careful not to look guilty, Jack followed Anya and the eloko away from the soiree and toward the back of the museum. She seemed oddly resigned to their fate—curious, as she could use magic to transport both her and Jack to safety. What could she be waiting for?

They were deposited in an office—perhaps the museum curator's, judging by the number of books and papers on the desk. The door slammed behind them.

"So...are we gonna make a break for it?" he asked.

Anya swallowed, looking nervous for the first time ever. "I... can't."

"What do you mean *can't*?" Jack asked.

"I mean..." She closed her eyes. "My magic, it's still not recovered from when we left Atlanta. Or Mobile. Or any of the other times. And I feel… I'm afraid if I use it right now, it might kill me."

Jack's mouth fell open. "You decided to tell me this *now*?"

"Well," she said, defensively, "I don't know, why haven't you noticed that something's wrong? I've been passing out after I use it!"

"How was I supposed to know that's a *new* thing?" he said. "I have no idea what your magic does or doesn't do. You don't *tell* me anything except to get on my case about shit." His eyes narrowed. "This has nothing to do with the talisman bullet or the curse, does it?"

She sighed heavily. "The only way I'll truly recover is if I return to Ath-kur. Athtar's land."

"So, you lied to me."

"I didn't *lie* per se," she said, wincing a little. "The curse is preventing me from going back to Ath-kur, which—"

"You know what, save it," Jack said, sitting back. "It's clear you still don't trust me, after all we've been through. After everything I've *given up* to help you."

"So?" Anya said, crossing her arms. "Go back to Atlanta and your partner. I don't need your help."

"Amazing how far you've fallen, Lady Anat. Partnering with a human?"

Jack froze, but Anya's face steeled as they turned to look behind them. Adelbert was something of a silver fox, with thick lips and blue eyes, complemented by his tightly fitting suit and Italian leather shoes. As he passed, Jack heard a faint bell clanging.

"How did you know who I am?" Anya asked, her voice filled with a strength Jack knew she didn't possess.

"It was odd to see my friend Medhi and his wife not only grow fifty years younger, but also Caucasian and blond," he said, casually taking a seat at the desk as if he owned it.

Jack caught the smallest of grimaces from Anya; she must not have even checked the names on the invitations. Then again, Jack hadn't either. Infiltration 101 right there.

"At first I thought it a lilin trick from Lord Maes. He's been most upset about the influx of elokos into his territory. But that would be odd, considering he gave me his word there would be no trouble, and one of his seconds as insurance."

"And you trust a lilin?" Anya said.

"The more likely scenario," Adelbert continued with a sly smile, "is that Lady Anat and her human servant were looking for information about elokos and their origins. And what better place to find that information than among my artifacts?"

"Who said we were looking for elokos?" Anya asked with a low, deadly purr. "Was it that son of a bitch Parras?"

"Parras?" Adelbert chuckled, as if the idea were absurd. "I daresay he's got his hands full with his brand-new kingdom. He's a child. He'll be dead as soon as the schism is closed."

"Then who?" Jack asked.

"The grapevine was rather long, but I believe the source was the kappa named Wani."

Jack's mouth fell open, and Anya sucked in a breath. "I don't believe it," she said. "Wani gave me his *word*."

"And *you* trust a kappa?" Adelbert replied with a saccharine smile. "They are loyal only to the highest bidder. And I daresay King Bael has more gold than you do."

Anya licked her lips, processing this information.

"There are rumors that you are not the fearsome creature you used to be," Adelbert said, turning his head to the side. "But to rely on lilin glamour to hide yourself? Bael will see right through it."

"Lucky for me there are a few thousand miles between us," Anya replied.

"More, I'd say, as your king has returned to his castle in the Underworld," he said. "There's quite a bounty on your head, my lady. Bael promises an entire country to any demon who brings you to him."

"Oh? Yesterday it was a city," she said, leaning back.

"City, country, whatever it is will be quite worth the trouble," he said. "Especially since you haven't moved to draw your weapons."

"What interests me more is why *you* haven't drawn a weapon, and why Bael remains in the Underworld." She tilted her head to the side with a quirked brow.

"I am quite content with my standing," he said. "My children are well-kept and have plenty of humans to pick from. I don't wish to draw the attention of Bael needlessly, but I will, should you fail." He tutted. "Although there might not be anything left of you to pick up."

"I'm growing impatient. Tell me what it is you want."

Adelbert bristled. "There's a councilman in attendance tonight. Fischer. I want you to get rid of him."

Jack started, but Anya showed no sign of emotion. "Why?"

"That's my business."

"Unfortunately, if you wish me to kill him, it's now my business," she offered casually. "That's the way it goes."

"Is it? Will Bael agree?" Adelbert asked with the same level of casual indifference.

"I think Bael will agree that it was *most unfortunate* of you to ask his lady to accomplish a task so easily done by one of your minions," she said, slipping into the voice she'd adopted with Bael. "He's quite particular about how and when I use my sword. He might have me use it on you."

The voice worked; Adelbert looked a shade less confident. "The councilman has instituted a series of regulations that will adversely affect some of the institutions we've come to rely on in Belgium. He's refusing to moderate his position. I'd like a different person in charge."

"You do realize they're just going to replace him with someone even worse," Jack said.

Adelbert turned to him, sizing him up for a moment. In the distance, Jack heard the clanging of bells, but he was too annoyed to be swayed.

"I agree with the human," Anya said. "If your goal is to get ICDM off your back, you'd be better suited doing it the old-fashioned way."

"My dear lady, this *is* the old-fashioned way." He templed his fingers together and pressed them to his chin. "Fine, I shall leave the particular methods of persuasion up to you. If you succeed in helping me change ICDM policy, I will let you walk free and not tell a soul you were in this city."

"How can I be sure that souls in your employ won't tell?" she asked.

"They believe you are a pair of wayward lilins who were encroaching," he said. "You may question them yourselves to see what they think. But if you decline my offer..." He lifted his cellphone to his ear. "I will have your king here in an instant. And if what I overheard is to be believed, I doubt even you could get away in time."

Anya was quiet for a long time. Was she actually considering killing the man? *Could* she kill him?

"I will need a weapon."

Jack's heart fell.

"You may have your pick," Adelbert said, standing with a smile. "But as insurance, I will keep your human with me."

She looked at Jack without any sort of familiarity. They might as well have been strangers. "Fine with me."

Jack had no idea if Anya was concocting a plan or if she was truly planning on killing the European councilman. Either way, he was in no position to stop it. Adelbert and Anya left him in the office, and a few eloko henchman came in to retrieve Jack.

"Get up, lilin," Rightie said, grabbing Jack by the arm. They must've thought him a neophyte, or at the very least, didn't think much of lust demons.

Jack went along peacefully, biding his time until he found an opening to make his move. The elokos wore no weapons except their size. And still, he was useless. Yet again.

He was getting pretty damned tired of that moniker.

He was Jack Fucking Grenard. He could trace his demon-hunting lineage all the way back to the eleventh century. He'd graduated magna cum laude from the internationally-recognized Academy for Demon Management. He'd tussled with some of the most fearsome demons in D.C. *and* Atlanta. Sure, he was without his knives, but he could improvise.

He *would* improvise. Because Cam would never forgive him if he died before she could scream at him.

His eloko guards returned him to the museum gala, presumably as evidence that he was still in custody. The event had continued on, oblivious to the impending assassination. Anya was now on Adelbert's arm, playing the part of an interested party as he introduced her around the room, edging closer to Councilman Fischer.

Jack's guards must've been given an order to look normal, because they gave him a wide berth, although their nearby presence was palpable.

"Fascinating piece, here, don't you think, Councilwoman?"

"No more fascinating than the last one."

Jack froze as María and another man with a thick Australian accent joined him in front of a set of vases. Jack kept his gaze on the vases showing the upside-down shields of the men walking toward a crude drawing of Biloko.

Unfortunately, he had no such luck.

"I don't believe we've met, sir," said the man, whose cheery disposition was at odds with María's grim expression. "Lucas Williams," he said, taking Jack's hand.

"Ah, Ben Jones," Jack said, lowering his voice a few notes and shaking both their hands. He waited for the councilwoman to recognize him, but she dropped his hand as soon as the handshake was finished.

"American, huh? And this formidable woman is Councilwoman María García, from Mexico."

"Very nice to meet you," Jack said, his gaze moving to Anya on the other side of the room.

"Ah, that's your wife, I take it?" Lucas said with a knowing smile. "That Adelbert's a charmer, but he's an eloko. No need to worry about him stealing your wife."

"He's a demon, Lucas," María said, her words sharp and biting. "We should all be worried."

"So...why are you here then?" Jack asked, unable to help himself.

María turned to him, and Jack's heart skipped a beat when her eyes narrowed. But she quickly turned to the art pieces. "Councilman Fischer asked me to accompany him. This is the largest known collection of eloko artifacts. Obviously, ICDM is concerned with preserving our demon-hunting history."

"Uh-huh." Jack could tell a lie when he heard it, but he had other things to worry about. Namely Anya, who was currently chatting up the councilman she'd just been hired to assassinate.

"We've been dealing with these demons for over three millennia, and we still aren't much further along than these sorry fellows," Lucas said, pointing at the vase. "Though from what I hear, there's some talk of a new weapon coming out of Atlanta."

Maria's frown grew more pronounced. "I doubt we'll be hearing more from there. Whatever you heard was overblown. My great-niece is assigned to that city. I assure you, the demons retreated of their own accord."

What? The question was so loud in his mind that Jack was sure María heard it. He was *positive* Cam had told everyone with an ear about her technology, especially her aunt. María wasn't a loving relative, but she had come to Cam's graduation and given her the macauhuitl club to take into the field. So what was going on?

"Question, Mr. Jones?" she asked.

"No, just...I heard something different about Atlanta," Jack said slowly.

"Demon Springs can be very chaotic times," María said, her brown eyes piercing his. "People see things they might not understand in the heat of the moment. Nothing new, other than the appearance of Bael, happened there."

Jack felt for the talismans around his wrist and forced a smile onto his face. "Of course."

"If you'll excuse us," María said, not waiting for Lucas to follow her away from the conversation.

But as Jack watched her go, the sound of laughter drew his attention to the other side of the room, where Anya was still chatting it up. Why hadn't she made a move yet?

More importantly, why hadn't he?

The talismans clinked against each other, and he formulated a plan. Just because María didn't believe the symbol-laden bullets had worked didn't mean they hadn't. Anya had nearly died from a wound to the shoulder.

His two guards, while still nearby, had grown more lax with their monitoring, which gave him time to case the room. Fifteen steps from him were examples of primitive weapons. A sword, a spear, and, most attractive, a bow and arrow. Not deadly to a demon. But add one of his talismans onto the arrow, and it might have some impact.

Jack hadn't shot an arrow since his junior year at the Academy, but he was feeling cocky—or panicked, he wasn't sure. Before he could make his move, he needed a diversion.

María and Lucas were still nearby, so Jack joined them over near the vases. As he walked, he pulled his bracelet off and extracted the green-coated piece.

"Councilwoman, I just wanted to apologize," Jack said, holding out his hand. "My wife and I have just flown in and we're a bit jet lagged. I don't want you to consider my question rude."

"Not at all," she said, although clearly she considered it to be so.

"I just—" And there it was, the elbow too far, the vase

toppled, *smash*.

As the horrified cries filled the room, Jack backed up feigning panic but really finding his footing. He had precious seconds to retreat, and if he didn't move quickly, he wouldn't make it in time.

He dashed across the room, jumping over the barricade, and landing in the center of the weapons exhibit. He yanked the bow out of the mannequin's hand and pulled one of the arrows out of the quiver. With one eye on the oncoming eloko guards who were screaming at him to stop what he was doing, he attached the anti-eloko charm to the arrowhead using the string and nocked the arrow.

Then he aimed, took a breath, and fired, moments before two thick shoulders slammed into his midsection, throwing him to the ground. He landed with a thump, steeling himself for fists and feet, but all that came was a bright white light. Then more lights, all over the room, as Adelbert's spawn reverted to human.

With a grunt, Jack pushed the unconscious guards off him and sat up, rubbing the back of his head before remembering where he was, what he'd done, and that he needed to get the hell out of there. He jumped to his feet, scanning the room for Anya. She was still next to Adelbert's corpse, staring at it with wide-eyed shock, as if she weren't quite sure what was happening. The look was shared across the entire room.

Except for María, whose gaze was so sharp on Jack he could've sworn she could see through his glamour.

Ignoring her and everyone else, he sprinted across the room

and grabbed Anya by the hand, half-hauling her toward the exits. She let him drag her, high heels and all, through the room and down the stairs, all the way into the street before she yanked her hand out of his.

"What the…what the *hell* was that?" she cried.

"That was me saving us," Jack said, gasping for air. "And the Councilman, while I was at it."

"Did you not stop to think that *maybe* I had a better plan?" Anya said.

"Better than me killing Adelbert and getting us the hell out of there?"

"Y-yes!"

Jack pointed at her, a smile on his face as his heart continued to pound from excitement. "You're a damned liar. You had no idea how you were going to get out of that situation. If you did, you would've done it."

"I…Well…" He could almost see the blush under her glamour.

"You, well, what?" Jack said with a proud grin. "Am I suddenly not so useless? More than just dumb questions?"

"Why didn't you leave me?" Her voice had lost its usual caustic timbre, and her gaze was no longer wide and surprised, but curious and untrusting.

"What?" Jack said after a moment.

"You could've run," she said. "Left me there. After what I said…"

"And why the hell would I do that?" Jack said, glancing

down the street.

"Because I lied to you, I've treated you like garbage, and… well, you would've had every reason to run," she said.

"You're right, you have treated me like garbage. And that's gonna stop right now," Jack said with a half-smile. Was she really that worried he would desert her? "But I told you, we're partners. And I'm going to see this through to the end. As long as you *quit lying* to me." He put his hands on her shoulders. "Now what the fuck is actually wrong with you? The truth, please."

"The truth is…" She licked her lips. "The truth is I've been using a lot more magic than usual. But with all this crisscrossing, I need weeks, not hours, to recover. If I can even recover at all."

"If it's killing you, why do you keep doing it?" Jack asked, a little softer.

"Because maybe…" She stared at the ground. "Maybe I was lying to myself a little, too. I didn't want to admit how bad it's gotten. Because that's just how much closer I've come to death. And I still don't know how I'm going to fix all this. If the only cure is to go back to Ath-kur…" She looked away, tears in her eyes.

The rest of Jack's anger floated away and his shoulders sagged as the first sirens began wailing in the distance. "It may not be the only cure. I promise you, Anya, we'll figure this out. Together." He held out his hand. "Deal?"

Anya stared at his hand and shook her head. "What's the point, Jack? We've found another dead end."

"Geneva," Jack said, craning his neck down the street to look for the oncoming authorities. "Break into ICDM and find out what sort of other goodies they have. I'll try not to break any vases this time."

"And what happens if we find nothing there?" Anya said. "We keep running, keep almost getting caught. For how long? How long until all these near-misses catch up with us?"

Jack heard the exhaustion in her voice. So he rested his hands on her bare shoulders. "Then why don't you try something new for a change? Trust me. Let me handle things for a little while."

"Jack, I appreciate what you're trying to do," she said. "But you're...*human*."

"And you aren't back to full strength. You can't use your demonic magic without nearly killing yourself, so you're about as weak as I am."

"I've got experience—"

"So do I," Jack replied. "And I haven't done a very good job up until now. For that, I'm sorry. But if there's one thing that always makes me work harder, it's trying to prove someone wrong." Jack smiled, as pride rushed through him. "And Anya, I'm going to prove you wrong about me."

CHAPTER FIFTEEN

Cam released a heavy sigh of relief when she turned off her car. She'd been driving for eleven hours straight—stopping only to pee and refill coffee. She hadn't even gone to her apartment in Atlanta, continuing until she reached ICDM HQ in Charleston.

Two hours into her drive from New Orleans, Frank called. He wanted her to come to Charleston to help out with the investigation. Kim, he said, would be dealt with, but Wani's death merited her appearance.

She pressed her forehead to the steering wheel and waited for her mind to catch up with her body. The drive had been long and monotonous, giving her plenty of time to devise reasons about why Jack might've been at the lilin bar or why they'd killed Wani. And she didn't know what she was going to say to Frank when she got to his office. She assumed he'd gotten the gruesome photos the New Orleans office had taken, plus the images from the other crime scenes. The slices were clean and precise—not something a regular demon could do.

But could La Colibrí be the killer? Cam wasn't so sure.

She also still wasn't sure about the charges they'd put up against her and Jack. What did the Division care if she'd killed Wani? He had no political clout, and everyone who might've cared that he was gone had ended up dead with him.

There was a rap on her window and she looked up, half-smiling at Frank who stood outside her car.

"Curbside service?" she asked wearily.

"I was on my way over to Karen and George's for dinner," he said. "I thought we could discuss your findings on the way. You can leave your car here. I'm sure we'll both be back bright and early in the morning."

"Back to what, though?" Cam said, letting some of her frustration seep out. "I don't even know where to begin. I feel like I'm always five steps behind them."

He offered a pitying look. "What you need is a square meal and a good night's sleep. Things always look different in the morning."

Cam's stomach rumbled and she nodded, stepping out to retrieve her bag and toss it into Frank's luxury sedan. She slid down into the plush seat, inhaling the scent of leather and the old-man cologne Frank wore. Although she wasn't ready to be moving again, she was grateful someone else was driving.

"Karen's been cooking all day, I hear," Frank said as they pulled out of the parking garage. "She'll fill you right up."

Cam yawned. "I ate pretty well in New Orleans. At least Jack and La Colibrí went somewhere with good food."

"La Colibrí?" Frank asked.

"Ah…hummingbird," Cam said. "You know, 'cause she flits around and only weighs about a hundred pounds."

"Mm."

"You know I don't think they killed Wani," Cam said, ready to get this conversation over with. "I know Kim doesn't agree, but…man, I can't see how Jack would let her go on a rampage. Demon or not."

"I agree with you," Frank said with a short glance. "Wani is a peaceful demon, as far as they go. Happy in his swamp, and very rarely causing any trouble. I can't think of a scenario where Jack would need him dead."

A flicker of hope ignited in Cam's chest. "Thank God. I was afraid I was the only one."

"You and I might be," Frank said with a grimace as the sound of a phone ringing echoed in the car. The hands-free screen read *Anne Navarro*.

"Great." Cam slid further into the seat.

"Chin up, Cam," Frank said, pressing the button. "This is Frank."

"Hello Councilman," said Director Navarro. *"Wondering if you've heard from Agent Macarro yet?"*

"I did," Frank said. "She's sitting right here with me."

Cam could've killed him; why couldn't he have just kept quiet? "Evening, Director," she replied dully.

"This will save us both an email. Can you share the latest from New Orleans?"

"There's not much to tell that isn't in my email reports."

"And those reports are pretty empty," Navarro said without hiding her annoyance. *"No sign of them at all?"*

"We've spotted them in London," Frank said. "They landed at Heathrow with false identifications. It was several hours later that we found the footage."

"Do you think they're staying there?" Cam asked, grateful Frank didn't mention the hundred laws Jack was breaking by entering a country illegally.

"No, it appears it was just a layover. We've lost them again, but the alert's gone out to our European offices. We're having our team scrub the videos, but so far, we haven't been able to find them once they get on the tube."

"Have you tried the train?" Cam asked.

"Hm?"

"I mean, if you know they got on the tube, then maybe they got off at the train station, King's Cross or whatever it is." She tapped her fingers against her chin. "I doubt they were staying in London, maybe if we search the footage at the train stations?"

"I'll pass that along, if they haven't tried that already," Frank said with a grandfatherly smile.

"But even so, they were sighted over a week ago. I don't think it's prudent for you to go to Europe, Macarro," Navarro said. *"In fact, I'm not sure it's prudent for you to be away from Atlanta. We've still got a hole in the middle of our city, and with Nunzia's death, it's*

been all-out war among the lower factions."

"Understood," Frank said. "Did the Los Angeles team arrive?"

"Yes, a few weeks ago."

"And the Shanghai team? The Jakarta team? The Toronto team?"

Navarro paused, as if sensing where he was going. *"We need all hands on deck to coordinate."*

"I'm sure you can get by without one person," Frank replied. "Besides that, aren't you using those lovely talisman shooters Cam made?"

There was an uncomfortable pause. *"I've been asked by the higher-ups to hold off on using them any more until Demon Spring is over."*

"Are you serious? Why the hell would they do that?" Cam asked, sharing a confused look with Frank.

"I'll check with my counterparts in the federal office to find out what the deal is," he said. "Until then, I'll see about getting some additional support for you guys there. Does that sound good?"

It probably didn't, but Navarro was hopelessly outranked by Frank. *"We'll make it work."*

"Excellent. We've got to run to an important meeting," Frank said as the car pulled up to the Grenard mansion and the mechanical gates groaned open. "Please contact my assistant if there's anything else you need." He ended the call and winked at Cam. "It's good to be the Councilman."

She smiled, but it didn't dismiss the queasiness in the pit of her stomach. "Why would they tell them to stop using the talismans? At the very least, they should be using them to defend against athtars."

"And we would, I suppose, if we'd seen any. But since Bael returned to the Underworld, there have been no sightings of any athtars at all. Unless, of course, we count Anat."

"That's…kind of strange isn't it?" Cam said, as they pulled up to the mansion. "You'd think with Bael running around, he'd let his minions out to wreak havoc."

"That doesn't mean he's not orchestrating something behind the scenes." Frank nodded to the front of the car. "Ah, we have a welcoming committee, it seems."

Karen, a beautiful pageant queen with perfectly styled brown hair and a vibrant smile, stood on the doorstep. Cam was barely out of the car before she was pulled into a bear hug, the kind that left her warm.

"Cam, baby," Karen said, cupping her cheeks as if she were a child, "you look half-dead. Let me get some food in you. I've been on the phone with your mother. She says I'm to feed you and make you rest, and then you have to call her."

"I will, I promise," Cam said.

The first time Cam had gone home with Jack, she'd been awestruck by his mansion of a home. The Grenards had been in the demon-hunting business for generations, and it was clear they'd profited greatly from it. Their home was one of the nicest in Charleston, a sixteen-room monstrosity with a gourmet kitchen and a grand ballroom. Teenage Jack had taken great pains to show Cam every oil panting and priceless sculpture, as if he were the prince of England.

Karen had appeared shortly thereafter and scolded her son for fooling Cam. That was, as she explained, the part of the house where ICDM dignitaries and ambassadors met with Frank. The Grenards lived in a smaller apartment-like area in the back, much cozier and kid-friendly.

Dinner was already sitting on the table, so Cam took her customary seat on the left. Jack usually sat across from her, but there was no plate for him.

George, Jack's father, walked into the dining room with a glass of red wine for Cam and a kiss to her forehead. "Good to see you, Cam," he said, taking the seat at the head of the table. Frank took the opposite, and Karen joined them to round out the foursome.

Cam's gaze slid to the spot across from her once more, but then turned to the steaming pile of potatoes and steak in front of her. Lucky for her, Frank did most of the talking, filling George and Karen in on the latest on their son.

"I hope he's taking care of himself," Karen said with a worried sigh. She hadn't touched her food. "I just wish he'd call or *something*."

"He'll come home," George said, almost as if he were saying it for his own benefit. "He's too smart not to. Maybe he knows something we all don't."

"Did he say anything to you about his time in the

Underworld?" Karen asked Cam.

Cam shook her head and swallowed a spoonful of potatoes. "I got five seconds with him before he left again. But he always had some sort of hero complex when it came to this demon woman." She sighed. "I think in his own mind, he figures if he can save this woman, he'll atone for Sara's death."

"My poor baby," Karen whispered. "He was acting strange when the two of you came to visit, but I thought he was just under stress because of the new job and Demon Spring. He hasn't been the same since Sara passed." She reached across the table to take Cam's hand. "Thank God for you, Cam."

She smiled, but she didn't feel it. "Do you need any help with the dishes?"

"Oh, sweetheart, no. You run upstairs and get your shower and get into bed." Karen kissed the top of Cam's head. "And don't you let me hear you getting up and working on that computer."

"Yes, ma'am," Cam said, standing. She tried to take her plate into the kitchen, but Karen was having none of it, fussing at her to get upstairs. Cam obliged, not really wanting to be on her feet anymore.

She'd been sleeping in the same bedroom since the very first weekend she came home with Jack. She put her suitcase down and checked the dresser, finding an old pair of pajamas. She'd shower in the morning.

Even though her head pounded from exhaustion, sleep still didn't come. Two tears slipped down her cheek. She wasn't a crier, but her emotional well was running dry.

And just like that, her phone lit up with her mother's face.

"Hola, mamá," she said, wiping the emotion from her voice for just a few moments longer. If Elena knew her baby girl was upset, she'd be on the first flight, and Cam couldn't handle having both *her* mother and Jack's hovering over her.

Maybe Frank was right. She'd get a few days of rest, then she'd reattack the problem with a clearer mind.

CHAPTER SIXTEEN

Forced to figure out a solution without her magic, and not ready to test his own skills at car thievery, Jack used a few hundred euro from Anya's stash to rent a car in the town. With Anya sleeping beside him, he drove all night, thinking about what their next move was, especially as their money wasn't as plentiful as he'd thought.

After stopping at a service station, and playing the role of Dumb American, Jack learned they were about ten miles outside Amsterdam. Using broken English and hand signals, Jack was able to get directions to a hotel in town, which he again paid for in cash.

"We normally need a credit card," the hotel clerk said with a thick Dutch accent.

"I know," Jack said, offering his most charismatic smile. "But my credit card has been cut off. Apparently, you have to tell your bank you're traveling abroad."

"Oh, yes, I've heard that." Her gaze slid over to Anya, sleeping soundly on the chair where Jack had deposited her. "Your lady doesn't look well."

Jack glanced over his shoulder where Anya was snoozing. "She's just pissed at me for the credit card thing. The bank said they would resolve it quickly, but it's been two days." He leaned across the counter. "I was going to ask her to marry me on this trip, but it's kind of been a comedy of errors."

That last little tidbit seemed to convince the clerk, and she took his cash without any more questions. After Jack got their room key, he wandered over to Anya on the couch.

"Honey," Jack said, gently shaking her.

"Mm?" she mumbled, cracking open an eye.

"Come along, dearest," he replied with a self-satisfied smile. "Time to go to bed."

She didn't move, so Jack hoisted her into his arms. The front desk clerk, who'd obviously bought his sob story, cooed as they walked by. He ambled up the stairs, positioning Anya so he could slide the key into the door and crack it open. After setting her on the bed, he returned to their rental car to retrieve their bags.

When he got back to the room, Anya was sitting up, a cross look on her face. "Where are we?"

"Near Amsterdam," Jack replied, putting the bags on the floor. "Told the front desk our credit card had been frozen by our bank so she wouldn't question why I was paying in cash."

Anya looked at the window. "Did you check for demons?"

"What, like, under the bed?" Jack chuckled and pulled off his shirt, deciding one of the many things he'd hunt down was a laundromat. "Go back to sleep, Anya. No one saw us arrive. No one knows we're here. No—"

He stopped when he turned and saw her curled up on the bed again. He covered her with the blankets.

"Thank you," she murmured.

"Get some rest," he said, gently brushing the hair out of her face. "I'll take it from here."

The next morning, Anya was still in the same position she'd been in the night before, but Jack was wide-eyed and ready to get down to business. All joking aside, he wanted to check the neighborhood for demons, just in case, and look for a way to make a quick buck.

Although he didn't have the sort of connections Anya had, he was bolstered by her ability to walk into New Orleans and find a job almost immediately, despite not having been there in a century. Maybe he would be as lucky.

The clerk at the front desk was different from the night before, so he was able to craft a persona as a single man. He asked for the best place for breakfast and got a handful, most in walking distance.

He got his fill of eggs and espresso while pretending to read the paper as he listened to conversations. Unfortunately, he had almost no knowledge of Dutch, so that quickly turned into a dead-end. He asked the waitress for the most tourist-y part of the city, and got directions to Dam Square. It was as he'd requested, full of tourist-trap shops and stereotypical Dutch memorabilia. He caught several English conversations, but there was nothing demonic about them.

After walking into a shop marked *Tourists*, Jack made a show of inspecting the goods as he cased the employees. A teenaged girl was at the cash register, looking bored. In the back, an older woman was restocking t-shirts. On the other side of the store, a twenty-something guy thumbed through postcards.

Jack plucked a coffee mug off the display case and walked over to the girl.

"Hey," he said with a smile.

She nodded, looking even more bored up close as she rung up his order.

"So…" Jack began slowly. "What's your favorite thing to do in the city?"

She turned to him, blowing a bubble with her gum. "I don't know. Go to the cinema?"

"Yeah?" Jack said, turning on the charm and leaning on the counter. Sure, she was half his age, but he was just trying to get information out of her. "Anything more thrilling than that?"

"Oh." She frowned and pushed his mug to him in a bag. "You're one of those Americans, huh?"

He knitted his brow. "What?"

"*Demon minnaar,*" she said then tapped her finger on the table. "Not demon hunter, what is the word?"

"Vigilante?"

"Lover," she said, after a moment. "The ones who go to Rosse Buurt and flirt with the *witte wieven*. Court death."

Jack cleared his throat, understanding about half of what she was saying. "One more time? What's a whit weaver?"

"*Witte wieven*," she repeated, slower. "I think you call them…lilies?"

"Lilins?" Jack said, forcing the smile off his face. "So what happens in Rosse Buurt with the lilins?"

"Head down there tonight and find out for yourself," she said. "Of course, if you make a mistake, the *jachtpaard* will be around in the morning to solve it for you."

"Uh-huh," Jack said, stepping away from the counter. He didn't want to ask too many questions. So, he said, "How do I get to Rosse Buurt?"

"Right now, in the middle of the morning, it's going to be empty. But around eight or nine tonight, that's when it all goes down. Take the train there," she said, holding out her hand. "That'll be fifteen euro."

Jack returned to the bed and breakfast, finding Anya still asleep. Careful not to disturb her, he pulled her laptop out and searched the web for the *witte wieven*, although it took him a few tries to get the spelling right.

He landed on a tourist-looking page with a photo of a beautiful woman, talking about the fun a person could have in Rosse Buurt.

An old legend says the lilins were women who'd been so twisted by a broken heart they turned into demons. Witte wievens lure impure men into the forests and kill them. A popular game for tourists is to see who's the first to succumb to the magic, as they are the one with the most impure soul.

Jack was pretty sure impurity had little to do with lilin miasma, but a talisman might be helpful. He kept it within reach as he took the train to Rosse Buurt later that night. The magic was palpable from the moment he walked off the train. A rather true-to-life mural of Freyja, the original lilin demon, was painted at the entrance to the train station. Her robes were open down the front, leaving little to the imagination, and her eyes invited Jack to keep looking. As the humans passed by, they paused, bowing a little to the demon, before continuing on.

"I don't want to bow," said a girl to Jack's right.

"You have to, or else Freyja will tell her demons to turn you into one," her friend said.

Despite her distaste, the first girl bowed demurely, while the second curtsied. Then, with a giggle, they ran off into the street.

Jack wasn't going to bow to her; rather, he recalled how *she* had bowed to Bael, and how those breasts had looked as she did. He shook himself, glancing at the talisman that had fallen from his grip. He replaced it against his palm, vowing to check it every so often to make sure it was still there.

Another train arrived, depositing more thrill seekers, so Jack fell in line behind them. There was a certain energy in the air from the humans; a devilish sort of glee that they were about to embark on an adventure frowned upon by most of society. Their smiles grew wider and their giggles more pronounced as they approached the center of the activity. Jack, of course, was blissfully desensitized to the magic. It was almost like watching a movie sex scene with parents—the action was there, but the desire was not.

Leaning against door frames and catcalling to passersby, the lilins were easy to spot. Although they shared lusty glances with the humans, theirs verged on predatory. Most of those newly arrived were too skittish to go inside, the girls hiding their faces behind their hands, and some high-tailing it out of the neighborhood.

The group Jack had been trailing from the train were deep in conversation, debating amongst themselves if they wanted to be brave and go inside. They couldn't have been more than twenty —and South African by their accents. One of the girls, tall with ropes of braids down her back, was the brave (or stupid) one, walking away from the group and into the bar. Her friends called after her, half-heartedly, then reluctantly followed—as did Jack.

The miasma blasted him in the face as soon as he entered, smelling sex and flowers. Jack pressed his talisman harder into his hand while forcing himself to think about the most unsexy thing he could think of—his grandfather in swim trunks. The image of the old, wrinkly man chased away the lust threatening to invade his senses, and Jack straightened, pleased with himself for fighting off the lure. Two women nearly knocked him over, each trying to tear the other's clothes off as they fell into a booth.

"Hey there, handsome," said a young man with spiky blond hair. Before Jack could stop him, the lilin ran his hands along Jack's chest, purring happily. "You look a little tense. You're in a good place. Relax—"

The look Jack gave him was enough to stop the seduction in its tracks. "What are you, ICDM or something?"

"No, looking for a job. Know of any?"

"Oh, you're a jachtpaard." He plopped down on a nearby poof and frowned. "So disappointing."

"What does that mean?" Jack asked.

"The ones who deal with the upside-down shield," he said, pointing to the symbol on the doorframe, before his gaze was drawn to a pair of young women walking into the bar. "Wait until the morning. There'll be a ton of whiny neophytes who say they were coerced and want their demonic existence undone. I'm sure you'll have your pick of jobs. And you'll get a stipend from the city government, too."

Jack could barely believe what he was hearing. "Really? The government sanctions this?"

"Oh, yes," he said with an emphatic nod. "The Netherlands is one of three countries not in the international coalition for dumb men. We were kicked out for embracing the glorious relationship between humans and demons." He looked around at the club of writhing humans and demons. "Demons turn humans, humans kill demons, and we just make more. It sure does bring in the tourism money."

"That's an awfully flippant way of discussing the death of

your demon brethren," Jack replied.

He shrugged. "If you're stupid enough to turn a tourist with money to hire a vigilante, you deserve to be beheaded." He puffed out his chest and stood. "Excuse me."

The lilin left Jack standing in the middle of the bar as he approached the two girls. Almost instantly, he had their attention, their eyes filling with lust and hunger. By the time Jack walked out of the bar, the three were crammed into a booth, having a wild time getting to know each other.

For a moment, he contemplated putting a stop to it. After all, the demon had said "a tourist with money," so there was still a chance he might turn these girls if they didn't have that kind of cash. But on the other hand, they'd walked into this part of town willingly, looking for a thrill. There were no innocents in this bar, and although it didn't make it right, it didn't make it wrong, either.

Jack, however, was starting to feel the stirrings of something pleasurable in his gut, so he decided to bow out of the room before he succumbed. He did find it ironic that the first thing he saw on the train back to his hotel was a warning poster about the dangers of cavorting with a lust demon, courtesy of the Dutch government.

It was nearly two in the morning when Jack finally arrived back at the hotel. He unlocked the door quietly, hoping not to wake Anya, but she sat straight up when he walked into the room.

"Where the hell have you been?" she snapped.

"Taking care of us," he said, pulling off his shirt. "I think I can get a job tomorrow and earn some money."

"You smell like a lilin."

He turned, halfway to unbuttoning his pants. "How can you *smell* me all the way over there?"

"You smell like sex and booze," she said, the frown deepening. "What kind of job? What are you up to? What happened to—"

"Taking care of you?" he asked, dropping his pants on the floor. "That's what I'm doing. We're low on cash. I'm going to get us more." He patted her head as he passed, which turned her frown into a full-blown scowl. "How do you feel?"

"Murderous," she replied. "Don't talk to me like a child."

Jack turned and smiled. "I'm not. I'm just feeling good."

"Cause you're high on lilin miasma," she said, lying back down. "Don't think I'm going to help you get rid of any of it, either."

"C'mon, don't be pissy," Jack said, climbing into bed behind her and sliding his hands up and down her curves.

It happened in less than a second, but Jack was keenly aware of the sharp knife pressed to his groin before he saw it.

"Hands. Off."

He released his hands and scooted away, chastened by the knife. "I thought you were saving your magic."

"It's worth it to knock your ass down a few pegs." She rolled over and placed the knife on the bedside table.

"Hey, at least I wasn't fucking everything that moves," Jack replied, putting his hands behind his head.

"What do you call that?"

"Uh…" What was that? Okay, so maybe he was feeling a little giddy from lilin magic. He and Anya didn't have the kind of relationship where he could grab her like that—previous sexual encounter or not. "I'm sorry. That was out of line."

She turned fully to face him. Jack's breath caught in his throat when she lazily raised a hand to his chest, trailing her fingertips up and down, down, down. "Maybe I could help you a little…"

That was all he needed, and he closed the distance between them. But instead of lips, he was met with the back of her head.

"What the hell?" he said.

"Goodnight."

Jack lay in the bed for a moment, angry and horny. But instead of barking up that tree again, he left to take a long, long shower.

CHAPTER SEVENTEEN

The next morning, Jack awoke with a lingering hangover and a larger cloud of disgust at himself for the way he'd acted the night before. He rolled on his side, almost wishing Anya was awake so he could apologize more. Instead, he took a moment to watch her sleep. Even in her dreams, she was on edge. He lifted a finger to smooth away the furrow on her brow, but stopped himself. It would be better to ease her worries by doing something to help.

The city was much calmer in the light of day, and the red light district was no different. Where there'd been a thick oozing miasma, now there was nothing but mist and morning air. The streets were empty, except for a few half-naked people sleeping against steps and in alleyways. Several shop owners were out front, sweeping the drink cups and glass from their walkways and looking barely awake themselves. Jack spotted the same spiky-haired blond from the night before and walked over to him.

"Oh, it's you again," he said with a yawn. "Go on in, there's three of 'em asking for help."

"Really?"

"Slow morning. There's usually fifteen," he said, sweeping a broken beer bottle into a dustpan.

Jack thanked him with a twenty euro note and walked into the bar, where there were, indeed, three young demons, looking horrified and hungover as they complained to each other. Luckily for Jack, they were all American.

"I can't believe this. My dad is gonna kill me."

"Maybe we should go after him ourselves," said the girl.

"Hi there," Jack said. "I heard y'all need some help."

They introduced themselves as Roland, Vihann, and Leighton, saying they were in Amsterdam on Spring Break and were set to go home the next day.

"Well, we were just here for a thrill, you know? They say, come to Amsterdam for the best sex of your life," said Leighton, a bright-eyed strawberry blonde with perfect teeth.

"Yeah, hasn't anyone ever told you not to sleep with a lilin?" Jack said.

Roland, a black teen wearing a perfectly pressed Lacoste shirt, rolled his eyes. "I mean, we all got the spiel during our first year—"

"Hang on, *hang on*." Jack slapped his hands down on the table. "Are you telling me you're *Academy* kids?"

They looked sheepishly at the floor.

"You three are a special kind of stupid," Jack said with a shake of his head. "Don't you know you're supposed to be fighting demons, not getting fucked by them?" *You're one to talk, Grenard.*

"Are you gonna help us or what, man?" asked Vihann, an Indian boy with long hair that hung around his ears. "If I wanted to get lectured by someone, I'd have called my parents."

Jack was tempted to ask who their parents were. After all, if they'd been accepted into the Academy, they were either related to someone or had exemplary grades. Considering that they'd just been turned into lilins, he suspected the former.

"Fine, I'll help you. Did any of you get a photo of your maker?"

They shook their heads.

"For fuck's sake," Jack muttered. "Check your Instagram, Snapchat, Tumblr. You idiots were taken and didn't want to broadcast it all over the place?"

"Well, obviously not. Our parents check that shit," Vihann said.

"Fine," Jack said, pinching the bridge of his nose. "What did your demon look like?"

"He was Dutch," Roland said. "Blond, blue-eyed guy. Maybe six-three?"

"Get a name?"

"Ryker," Leighton said quietly. "Or Striker. I heard one of his guys calling him that."

Shit. "He had guys? As in, employees? Seconds?"

They nodded.

Jack sighed and sat back in his chair. He was now firmly convinced that these three had been targeted because they were Academy cadets, and they'd been turned by a powerful demon—or at least, one with enough clout to have seconds. Under normal circumstances, demons didn't usually target Division families like this. But with Demon Spring and the upheaval in the US, Jack wasn't sure he could trust past history anymore.

"Okay, how much money do you have?" Jack asked.

"M-money?" Leighton squeaked before bursting into tears. Jack knew enough rich girls in Charleston to see right through them. He waited, with his arms folded across his chest, for her to realize they weren't working on him.

"Fine." She sniffed, wiping her cheeks. "I can pay you a thousand dollars."

"Mm..." He gave her a once over. "I see a Coach bag. I think you can do better than that."

"That's all I have!" she said. "Or else I'm going to have to call my parents...." Jack tilted his head toward her and she burst into tears again. "You don't understand. My dad is on the *Council.* He can make you help us."

"Oh really? What's his name?"

"G...Grenard?"

Jack had to laugh. "No, honey. You aren't a Grenard." He leaned in closer to the three of them. "I hate to break it to you, but the Division doesn't care who your mommy and daddy are.

If you've been turned by a demon with some connections, they won't be stepping in to help you. And you'll be demons for the rest of eternity."

Vihann spoke first. "My mother's the weapons aide to the Middle Eastern Councilman—"

"Myra?" Jack said, incredulous.

"Y-yes, how did you know?" Vihann asked.

"I know things," Jack said, trying to keep the frown off his face. He'd met Myra in Charleston a few months ago; she'd been the aide working to get Cam a job in Shanghai. "So what are you going to offer me?"

"I already called my parents," Roland offered, earning a cry of horror from his compatriots. "They're willing to pay you twenty thousand dollars."

"Sold," Jack said then eyed him. "And who are your parents?"

"Mom is the Division Director in New York City," he said, staring at the ground. "Grace Dewberry."

Jack had met her once before, as part of a city-to-city task force he and Cam had been asked to sit on. She was a tough nut to crack, and he didn't blame the kid for breaking so easily. Jack wouldn't want to see her angry.

"Show me proof," Jack said.

The three kids looked at one another, then Roland reached for his cell phone. The boy's pained expression worsened when the other line picked up.

"Roland? Roland, is that you?"

"Hey, Mom," Roland said. The barrage of anger from the other side was audible to everyone in the room, and Jack felt sorry for the boy. Finally, he admitted that Jack was the real deal, and they were trusting him. He handed the phone to Jack.

"*So how do I know you aren't going to take the money and run?*" came the angry voice on the other side of the phone.

Jack considered coming clean with his identity, but that might cause more problems. "I won't. I've been around ICDM for a long time, and I used to put away a lot of demons for the Division. I'll get your kids back to normal."

He tried to sound sincere, and it appeared to have worked. "How do you want to do this?"

"Wire half the money to your son to give me in cash. When I complete the job, wire the rest for cash too."

"No bank account?"

"Ah, trying not to leave a paper trail?" Jack said with a laugh. Anya might've used her tech guys to create a new account she could access, but he didn't have the resources for that. And he also didn't want to ask her for help. This was his rodeo, and he wanted to be in charge.

"Your terms are accepted. How long until you can complete the job?"

"Get me the money by tonight, and I'll see what I can do."

Anya didn't ask why Jack was strapping on his weapons as night fell, but she watched him with a sleepy curiosity that put him on edge. Still conscious of overstepping his bounds the night before, he tried his best to engage her with respect.

"Know anything about a demon named Ryker?" Jack asked. "Lilin?"

"Name's not familiar," Anya replied. "Is that who turned them?"

"Yeah, the kids said it was a demon with 'guys,' so I'm assuming he's not your run-of-the-mill lowlife." Jack pulled his knives out of the bag and strapped them to his legs. "So, hey… do you feel up to coming?"

She smiled triumphantly in the mirror. "Why? Need backup?"

"No," he said, enjoying how her smile disappeared. "I don't want to carry around ten thousand dollars while I'm demon hunting." He stood and tried to look innocent. "Feel up to that?"

"Ten thousand dollars? Is that for the whole job?"

"Twenty grand total."

Her eyes bulged. "You caught a whopper, didn't you?"

"Is that good?" Jack asked. "I wasn't sure what the going rate was."

"I rarely take a job over five thousand. Any more than that, you're usually looking at someone with connections."

"Yeah, the three kids are Academy cadets. I know their parents," Jack said.

"You shouldn't take the job," Anya said firmly. "The risks are too high. If they know you, they—"

"Hey," Jack said, holding his hands in the air. "Let me

handle this, okay?"

"You're going to fuck it up—"

"Then let me fuck it up, and then let me fix it," Jack said. "You don't even have to be involved. You can take the money and bug out of the city if you want." She didn't respond immediately, so he turned to look at her. "What?"

"You'd just let me leave?" she asked. "What if I didn't come back?"

He shrugged. "Maybe I'll make a new career out of helping stupid kids in Amsterdam. Would be more fulfilling than my Division job, and apparently I get a stipend from the government." He smiled. "But I'd like it if you came back. I want to figure out why you're still cursed."

That earned the smallest of smiles from her. "I'll get the money. But if I don't like it—"

"You are free to go."

Jack met the three kids in the alleyway beside the lilin bar once the sun had set. Anya, concerned about the lilins recognizing her, kept to the shadows. The miasma was thick again, although neither Jack nor the kids were in any mood to partake. They sheepishly handed over an envelope.

"Is it all there?" Jack asked.

Roland nodded. "Mom said the rest of it will be ready when you finish. How long do you think it'll take?"

Jack shrugged. "Who knows? A lot longer than getting transformed by a demon, that's for sure."

"We could do without the lecture," Leighton replied.

"Could you?" Jack said. "Because what's to stop me from walking away with this money and not helping you? I suggest you knock off the attitude, princess."

She demurred, looking at the ground.

"Yeah," Roland said. "What is to say you won't do that?"

"Well, I guess you're going to have to trust me," Jack said, stuffing the envelope into his back pocket. As soon as he removed his hand, the envelope was gone. He just hoped he trusted Anya not to run away either. Otherwise he'd be stranded in Europe with no money.

"Go back to your hotel," Jack said. "If I finish the job tonight, you'll know. And I'll be by to collect the rest of my money."

With a final glare, he turned from them and headed toward the bars. It was still early, but there were already partiers having their thrills. He found his lilin friend and waved him over.

"Back for fun?" he asked with a hopeful smile.

"Hardly. Know anyone named Striker or Ryker?"

"Uh, those poor devils," he said with a shake of his head. "He's the second to the demon lord. Surprised he lowered himself to a bunch of kids."

"They're special kids," Jack said without divulging more details. But this was a problem. Jack was already shaky in a fight, he wasn't keen on getting into it with a lilin second.

"Well, Striker doesn't descend amongst us peasants often. You'll probably find him across the street in his apartment."

Jack patrolled the street a few times, keeping his distance from the apartment as he built himself a mental map. There was one street entrance to the apartment, but a wall of windows staring down on the street. He couldn't see very far into the apartment, so he had no idea how many people Striker had up there. He'd be going in basically blind.

"What would Cam do?" he asked himself. A better question: what would the old Jack do?

He stopped midway down the street, remembering every harebrained scheme he and Cam had thought up to outwit the noxes. There were back-alley brawls and big shows of force, but also covert operations. And sometimes, he and Cam just walked right up to the demon nest and banged on the door, demanding to see contracts as part of a surprise inspection.

A smile curled onto his face as he walked toward the apartment.

Bang, bang, bang.

"ICDM surprise inspection. Open up."

So it wasn't his most brilliant plan, but it was a plan, and it would hopefully get him inside.

The door cracked, and a very surprised young woman appeared. "I'm…sorry?"

"ICDM surprise inspection," he repeated. "I'm on loan from the US Division and they sent me here to investigate."

She opened the door wider, glancing back at an older man sprawled on the couch. She spoke to him in Dutch, and the man laughed, although not in a threatening way.

"Let the poor bastard in," he said with a wave.

Jack walked inside, hoping his ruse would work, but not sure what he was going to do from there. "I'll need to see—"

"Oh, dear friend," the demon presumably known as Striker said. "Your new colleagues have played a very nasty trick on you."

"They have?" At least it was easy to play dumb.

"Things are a lot different here in the Netherlands," he said. "We don't have your ICDM laws on contracts or any of that. There's no surprise inspection, no hoops to jump through."

"Oh." Jack probably should've guessed that from what he'd known of the country. "No wonder they sent me out on my own."

"You're amongst friends here," Striker said, offering Jack the seat across from him. "You may tell your boss Jansen that I handed over all my contracts, and you approved them very American-like."

Jack half-smiled and took a seat. The smell of flowers tickled his nose, and he straightened. "I take it this happens a lot?"

"From time to time. I'm surprised ICDM is still sending agents to the country. I thought they were formally kicked out of the coalition for not adhering to their strict rules?"

There was a question in his words—one Jack didn't have the answer to. Then again, the miasma had grown thicker in the room, so perhaps Striker was just hoping Jack would start babbling. "There are sanctions, I think. But I submitted a request for a trip almost a year ago, and it took this long to get approved.

Maybe they forgot to cancel it."

"Maybe, maybe. Or maybe you're just lying to me."

"That is also an option," Jack said. He was starting to question the brilliance of coming in here without backup then questioned himself for questioning himself. He never used to think—he just did what he felt was right and hoped it worked out.

"What I don't understand is why you haven't fallen victim to my lure yet," Striker said quietly. "Do share your secrets."

CHAPTER EIGHTEEN

Jack had felt the magic, but it hadn't taken root. Either he'd become accustomed to miasma in the past few weeks, or this demon wasn't nearly as powerful as the ones he'd been dealing with before. If it was the latter, that boded well for him.

"Well?" Striker said, swirling his wine around in the glass. "I've had many a jachtpaard in here, and most have succumbed with much less effort."

"I guess I'm a little different," Jack said. "Why did you target the Academy kids?"

Striker chuckled and sipped his wine, reminding Jack strongly of a cheesy movie villain. The only thing he was missing was a white cat named Mr. Bigglesworth.

"Do you know why we let the jachtpaard kill our spawn?" Striker asked. "Because for every one they kill, we make three more. Some new lilins live just forty-eight hours—transitioned

194

one night, spawn the next, dead by morning at the hands of a vigilante. The government tells the tourists they're on top of the situation, and we get our new lilins every night."

"And the kids? Why target them?"

"I've got an eye to expand business into the United States now that that blowhard Nunzia is out of the way. They will be a nice leverage as I make my way through the US Division."

"Good luck with that," Jack said.

"Don't worry about the children. They'll be happy here. Rosse Buurt is so thick with lilin magic, it's practically the motherland, Liley, herself. Freyja would be proud to see the empire we've built in her name."

"Don't let Bael hear you say that," Jack said with a chuckle. "I hear he gets pretty pissy with demons who claim towns for their own."

Striker faltered, showing the first bit of concern. "King Bael is, of course, the king of the five realms, including Liley. We only live here because he allows it."

Jack had to laugh. "Save your groveling. I'm not allied with Bael any more than you are."

"Then who, exactly, are you?" Striker asked.

"I'm a man who's been paid a lot of money to get some results, and I'd like to get those results," Jack said, glancing around the empty apartment. "And you seem a demon lord without the usual muscle."

Striker stood and reached behind his Swedish-looking couch, revealing a cutlass that seemed both sharp and decorative. He held it in front of him, admiring it for a moment as a teenaged boy does his manhood.

"Swordplay is a lost art. Now, it's all guns and cyber hacking, or whatever the newest technology is. Demons stand around waxing poetic while they fill a room with their magic, trying to outdo each other." He sighed. "But you seem the kind of man who would die honorably if he won't be taken by a lure."

"I'd rather you just try the miasma," Jack said, gripping the handles of his knives.

Striker smiled. Then he struck.

Jack unsheathed his knives almost too late, catching the demon's sword between them before it cut him in half. Striker stepped back, nodding with some approval.

"You are well-trained," he observed. "But I still have a few centuries of experience on you."

Jack jumped over the couch, and the lilin followed, swinging his sword wildly. Jack could only defend himself, struggling to find his feet and his rhythm as the lilin pressed inward.

His calf landed against a low table, and he lost his balance, falling backward. The point of the sword wasn't far behind. The world slowed as his impending death…

No, it just slowed.

And he didn't hit the floor either; rather, a pair of strong, small arms held him, and a warm breath brushed against his cheek.

"A-Anya?" Jack said, looking over his shoulder. "What are you doing here?"

"You're obviously in need of assistance," she replied, helping him to his feet. "I've been monitoring you."

Jack stepped away from her, minding the slow-moving sword still sliding through the air at a snail's pace and Striker's face stuck in murderous glee. "Why?"

She gestured at the lilin with a bored expression.

"I'm handling it," Jack insisted.

"You were about to *be* handled," Anya said. "I shouldn't have let you come here by yourself. It's clear you aren't—"

"It's clear that this was my call," Jack said with more than a little anger. "If he kills me, you've got the money. You can disappear."

Her brows knitted together. "But—"

"Anya, I need to do this by myself," Jack said. "Believe it or not, I used to be pretty good at this sort of thing. Maybe I just need to get my ass in trouble to get rid of whatever mental block I have." He sighed, tapping his knife against the sword tip. "Because I've tried *literally* everything else. And nothing's worked yet."

Her gaze was steady and disconcerting, but finally, she nodded. "Fine. You may handle this on your own. If you die—"

"Feel free to continue without me," Jack said with a hopeful smile. "But if not, I'll see you back at the hotel room."

The world sped back up and so did the sword.

"W-what just happened?" Striker said, blinking.

"Wouldn't you like to know?" Jack said, knocking away his sword with ease. He shook off the notion that Anya was still watching him, as it both unnerved him and gave him a false sense of security. If he was truly going to save himself, he needed to do it without her help.

But he'd take the effect her presence had on Striker, who was sporting a light sheen of sweat on his head. He spun around the room as if Bael would appear at any moment.

"What's the matter?" Jack taunted, inching closer. "Expecting someone?"

Striker snarled and tossed his sword into his other hand. Right, left, Jack pushed away his blows, standing his ground, even as the sword came dangerously close to his head. Jack caught the sword between his knives, and with a heave, knocked it out of the demon's hands. Before it had even clattered to the ground, he crossed his knives at the demon's neck to level the killing blow. The lilin landed a sucker punch in Jack's stomach, and he fell backward and landed hard on the ground. But this time, Jack sprang to his feet, ready for the next volley.

The lilin chuckled, wiping his brow. "You'll have to do better than that. I have survived thousands of *jaachtpaards* like yourself. You may have some tricks, but you are no different than—"

He choked on his words as Jack plunged one of his knives into the demon's chest. Striker looked down at the handle, and then with a low grunt, pulled the knife out of his chest and threw it away. Blood pooled at the wound but it was more a curiosity than a danger.

"What was the point of that, other than to ruin a perfectly good shirt?" Striker asked.

"This," Jack said, dropping his bracelet to the ground. He slammed his hand and the anti-lilin talisman against the athtar's chest, shoving the iron coin into the wound.

Striker released a guttural wail then fell forward, face-down on the carpet. A moment later, he released his final breath.

Lights flashed like fireworks outside the nearby windows as Striker's spawn turned back into humans. Jack picked his discarded knife off the ground and wiped the blood on the shag carpet.

"Well done."

Anya sat on the windowsill, as comfortably as if she'd been there the whole time. As usual, Jack couldn't read her expression, although he thought she looked a bit pensive.

"Thought you were headed back to the hotel?" he asked, slipping the knife back into its holster.

"Decided to watch the show. A tad verbose for my tastes, but you survived anyway."

Jack lifted his bracelet, where only three talismans remained —a nox, a kappa, and an athtar. He should probably draw the symbols out before he lost all of them.

"Do you feel better?" she asked, kicking the demon's corpse.

"No." And that was concerning. Twice now, he'd had to rely on the talisman magic instead of his own fighting skills. Was it simply a lack of training or was there something else going on?

"Take the win, Jack," she said softly, coming to stand next to him. "You did what you wanted to. Doesn't matter how it happened."

How he wished he could. "I'll head over to the hotel and get the other half of the money from the kids. Hopefully, they're good for it."

"Hopefully," Anya said with a small chuckle. "You could always skip town without it? We don't need it."

"I could," Jack replied with a sly smile. "But it's not about the money. I want to impress upon these kids the severe stupidity of what they've done. And that includes making sure they pay up."

Striker's death had emptied Rosse Buurt completely, a far cry from the previous few nights. Jack wondered how many lilins on the street he'd just converted back to humans—and how many more would return to their demonic state in the coming nights.

His lilin bartender friend waved at him with a chipper expression. Jack could only assume he was from another maker, because he looked more than a little pleased. Jack didn't stop to ask why; the last thing he wanted was to get involved in an intra-lilin spat.

The kids were staying in a swanky hotel in the center of the city. Jack didn't bother changing or removing his weapons, opting to show up bloody, disheveled, and armed—if only to drive home his lesson.

He knocked on their hotel door and heard muted conversations inside. Were the kids about to stiff him? Did they think the three of them could take on a grown man? Well, considering his track record until then, they might be able to.

But the door opened, and something far, far worse ran through Jack's mind.

"J-Jack Grenard?"

Myra, Vihann's mother, was on the other side of the door. An Indian woman in her mid-forties, she'd looked more terrified mother than powerful government bureaucrat.

"Uh…" *Shit, shit, shit.*

To Jack's surprise, she grabbed him by the arm and pulled him into a strong hug. Words of thanks bubbled from her lips as she held on for dear life.

"I take it they're back to normal?" Jack asked, carefully extracting himself.

"Yes, thank goodness," she replied, wiping her eyes. "But I don't understand. I thought you were on the run with a demon? Why are you here?"

"Uh… well, if it's all the same to you," Jack said as a blush rose on his face, "I'd appreciate it if you wouldn't tell anyone about this. About me."

"As if we would," said a new voice from the other side of the room.

Jack winced. The three kids were seated on the bed, dazed and pained, but otherwise fairly normal. In various other chairs were their parents: Myra's husband, Roland's father (who'd spoken), and both of Leighton's parents.

"As if we'd broadcast this embarrassment," said Leighton's mother. "An eloko or a kappa, sure, we might be able to play this off. But a lilin?" She threw another glare at her daughter. "For shame, Leighton."

Well, Jack was glad the kids were getting their due punishments.

"Besides that," Myra said. "We don't want to get involved, not after what's been happening."

"What's been happening?" Jack asked.

Myra paused with a furrowed brow, as if she weren't sure if she wanted to say. "It seems demons are dying after they come into contact with you. A lilin in New Orleans was decapitated. As was Wani."

Jack's mouth fell open. "Hang on, *Wani is dead*?"

Myra nodded. "Your partner, Cam, found him and his entire house slaughtered. It was very clearly done by an athtar. Actually, ICDM is rather hoping you might be able to shed some light on it."

Jack took a step back, processing. "When we left him, he was alive. We helped him with a little favor in exchange for some information. That's it. Are you sure it didn't look like an eloko or anything like that?"

"If you met him, you know. He was an old demon. It would've taken a very powerful creature to kill him."

And therein lay the rub—maybe. Anya wasn't a powerful creature. She had nearly gotten them both killed in Brussels because she'd overexerted herself. She had no cause to kill Wani before then, other than to silence him. Not only that, they'd left New Orleans shortly after that because—

"It wasn't her," Jack said, as dread slipped into his stomach.

"Anya felt another athtar moments before we left New Orleans."

Myra grew pale. "Another athtar? Bael?"

"No," Jack said. "At least, I don't think so. But that would explain a few things."

Like how Adelbert had known what they were looking for. It wasn't beyond the realm of possibility that the athtar had cornered Wani, tortured him for information, then killed him anyway. In fact, it almost seemed too plausible. And a little horrifying.

"Jack?" Myra asked, breaking the silence.

"Even more reason not to say anything," he said. "Not even to your friends, not to your spouses. Not to anyone not in this room. Because whether or not Anya killed Wani, Bael is the one who's on our trail. And I don't think any of you want to meet him."

"Is that a threat?" Roland's father asked.

"A suggestion? These three look like good kids—if not a little stupid," Jack said. "If I hadn't had Cam keeping me on the right path, I might've ended up in the same position. I don't want to see anything happen to them."

"So does this mean we get to keep our money?" Leighton's father asked.

"Nope," Jack said, swiping the envelope off the table. "I'd make your kids work it off. Summer is coming up. It would do them some good to get a part-time job."

With that, he headed for the door, but Myra stopped him with a gentle hand to the shoulder.

"Your family has been worried sick about you," she said. "Can I at least tell them you're alive and well?"

Stick that knife in deeper, why don't you? "I'm sorry, but no. Nobody can know."

"Not even your partner?" Myra asked.

Jack hesitated, torn between complete anonymity and throwing Cam a lifeline. At the end of the day, he chose the latter. "Yes. But you have to do it in person, alone, outside of ICDM or the Division. And you have to make her *promise* she won't tell a soul either. I don't trust that Bael doesn't have spies in the organization. The last thing I want is for him to find out you've been talking with me."

"So what if he does? You're no better than these kids, cavorting with a demon," Leighton's father said. "You deserve what you get."

"It's not me I'm worried about," Jack said over his shoulder. "It's your kids. Thanks for the cash."

CHAPTER NINETEEN

When Cam was working a particularly difficult case, she usually had a few tried and true methods to break through. The first was brainstorming with Jack. They'd sit in their office and throw around ideas from the realistic to the ridiculous until they put together a plan of action. But since Jack wasn't there, she found brainstorming wasn't nearly as productive.

The other method, which she'd perfected in the final grueling years at the Academy, was to inundate herself with as much data about a certain topic as she could possibly take. Then, once she was fully apprised, she would synthesize and answer the question (plus an additional twenty pages of footnotes).

After two days of forced hiatus from active work thanks to Karen, Cam was finally allowed to return to ICDM headquarters. And this time, Cam had a plan.

Since there was no way for her to know where Jack and La

Colibrí were, it was useless for her to putter around Europe, as nice a vacation as that would've been. Instead, she would focus on their end goal. If she managed to solve the mystery of La Colibrí's curse before they did, she could predict where they'd be. It might not have been her most brilliant plan, but it was better than sitting around and waiting for news. By the third day of research, she was no further along in understanding curses, talismans, or anything of the sort, but she had a very good understanding of what had happened during the Demon Springs of the fifteenth century. It was a feat of authorial greatness that the writer could've made the horrific slaughter of hundreds seem banal.

She closed the book, yawning and pressing her fingertips against her forehead. There were probably better ways to find information, but this felt good. Reading for hours on end meant she wasn't able to dwell on the shitstorm swirling in her inbox. Emails from Kim and Navarro, each pressing her for information on what she was doing—and when she'd be coming back to Atlanta.

Wrenching her focus away from her wandering thoughts, Cam took a swig of her cold coffee and turned back to the book. She'd just finished reading about the attack on Geneva in 563 A.D., where a kappa had flooded the nearby lake and taken thousands prisoner. In the aftermath, the Europeans went on a rampage, stamping out anything that might be seen as demonic through witch burnings and the like. Most of those killed were humans, which led Cam to believe there might've been something more than mistaken identity.

This post-Demon Spring hysteria wasn't limited to just Geneva, it seemed, but everywhere in Europe that had experienced the influx of demons. In fifteenth century France, ten people were burned alive, accused of demonic possession. Only there weren't any records of demons nearby. Those killed all bore a similar tattoo—an inverted shield in a circle.

Cam doodled the symbol on her notebook. She'd seen it before, but couldn't place her finger on where.

"Hey, Patrick?" she called once more.

"Yes?" came the tired voice of the head archivist from the other side of the room.

"Do you guys have any way to search symbols?" Cam asked.

He appeared around the corner, holding another stack of books that he placed next to the others Cam had on her to-be-read list. "I don't believe we have that capability here, no. What did you find?"

"Not sure if it's anything," Cam said, showing him the book. "Just some mention of ten people burned alive because of this symbol. To the fifteenth-century French, it meant they were demons."

"Hm," Patrick said, pulling the paper to him. "This symbol looks vaguely familiar. Then again, it's not all that complex, so it might just look common. It might be some kind of early human symbol for demons."

Early humans—*that's* where she'd seen it before. Cam swiveled to her laptop, searching for the report from the Belgium art museum where an eloko demon had been killed mysteriously. She browsed through the photos of the broken artifacts quickly, then stopped.

"Look at that," she said to Patrick. There was still an intact painting on one of the bowls, depicting a group of warriors marching toward an eloko demon. But what had caught Cam's attention was their shields.

"Inverted," Patrick said with a nod. "Do you think...?"

"I think it's the closest thing I've gotten to a break yet." Cam searched the archives for information on the pottery, but there wasn't much other than the name and where it was found. "And just like that, the break is over."

Patrick chuckled and handed her the drawn symbol. "Why don't you run this up to Councilman Grenard? Search engines can only give you so much. Sometimes, you need a pair of human eyes and a human memory to get the job done."

The sun hung low in the sky when Cam got off the elevator at Frank's office level. She could've sworn it was only ten in the morning, but time seemed to fly in the windowless basement. Frank's assistant was at his desk, and he glanced at Cam for a moment before waving her inside.

"Ah, Cam! Come to drag me away from my work?" Frank asked when she walked through the door. "Or care to share a glass of whiskey while we continue?"

"Latter, please," she said, taking a seat on his couch.

Frank wasted no time, walking to a cabinet marked Top

Secret and pulling out a bottle of whiskey and glasses. He set them on the table and poured, toasting the two of them before taking a seat across from her.

"Any news from Jackie?"

"Not since the last report from Brussels," Cam said. "Anything on your end?"

"There's talk he might've been behind a dust-up in Madrid, but we're still canvassing the local hostels for anyone matching his description." Frank's smile had begun to wither and he took another long sip.

"So, you know I've been trying to figure out this curse thing, right?" Cam said after a long pause.

Frank nodded. "Did you find something?"

"Maybe." She wished she had something more concrete, but she pulled the symbol from her pocket. "This was in a book about some demon burnings in the middle ages. A village burned them alive because they bore this symbol."

"Ah." Frank's grimace was unmistakable, and a small spark of hope flared in Cam's chest.

"You've seen it before?"

"Unfortunately, yes. And unfortunately, I doubt this relates to our athtar." Frank spun the paper around and handed it back to her. "This symbol belongs to a small group of people who don't quite believe in what we're doing here at the ICDM."

"Do they think we're too strict?" Cam asked.

"The opposite. They don't think we go far enough," Frank said. "I'm sure you've run across vigilantes in the field, right?"

"Rarely," Cam said. "But I'm familiar with them."

"It's not that much of a problem here," Frank said. "The biggest concentration is really in the Netherlands. They condone the behavior, even providing stipends to those who kill demons extrajudiciously." He shook his head. "ICDM has been on the outs with the Dutch government for some time. The demons there don't mind, but the demons elsewhere do. It's why we set up an international coalition in the first place. If we all play by the same set of rules, it makes our demon cohabitants easier to deal with."

She could almost hear Jack's snort of derision. Cohabitants was a bit of a stretch—more like demonic overlords. Cam had been around long enough to know that ICDM was less about demon management and more about human management.

Frank shook his head, as if the very concept was insane. "The Dutch government says they have a demon transformation problem. Tourists flock there, they say, to experience their lilin lust district and many are turned after drinking too much. Their thinking is, if they show they're working to mitigate the problem, their tourism industry won't suffer."

"I...guess," Cam said with a shake of her head.

"It's not something we should subscribe to," Frank said. "But this group is strictly human. I doubt they have anything to do with Jack or your talisman search. It's mostly conspiracy theories."

"Frank, I'm...well, I'm grasping at straws here," Cam said. "I've been reading for weeks without success. This...this is the first thing that *might* be useful."

Frank nodded, but didn't look convinced. "What do you need from me?"

"I guess…permission to keep looking," Cam said. "And maybe another email to Kim and Navarro."

"You could transfer, you know," Frank said. "Work here permanently."

"I'm not ready to make any decisions about anything," Cam said. "I want to get Jack home first. Then we'll figure it all out."

"Cam," Frank began, as if he wanted to offer some sage advice. She was grateful when he didn't, instead saying, "Go home for the night. I'll see what I can find about the vigilantes in the morning."

CHAPTER TWENTY

"Wani's dead?"

Jack hadn't told Anya about Wani immediately. In the first place, they'd been more focused on getting the hell out of Amsterdam. They'd been there over a week, and even Jack was starting to get antsy about the way the hotel clerk had recognized him. Perhaps Anya's paranoia was rubbing off on him.

But when they finally settled onto their evening train, he told Anya everything he'd found out from Myra.

"And they think I did it?" she said, softly. "Well, why wouldn't they?"

"Did you…" He swallowed. "Did you?"

She lifted her head, with an incredulous look on her face. "*And when would I have had the energy to do that?*"

He lifted his hands in surrender. "I just had to ask. You are worried about Bael finding us."

"He found Wani instead," she said quietly.

"Do you think Bael did it himself?" Jack asked.

She shook her head. "He rarely gets his hands dirty."

There was more to unpack there, but Jack set it aside for now. "Do you think they're on our trail? Should we be worried about Amsterdam?"

"I haven't felt an athtar since we left New Orleans, so I think we're safe," she said, then cast him a dry look. "Assuming your new friends don't go and fuck it up."

"I told them not to say anything," Jack said.

"I told Wani not to say anything, too. And he obviously did."

"But I mean…why kill him?" Jack asked. "If he gave up the information, why not let him live?"

"Why *not* kill him?" Anya said with a shrug. "To an athtar, everyone is expendable. Including the lesser demons." She softened as she looked out the window. "I'm sure Wani thought Bael would be merciful, but he was killed for one reason alone: he knew Bael wanted me back, and he still let me go."

Anya's explanation made sense, and at the same time, it didn't. Why would Bael go to the trouble of killing a kappa in the swamps who nobody ever saw? Bael didn't just kill without cause, no matter what Anya said. He was the kind of demon who wanted to make a statement with each slaughter.

Jack shifted and winced, gingerly touching the bruise Striker had left. It was a glorious shade of purple, and the pain relievers must've just worn off. He stood to get more out of his bag.

"I'm amazed you've survived this long. You can't fight worth a shit," Anya said.

"I hadn't used my knives in a while," Jack said, shaking out two pills from the bottle and stuffing it back inside the bag. "I spent three years in accounting. I'm still rusty, it seems."

Her eyes narrowed as if she were scanning him for signs of falsehood. "That's not what it is. Unless your abilities in the field were grossly overstated in your Division records, you shouldn't be *this* bad."

"Guess I just am right now," Jack said, slinking down into the chair. "Would you like to keep insulting me, or can I take a nap?"

"Nap away."

As usual, their train tickets were to a different city—Munich—so it didn't really surprise Jack when they got off in Stuttgart, Germany. What did surprise him was that Anya kept walking out of the train station, both their bags in hand.

"What's up?" he asked, looking over his shoulder. "Are we being followed?"

"No," she said with an almost playful smile.

Playful? That was new.

She offered no further information or discussion, but it was clear she knew where she was going. The city was vibrant with new construction and shops, parks and lots of cars.

Finally, after walking through what was probably half the city, they found a small alley of old buildings. Anya stopped in front of a normal-looking apartment complex, pressing the doorbell to call the owner.

"Are we staying at an AirBnB this time?" Jack asked with a small laugh.

Anya glanced at him over her shoulder. "No."

The door clicked open and Anya walked through as if she owned the place. If she did, that would explain her familiarity with the city. Inside, there was clearly construction happening, with plastic, ladders, and paint cans sitting against the walls. The elevator door was wide open, but Anya headed for the stairs, climbing them without breaking her stride.

The staircase ended inside what would eventually be a penthouse apartment. There was no furniture inside, nothing on the walls except for... a lot of weapons. Spears and swords, looking too ancient to be useful. Unfinished blades and whetstones were scattered around the floor, along with leather hides and ropes.

"Where are we?" he asked.

A small growl echoed out of one of the dark rooms. Jack reached for his knives, sensing the demonic miasma pouring from the opening. There was no mistaking it—a nox.

"Did you bring me a toy, Lady?" came the raspy voice.

"Stop with the theatrics," Anya replied, bored. "Show yourself."

Jack had expected a fully transformed nox, but a human-looking woman appeared instead. She slunk in the shadows much as a cat would, her yellow-green eyes reflecting in the limited light.

"Jack," Anya said, glancing at him. "Meet Oce. One of the only nox demons I'm on good terms with. She's a brilliant weapons master, and she will find you a suitable weapon."

"Wait a minute," Jack said (the cattish woman squealed "American, too!"). "Is that why we stopped in this city? I don't need new weapons."

"I'll be the judge of that," Oce said, stalking out of the shadows. It was only Anya's cool, calm demeanor that kept Jack from running in the other direction. She stopped in front of him and inhaled deeply. "I love humans. The fear is addicting."

"Oce," Anya warned. "He shares my disdain of your demonic brethren. Be kind."

"Draw your weapons, human," she whispered, pulling a pair of long swords from her hips. "I want to see how good you are."

"Why?"

"So I can ascertain your problem."

"I don't have a—"

The nox let out a cry and lunged with her sword. Jack scrambled out of the way, fumbling for his knives. She hacked again, barely missing his shoulder. Finally freeing his left knife, he parried another strike, and she fell to the ground, rolling and waiting on her heels.

"Mm-hm," the nox said, perched on her heels.

"Mm-hm, *what*, you crazy demon?" Jack panted, pulling the second knife out.

Her eyes lit up with glee, and she pounced, this time with a second sword in hand. Jack watched them come in slow motion, caught in indecision of which to defend against. Either way, one of them was going to hurt.

At the last moment, the swords disappeared, replaced by a combat boot to the gut. Jack cried out as he fell backward, opening his eyes to see two pointed swords inches from his face.

"Tell me, human, have you suffered a loss?" Oce asked, her eyes more curious than murderous.

"Y-yes," Jack sputtered. "My wife. Killed by noxes."

"Were you there?"

He swallowed, unable to tear his gaze away from the yellow-rimmed eyes above him. "No. I was the first...I saw the aftermath."

"And your knives, do you think they failed you?"

"W-what?" Jack said. "I wasn't even home—"

The sword points disappeared. Oce sauntered back to Anya. "You were correct to bring him. He's got a lot of baggage, that one."

"Well, no shit," Jack said, standing. "But I like my knives—"

"Then why do you hesitate while you use them?" Oce asked. "I can see every thought. I can smell the panic. And grief—so much grief. A warrior of your caliber shouldn't fear a simple sparring match."

Jack pushed himself to his feet, looking down at his trusty knives. "I can get better..."

"There's no doubt, my pet." The nox unlocked a large metal door with her nail, revealing an arsenal that would've made Cam salivate—knives, swords, crossbows, archery equipment, spears, mallets, even a few machine guns. The nox reappeared with a long, thin sword in her hand, a perplexed look on her face.

"Perhaps we will try a single," she said, tossing the sword at his feet.

Against his better judgment, he picked up the sword and handled it awkwardly for a moment. It was almost too light for the length, whereas his knives were short and to the point (literally). Oce must've agreed with Jack's assessment, because she took the sword from him and put a crossbow in its place. But that didn't work either, as she snatched it away before Jack could even handle it. She tapped her long, black fingernail against her chin and disappeared into her armory. She tried a curved sword that was too heavy, a spear, a broadsword, a cutlass, and…decided none of them were correct.

"Perhaps I am thinking too far out of the box," she said, appearing with a pair of knives different from the ones Jack used. They were lighter, a bright silver instead of dull steel. The grips were leather, whereas Jack's old knives had been a more modern plastic.

"You like these," Oce said with a nod.

"Yeah, I kind of do," Jack said, turning them easily in his hand. The leather slid across his hands like silk, and the balance was nearly perfect—unlike his old set that probably needed an adjustment. His heartbeat rose in anticipation of using them in battle—seeing how they differed from his old set.

A light flashed, and Jack reflexively braced the knives above his head to catch the sword. Oce grinned madly, sliding her sword against the metal of his knives with slow precision. Then she came again, swinging wildly. Jack forgot to think, knocking away each of her strikes and reveling in the way these new knives worked in his grip.

The tip of the knives hit flesh, and he recoiled, shocked.

"I'm sorry!" he said, as red pooled on the nox's arm.

She seemed unbothered by it, raising the cut to her lips and licking. "It'll heal. You, my love, are wonderful."

"He's better than he was," came Anya's bored volley. She pushed herself off the wall and sauntered over to them. "This will do."

"As to the manner of my payment…" Oce asked, looking at Anya.

Anya tossed down a wad of euros. "Is that sufficient?"

"Mm…not this time, my love," Oce said. "I would like something else. Information on this new demonic weapon."

"Dem—You mean what my partner did in Atlanta?" Jack asked. He forced himself not to reach for the remaining talismans around his wrists. "That's what we're trying to figure out."

"You hurt an athtar with it," she said, her eyes lighting with pleasure. "I want to know what it was. Otherwise I will take my knives back.…*with interest.*"

Jack looked at Anya, who was pissed but shrugged. "Tell her what you know."

So he did, explaining the connection to the ancient Mexicans and how they'd been in Cam's family for generations. She purred with excitement when Jack told her that Cam had engraved the symbol on an iron bullet.

"Fascinating," Oce said. "I should pay a visit to this partner of yours…"

"No," Jack said, surprising himself with his ferocity. "Don't talk to Cam. Don't even—"

"Oh, pet, I'm not going to hurt her. She sounds fascinating. I would love to fight her." She chuckled and licked her arm again. "Preferably without her talisman bullets."

"Enough," Anya said, with a cutting glare to Oce. "Are you satisfied with our barter?"

"I suppose." She pouted. "But I wanted to play with your human some more."

"You know I can't stay long," Anya said. "And you know, if you tell a soul—"

"You'll find my demonic tail and feed it to me. Yes, my love, I *know*," Oce drawled. "Three hundred years, and I have never told a soul about our special friendship."

"That's because it's not a friendship, you yellow-eyed mongrel," Anya said, her demeanor changing in an instant. "You provide services, I pay you for them. That is it. I use you because you are the best at what you do in this miserable human realm. When you are no longer useful—"

"You're painful, athtar," Oce said, turning her back and walking back to her arsenal. "Be gone with you. I do not wish to look upon you anymore."

Anya grunted and threw down a wad of euros. "Leave your old knives," she ordered Jack.

"Why?"

"Because you no longer need them. You have new weapons."

"But..." Jack swallowed, staring at the discarded pieces of metal. He was overly attached to them, after all, even though his new weapons were lovely. A gift from Frank when he'd graduated the Academy, they'd been forged in Shanghai at the weapons institute. They'd saved his life (and gotten him into trouble) more times than he could remember. Much like Cam, they were familiar friends who'd turned into strangers after the world imploded.

"This is why I brought you here," Anya said, lowering her voice. "Your weapons carry too much emotional weight."

"Hah!" came the biting laugh from the arsenal. "And you're one to talk. I know what you carry in that bag."

Anya glared at the voice and picked up the duffel bag. "Let's go."

Jack forced himself to turn and leave the knives on the floor, knowing that this was a good, helpful move, but hating the pain that came with growth.

CHAPTER TWENTY-ONE

Since they'd missed their train, they grabbed a hostel in town for the evening. Jack and Anya pulled the same frozen-credit-card excuse, although this time, Anya was awake to play the part of the angry girlfriend.

"You don't have to call me a fucking idiot, by the way," Jack said as they ascended the stairs with their keys. "That's hurtful."

She actually smiled, and it brought a lightness to her face that Jack hadn't seen before.

Inside the room, Jack lay in bed and played with his knives as he got used to the subtle differences. After a while, he forgot how his old knives had felt—which scared him a little.

Anya had said little, but she'd gone out to retrieve dinner, saying she'd also do a sweep to make sure "that mangy animal" hadn't sold them out. She returned with a bag of fast food, and the dark cloud over her face that had been present since they'd left Oce.

Jack was feeling somewhat brave, so he thought he'd poke the bear a little. "So…I thought you didn't have any friends?"

She glared at him. "I don't. Oce is a business associate."

"She said friend," Jack said, sitting up and putting his knives in their sheaths. "And you've known her for three hundred years?"

Anya swallowed her bite with a haughty expression. "She is as I said. Good at her job and worth my time."

"She's the first person I've ever seen you have a semi-normal relationship with," Jack pressed. "Care to share more?"

"Will it shut you up?"

"Possibly."

"Fine." She stuffed her mouth full of french fries and swallowed. "Oce and I met before I was cursed. She had a reputation for herself as a weapons master. She had hopped between the Underworld and the human realm, spending a decade in different places and learning how the humans and demons fought. I occasionally call on her to forge me a weapon or two."

"And you're not worried about her meeting the same fate as Wani?" Jack asked.

Anya shrugged, although a bit of emotion slipped through her mask as she chewed. "She's survived this long."

"But things are different," Jack pressed. "Bael's hunting for you now."

Anya flinched but recovered quickly. "Usually after Oce and I meet, she returns to the nox den in Mexico City. Then, after a few years, she'll re-emerge in another city on the hunt for new weaponry."

"And..." Jack swallowed the hamburger bite. "What was that about what you carry in the bag?"

Her eyes flashed, and Jack prepared himself for a catty remark. "Sharur," she said quietly. "The sword Bael gave me in Atlanta."

"Why don't you use it?"

"I don't...like using it," she admitted quietly. "Bael did. He thought it was symbolic, covered in jewels and gems as it is." She loosed a shaky breath. "Much like you and your knives, I can't wield it without feeling a great deal of emotion. So I opt not to."

"It's the one you used to kill Mot and Xo, right?" Jack asked.

She nodded. "They deserved it. But...maybe others didn't. Either way, when I hold it, I can't bring myself to even lift it. Not even when Bael is telling me to." She reached for the charm that no longer hung from her neck. "It's been a few weeks. How long is this curse supposed to linger?"

Jack didn't say what he was thinking; instead, he offered an affirming smile. "We'll find out the truth."

"Then what?" she asked. "Do I go back to Bael? Is that what you want?"

Jack sighed. "It doesn't matter what I want. You need to do

what feels right."

"What would happen if I broke this curse and turned back into the woman I was with Bael?" she asked, a bit of desperation slipping into her tone. "What if I turned back into the Lady of Destruction?"

You might find her less destructive than you thought. "We'll cross that bridge when we get to it."

"Jack?" she asked, looking up at him with wide green eyes. "Why are you helping me?"

"Because you need it," he replied softly. "Just like you helped me today. You're right. I might've gotten myself killed the way I was using those knives."

She reached across the table and swiped a handful of his fries, as hers were gone. "I have to say, I was actually pretty impressed. Not many human men could stand against Oce. And she wasn't pulling any punches, either." A smile blossomed on her face. "I now understand why the Division called you one of their most promising agents when you graduated."

"Oh?" Jack perked up. "You know about that?"

"I researched you when you first started sticking your nose into my business," she said, although there was a teasing smile on her face as she took more of his fries. He pushed the entire pile over to her. "Up until now, I thought it was just nepotism. But now I think you might've earned that title."

"Glad I finally made an impression," Jack said with a sad smile. "I was promising. Once."

"You still are," she said, toying with a fry. "Do you think

you'll go back?"

"Nah. Nothing to go back to, you know? Even with Frank on the Council, I doubt anyone would give me a job after what I've done." He stared at the window. "I liked what we were doing in Amsterdam. Helping people who need it, regardless of the law. Sometimes I feel like ICDM is more about helping demons than humans."

"You aren't wrong," Anya said. "But I don't think it's as simple as that. Sometimes, you have to appease your tormentors for the greater good."

Jack slipped his fingers across his talismans. "Or we just kill the tormentors so they'll leave us the hell alone."

She cracked a smile. "You could do that too."

Finally, after another long train ride, they reached Geneva to continue the search for Anya's curse at ICDM headquarters. The city was familiar to Jack, and a welcome respite from all the running. During the summer months, his parents had sent him along on every business trip Frank took to the world headquarters. At the time, it was a fate worse than death (after all, he could've gone to lacrosse camp). Now, after traveling all over Europe, Jack was a little relieved to be somewhere he knew.

Anya didn't share his relief, leading him straight into the museum and waiting in the park across the street until the crowds at the museum were thick enough for them to blend in. Jack bought them a pair of knock-off ICDM hats to wear inside the museum, then joined Anya on a park bench with a view of the museum courtyard. There was already quite a large crowd assembled, from young kids chasing each other up and down the steps to older tourists who snapped photos of the large columns. The park was less crowded, but there were still a few joggers and older couples walking hand-in-hand.

"What are you grinning about?" Anya asked.

"Just people watching," Jack said.

"I guess," she muttered. "I don't like sitting out in the open like this."

"Do you feel any athtars?" Jack asked, watching a small bird hop along the park path. "Or any other demons?"

"No, but that doesn't mean they won't show up."

"How would they know where to go?"

"They could just recognize us."

"Then let's use some glamour."

"No, I don't want to use glamour," she snapped. "I don't have that much left and I don't want to waste it."

Jack tilted his head toward her. "We can either sit here and watch, or we can go somewhere else and watch, or we can just go in now. But you sitting here worrying isn't doing anything but making yourself crazy."

She opened her mouth to answer, then crossed her arms, sitting back on the bench. After a moment of fidgeting, she stood up. "I'm ready, let's go."

Once inside the large front hall of the museum, Anya grabbed a pamphlet from the front desk and joined him on a bench underneath the giant ICDM banner to figure out where they needed to go.

"This museum makes no sense," Anya whispered.

"Well, it's not like we'll find an exhibit on early demonic curses," Jack said, peering over the map with her. "We could try either the exhibits on the emergences, elokos, or ICDM weaponry?"

"You go to the elokos," she said. "I'll start with the emergence exhibit. We can meet at ICDM weaponry in twenty minutes?"

"Make that forty. We might find something in the nox section, too."

She nodded and left him on the bench. Jack scanned the room to make sure no one had been watching them then set off for the other side of the museum.

The museum had been boring when he'd been an incorrigible teenager, but now, he regretted not paying better attention to the exhibits. Knowing what he did now, he might've benefitted from all this knowledge. Or at least, he might've done better on his history exams.

He started in the eloko area, which had a fairly accurate painting of Biloko right down to the grassy hair and potbelly. But the exhibit, as a whole, was a bust. Jack was dismayed to read the following under the "emergence" section:

The first eloko sightings occurred in the third or fourth centuries, A.D. in what is now the Republic of Congo. Unfortunately, the hunter-gatherer peoples of Central Africa kept mostly oral records until the twelfth century, so the exact date, time, and locations are unknown to all except for Biloko himself, and the humans he first turned.

"Damn," Jack said under his breath.

He didn't have much luck at the nox exhibit, as there was no mention of the talismans. But he didn't expect to see anything either. Not until Cam got around to showing the world her new, old-fashioned weapon.

Anya was waiting for him at the ICDM weaponry exhibit with a frown on her face. "Anything?"

"Nope," he said. "You?"

"No, but I did see something interesting." She lowered her voice. "I went behind the exhibit walls and found a huge research laboratory. Maybe what we're looking for is back there," Anya said, gesturing to the exhibits of swords and other weapons. Jack spotted the door she'd slipped through. It was clearly marked 'employees only' with the ICDM logo, and had the telltale thumbprint scanner of most secured areas in ICDM.

"Are you sure you should be using your magic?" Jack said. "You just got better."

"Moving a few feet is nothing," she said. "But it would be better if we came back at night. I would rather use none if I can."

"I agree," Jack said as they headed toward the exit. It was still early afternoon, and the sun was shining on a perfect spring day. As they walked down the stairs, Jack tilted his face upward toward the sun, enjoying the warmth and the breeze on his face.

"What are you doing?" Anya asked, three steps ahead of him.

"We need to get back to the hostel and prepare for tonight."

"Do we, though?" he asked, looking at her. Perhaps it was the weather, or perhaps just being in a familiar city that didn't bring out his grief, but Jack didn't want to go back and sit in a dark hostel room, waiting for something bad to happen.

She blinked, clearly at a loss for words.

"It's been a while since anyone's been on our tail," he said, joining her. "After all, you thought it was safe enough to see Oce, right?"

"I don't follow."

At that, Jack had to laugh. "I thought maybe we could go out to dinner tonight. Or do something fun for a change. I don't know. I'm in a good mood."

"We have athtars hunting me, and demonic bounty hunters and the entire ICDM looking for us and you want to go get *dinner because you're in a good mood?*" She shook her head. "Are you *insane?* A whole city is being offered for our capture. A whole damned city. And you want to do something *fun?*"

"I know we're under a lot of stress," Jack said. "But we're probably going to leave after we case the museum, right? So why don't we just take the two hours we have and instead of sitting around the hostel eating another bag of takeout food, let's get a square meal? It's fondue, and it's really good—"

"It's too dangerous," she said. "We need to go back to the hostel where it's safe."

Jack wasn't taking no for an answer. "*You* can stay where it's safe. I want to eat a big bowl of melted cheese. I think we've earned it."

She blinked. "Is that what fondue is?"

"Yeah." Jack had to laugh. "You've never had it before?"

"I don't indulge in food, but..." She licked her lips, looking uncertain. "Where is this place?"

"Far, far away from ICDM headquarters," Jack said, looping an arm around her shoulders. "Promise."

To his surprise, she left his arm around her. "It had better be a damned good bowl of cheese."

Anya was not disappointed, her eyes growing to wide when the pot of steaming white melted goo appeared between them. One bite, and she was as suckered as a human on lilin miasma. She even started making the same sounds, too.

"I'm glad you're happy," Jack said with a hearty chuckle as she moaned in pleasure. "But you might want to keep it down. People will think we're doing something indecent over here."

"This is indecent," she said, swirling a carrot into the gruyere and white wine mixture. "I'm surprised Freyja hasn't imported this yet. This is...this is amazing."

"I'm glad you think so highly of our lowly human inventions," Jack said, enjoying his at a much slower pace.

"You know," she said, between bites. "I do remember coming to this city. Before it was a city."

"Let me guess, Demon Spring?"

She chuckled a little darkly. "Yeah. It was...well, it was. I want to say it was the fifth or sixth century. A kappa demon here caused a flood, so I don't know what it looked like before that."

Jack dipped a piece of bread into the mixture. "I think it's a shame you never slowed down enough to watch the evolution of humanity. You've been all over the world, and you don't even have a favorite city."

"That's not…entirely true," Anya said, averting her gaze. "Since I've been cursed, I've appreciated cities. I like Toronto a lot. And Seattle, but only for the coffee."

Jack smiled. "You like coffee?"

"I'm rather a snob about it, unfortunately." She looked down at her hands. "But I'll take a cup of gas station garbage when I'm exhausted."

"Yeah, me too," Jack said. "You know, I think this is the first real conversation we've ever had."

"Don't get used to it," she said. "We have a mission, and I won't have you screw it up because you're stuffed on good cheese and bread."

"Speak for yourself," Jack said, using his fork to stab one of the small pieces of bread on her plate.

She batted his fork away. "Oce is a novice swordsman compared to me," Anya said with a playfully dangerous glint in her eye. "I would watch your fork, sir."

Jack didn't doubt it, so he relinquished his claim on her bread and opted for broccoli instead. "So do you think Oce was serious about finding Cam?"

"Your partner will be fine," Anya said with a wave of her fork. "Oce is fond of humans like a child is of a toy. I don't believe she's ever spawned herself—or killed a human, either."

"You know an awful lot about her for being just business associates," Jack said, testing the waters of this new, calmer Anya.

To his surprise, it was sadness, not anger, that fell across her face. "It's for her own good, really."

"What? To not be friends with you?" Jack asked.

"The only friend I've ever really had was a kappa servant," Anya said, her eyes growing distant. "I don't even know why I decided...maybe she just had a kind face. I knew Bael would disapprove—he didn't like me being cordial with anyone but him. I kept it a secret as long as I could, but eventually Bael found out. He acted like it didn't bother him at first. Then, over the next few weeks, he kept mentioning it. He'd ask about her, if we'd talked about him and what she'd said. He got angrier and more accusatory. One day, he asked me if I was in love with her."

"Were you?" Jack asked.

"Bael was the king of the demons, how could I ever be in love with anyone else?" she said with a helpless shrug. "Besides that, Ayumi had her own lover, and they were quite happy together. But Bael didn't believe a word I said, just maintained that I was going to leave him for this...this *kappa*." She sighed. "The next Demon Spring, he came to the human realm with me. He brought Ayumi and told me I had a choice."

The same choice he'd given her a few weeks ago. "Kill her or kill a thousand humans?" The king of the demons was jealous of a serving girl. How ludicrous.

She nodded and kept her gaze on the table. "Not just any humans, either. He'd assembled thousands of children, some barely toddling. It was cruel, even for a demon. So I...I killed Ayumi." She swallowed hard and Jack had no doubt she remembered every second of it.

But from the tone of her voice, that wasn't the end of it. "Then what happened?"

"He killed the children anyway," she whispered.

Jack sat back, words of disgust and anger brimming to the surface. But he wasn't sure she'd be receptive to them.

She heaved a heavy sigh. "Oce is better off if she remains purely an associate and nothing more. I couldn't forgive myself if anything happened to her. If Bael killed her because of me."

"You...of course realize Bael's insecurities are ridiculous?" Jack said after a moment. "Sara was never jealous of Cam and me, and we were closer than siblings. She never made me choose between—"

"It wasn't like that all the time," Anya said quickly. "There were centuries of greatness. After...after Ayumi died, Bael was wonderful."

"Of course he was."

She glared at him. "He was kind and generous to the demons in the underworld. He even let Mizuchi return to the human realm to claim some more, as an apology for Ayumi. He wasn't angry—"

"Because you weren't pissing him off," Jack replied. "What I hear is this: Things were good as long as nobody made any sudden moves."

"You don't understand," she said, standing. "When you live as long as I have—"

"I don't think I have to live more than thirty years to see when someone's being manipulated. Even a demon as powerful as you are."

Anya's anger returned in a flash. "I'm tired of this conversation. If you bring it up again, I will behead you. We've wasted enough time."

Jack held up his hands in surrender. "Fine. I'll get the check."

CHAPTER TWENTY-TWO

Jack was almost a little giddy as he latched his knife holder around his waist. While it would be best if they didn't get used, he was excited to use his new knives. He stood in front of the mirror and pulled them, enjoying the singing sound they made as they came in and out of his holders.

"You'll probably need this instead," Anya said, handing him a case.

He opened it. "A gun?" Jack said with a raised brow. "Seems an awfully human weapon."

"We're going to be dealing with humans tonight," she said. "I don't think you'll need to use it, but...you might. At least then, they won't be able to trace it to us. I doubt anyone would expect you to use that."

Jack unhooked his belt and added the gun holster to it. "If you say so."

The streets were emptying at the late hour, so they moved swiftly toward the headquarters buildings. After finding a hiding spot in an alley nearby, they waited until the latest patrol had passed, then dashed to the wall. There, Anya used her magic to slide them to the other side of the fence. They crept toward the building, getting as close as possible to keep the magic to a minimum.

"I think this is it," Anya said, looking up at the side of the museum wall. "We were on the west side of the exhibit halls."

"And you're sure this won't be too much for you?" Jack asked.

She grabbed him by the hips and pulled him to her. Her eyes glowed black as she exhaled. The world slid under his feet, and the dark night winked into bright fluorescent lights. The lab came into focus, and Anya's eyes returned to normal.

She released him, looking no worse for wear. "What do you think?"

"We'll see how quickly you fall asleep tonight," Jack said with a smirk.

The lab was eerily sterile, brightly lit with stainless steel tables covered in papers and scientific equipment. There were files and notepads scattered around the room, and a few computers that had been switched off.

"So what are we looking for?" Anya asked, sitting down at

one of the computers and pressing the mouse buttons a few times. When the machine didn't turn on, she moved to the folders next to it.

"Your guess is as good as mine," Jack said, sitting down at another computer. It was locked, accessible by ICDM ID only. "Damn. Do you think there's anyone around with a log-in?"

Anya shrugged. "I'd prefer not to involve anyone if we—"

The door to the lab opened, and a young female doctor with pale skin and blonde ringlets walked inside. She stopped mid-stride, looked up from her folder, and opened her mouth.

Jack reached for the gun at his side and held it up. "Don't scream!"

She released a small squeak, her face blotching red. Her gaze frantically jumped between Anya and Jack as her breath quickened.

"We aren't going to hurt you, just don't scream," Jack said, releasing his grip on the gun and letting it dangle from his fingers. "I promise you. But please come inside."

She took a tentative step, then another, her eyes wide and fearful. "W-who are you?" she asked in a heavy accent.

"We're just trying to find some answers," Anya said, pushing herself off the desk.

The girl turned and her eyes bulged. "It's you! A-Anat!" She looked at Jack. "And you! The Grenard man!"

"Yeah," Jack said, putting the gun away. "It's us. But I swear, we aren't here to hurt you. What's your name?"

"Dr. Stalder," she said quietly. "I'm the assistant to the head researcher here."

"And what are you researching?" Jack asked.

She swallowed, seeming to calm down the longer they stood there. "We're excavating sites in Syria to find out where the first demon emergence happened." She turned to Anya and bit her lip. "I have to say...L-lady Anat, considering you've been the subject of my entire career, it's something of an honor to meet you."

Anya crinkled her nose. "It's really not."

"Anya," Jack said with a shake of his head. She, perhaps, had no idea, but there really *were* people who'd dedicated their careers to things she found mundane. "Dr. Stalder, are you only looking at the first Demon Spring? Do you know of anyone doing research on the first one in the Congo?"

She shook her head. "No. I mean, not to say there aren't people looking at it. But I don't really know more than what's in my department. The research institute is broken up by region, much like the Council. We rather stay in our own bubbles, you know?"

"What do you know about the first eloko sighting?" Jack asked. "Anything?"

"Only that it took place in the Congo," she said. "The stories of the first eloko were handed down orally, so we don't know *for sure...*"

Anya slumped in a nearby chair. "That's it, then. Another dead end."

"Maybe not," Jack said, holding up his hands. "Have you

ever heard of anything like a curse or a talisman used to ward off demons?"

Stalder shook her head. "Not anything real."

"What *not real* thing have you heard?" Jack pressed.

"There's always been a lot of talk about talismans and whatnot, but nobody's ever proven they really work. Scientifically, I mean," she added, with a nervous look at Anya. "B-but..."

"But?"

She heaved a sigh. "I never took any stock in it, but when I was a little girl, I used to hear stories about a group of people who worked outside the ICDM boundaries."

"Vigilantes," Anya drawled. "I'm one of 'em."

"They aren't lone actors, though. It's a group of people. They're all over the world, if you believe the rumors. I don't know anything about what they do, but I know...I know that ICDM bans any and all talk about them."

Jack quirked a brow. "I've never heard of anything like that."

"Your grandfather probably has," she said. "But they don't like us even acknowledging it exists. It was one of the things they impressed on us when we started the anthropology program here. Any talk of human magic is to be treated as smoke and mirrors."

"That I've heard," Jack said. "Any idea where we might find these magical humans?"

"We may have some information in the archives," she said, turning to the computer. "I do have access to that, in any case."

"See?" Jack said with a meaningful look at Anya.

"It says they're…well, that's odd." Stalder sat back. "We do have a lot of books on the early human vigilantes. But it looks like most of those books have been requested by and already shipped to the Charleston office."

Dread mixed with exasperation filled Jack's mind. Typical. "Cam."

"Who?" Stalder asked.

"My partner," Jack said, resting his hands on his hips. "I'm not surprised in the least."

"What the hell is she doing?" Anya asked.

"I would hope it's the beginnings of her research into weaponizing the talismans. But my gut tells me she's trying to out-research me to figure out the mystery and be waiting when we do." Jack laughed, a little nervously. "She does that."

"Then we'll just have to take her research," Anya replied heavily. She turned to the young scientist. "Are you going to tell anyone we were here?"

The woman shook her head so fast her curls bobbed. "N-no…"

"Good girl. You get to live," Anya replied. "Let's go. We've been here long enough."

Jack thanked the doctor, slid her a hundred euros, and followed Anya out the door.

"W-wait, Lady," the doctor cried, stepping forward with a map in her hand. "If it's not too much trouble, do you think you could remember the site of your village? We've been unable to find the exact spot."

Anya's eyes flashed, perhaps remembering the torture she'd endured before Bael had found her. But she softened and took the map from the doctor, her brows knitting as she scanned the map of the Mediterranean.

"Things have shifted," she said with a shake of her head. "Ugarit was the name of the village—"

The scientist's eyes lit up. "I know exactly where that is." She pointed to a small inlet just south of Turkey. "Here?"

Anya squinted at the map. "I don't know exactly."

"It's a start," the scientist said. She took Anya's hands and squeezed them. "Thank you, Lady Anat. Your generosity is most appreciated."

Jack beamed at Anya, who was blushing. "Uh…it's no big deal, really."

"C'mon, we've got to get going," Jack said gently, more to give Anya a chance to escape without being embarrassed further by the star-struck scientist. "Thank you, Doctor, for your help. Anya, if you'll do the honors?"

"Right," she said, taking his hand. This time, the eye-blackening and time-moving seemed almost an afterthought, and the fluorescent lights turned back into the night sky.

Anya released his hand and put her hands on her hips. "That was weird."

"What? You know humans like to study history," Jack said. "I bet if you go back and tell that scientist everything you know about when Bael emerged, she'd give you her firstborn."

Anya actually laughed, a disbelieving look in her eyes. "I hate to break it to her, but I *destroyed* that village."

"Oh, well," Jack said with a shrug. "Maybe you could lie a little bit to her. Just to make her career worthwhile."

She smiled, but then it faded. "Something's wrong."

"What—"

She took his hand, and with a single exhalation, they were back inside the laboratory. Only this time, they stood in the hall. Jack stared into a security camera, shocked that Anya would give away their position so carelessly. But by the nervous look on her face, Jack was pretty sure whatever she was feeling trumped the ICDM security concerns.

"What is it?" he whispered.

"Ssh," she said, pressing herself against the wall. Carefully, she cracked the door open.

Dr. Stalder's voice echoed out. "P-please, I didn't do anything. I won't tell a soul!"

"What's—" Jack started, but Anya silenced him with a hand to the mouth.

"I know you're there, Anat. I can feel it the same way you felt me." The voice was male with an Irish accent. The power reverberating in it was as intense as the original demon himself. Anya was as still as a rock.

"Every day that passes means more punishment from the King of the Mountain. His patience is not infinite, although it's much longer where you're concerned." Annoyance dripped into his voice. "Of course, I could kill you myself and tell him the humans did it. A century in the human filth has made you weaker than even I thought possible. One blow would do it." He chuckled. "But we both know you'll come back to Ath-kur before too long. What else is there? To live with them until the lack of demon magic kills you? I can't imagine a worse death."

The monologue was running a little long, which told Jack what he'd already suspected: this new mystery man was an athtar. Anya's face was a mixture of fear and hesitation, as if she wasn't sure she wanted to engage. Jack wasn't even sure why she'd come back in the first place.

The strangled cry of the scientist pushed her out of the shadows.

"Let the human go," Anya demanded, brandishing her swords. "She's done nothing wrong."

"They said you were screwed in the head lately." The man with fire-red hair and blue eyes stared maniacally at them, the struggling scientist still in his grip. With barely a glance, he released her, and she bolted from the room as fast as her legs could carry her.

"What do you care if I kill a human? Still cursed?" he asked.

"Maybe," Anya replied. "More interested in what you're doing here."

He smiled, his gaze sliding to Jack for a moment before returning to Anya. "If you think I'm here to drag your sorry arse back to Bael, you're sorely mistaken. I'm merely enjoying my time in the human realm until the portal closes."

"Conveniently showing up where I am?" Anya asked with a

lifted brow. "On the other side of the world from the schism? Shouldn't you be terrorizing Atlanta?"

He shrugged and looked at Jack. "And shouldn't you be hanging off Bael's arm instead of this pathetic human's?"

She didn't even flinch. "I might just get back there once I find out the story behind this curse, and believe me, I will remember your insolence."

"You have no power over me in this human realm," he said. "And the longer you stay away from Bael, the shorter his patience becomes. When the breach closes, that will be the end of his grace. After that, he might just give me the pleasure of killing you myself."

"You could certainly try," Anya said with a chuckle.

"I can see your life force melting away with each passing second," the other athtar said with a hearty laugh. "I have been breathing in our glorious athtar magic, growing stronger."

"Even on my weakest day, you are no match for me," she replied.

Bullshit, Jack thought, but was caught between watching their battle of egos and wondering when he should make his move. The athtar talisman sat against his wrist, and the gun in his holster. Unlike Adelbert, this demon would be almost impossible to hit.

But Jack had to try. There was no way Anya would be able to defeat him in her current state.

"You simpering whore," the athtar replied. "Bael hasn't even noticed your absence over the past century. He is showing you mercy and you throw it in his face."

"So little you know, Ekur," she snarled back. "A whole universe existed before you came along, and so shall it be after you die."

"Are you going to be the one to do it?"

Jack undid his wristlet and opened the barrel of the gun as quietly as possible.

Ekur laughed. "Oh, my dear Anat. Your human has decided to shoot me. I wonder, shall he hit me?"

Anya glanced at Jack, her eyes lighting up in understanding. He gave her a brief nod.

And that was all it took, for the next thing Jack knew, the earth moved beneath his feet, the lights blinked to darkness, and Anya slumped against his chest, a hot gun in her hand.

"W-what just happened?" Jack asked.

"I killed him," she said, unable to remove her face from his chest. "I...I overpowered his magic. Froze him in place, then shot him with the gun."

"So why are we here?" Jack asked, looking around the dark alley. "And where is here?"

"Bael will know the moment he dies," Anya whispered, almost soundlessly "He will know it was me. He'll be there in a second. And he'll be *pissed*."

Jack swallowed. That they'd been so very close to being discovered sent chills down his spine. "I'm sorry, I didn't know what else to—"

"You did perfectly," Anya said, relaxing more into his arms.

Almost by instinct now, he hooked an arm under her knees and lifted her. She leaned her head against his shoulder, her eyes fluttering as she struggled to stay awake.

"So how did that go down, exactly?" Jack asked. "How do athtars fight each other?"

"It's a battle of who has more control over time," she replied softly. "I may not have a lot of magic, but what I have is very old compared to him. He's a neophyte."

"Hang on, he's a *new* demon?" Jack asked.

"As far as athtars go. He was turned about two hundred years ago," Anya said, nestling into his shoulder and closing her eyes. "Unless Bael changed someone else, he's the newest of them."

"So what you're telling me is that if we happen to face any other athtar, they're going to be more powerful than the one you barely beat?" Jack asked nervously.

"Barely is a bit of an overstatement," she said with a soft glare. "Ekur thinks highly of himself. As do all athtars. It's what draws Bael to their human selves. Ekur was a disgraced human prince in Ireland when Bael found him. Bael liked how he maintained his pride while the citizenry threw mud at him." Anya half-smiled. "So Ekur took his revenge on them and worships Bael for giving him the power to do so."

"Bael-worship seems to be a common affliction amongst athtars," Jack said. "You're sure he's dead?"

Anya nodded, her eyes growing sad. "I don't like killing athtar demons. Bael used to…when they'd piss him off…"

"You did what you had to," he said quietly. "If you didn't

kill him, he would have killed you, right?"

She nestled against him, pressing her forehead to his chin. He waited for her to respond, or to fall asleep, but she remained motionless, staring ahead as if she was replaying Ekur's death in her mind over and over again. So Jack held her, knowing just being there was all he could do for her.

CHAPTER TWENTY-THREE

Funny thing about searching for information: use the right word or phrase, and it's like the world opens up.

That was how Cam felt when she received the box of old books from Geneva, detailing the interactions with these underground vigilante organizations, the ones who'd used the symbol in the olden days. She wasn't looking forward to reading about burnings, hangings, and the like, but hoped to find a nugget of information about the group themselves.

Frank seemed to believe that if there'd been any human magic amongst the group, it had been stamped out thanks to the ICDM forerunner's policy on the subject. The vigilantes who existed now were mostly bounty hunters and mercenaries, and most of ICDM's documentation on them were wanted posters.

Cam had no reason to doubt Frank, but conceded he was probably a little biased. After all, humans and demons got along thanks in no small part to his and the council's carefully balanced politicking. It probably didn't make his job easier to have to cover up for all these extra killings.

But while she didn't blame him, she also didn't believe he was looking at the facts without tinted glasses. Cam, on the other hand, was willing to explore all avenues.

Even if those avenues were log books from the sixteenth century, detailing gruesome actions on behalf of the French and Spanish demon management brigade.

Cam pulled on a pair of latex gloves as she pawed through the old book, feeling Patrick's stare on the back of her neck. She was no amateur, however, and took care to turn the pages, jotting down notes on her laptop.

It was as detailed as she'd expected, with some hand-drawn images that left little to the imagination. Most of those found guilty of demonic possession were probably not demons at all and weren't associated with the inverted-shield symbol.

After hours of reading, she finally stumbled upon an entry in a Spanish logbook mentioning a tattoo. The witches in question had all borne the mark, and had been sent to Cuba to fulfill their punishments. She searched the archives on her laptop for mention of "witchcraft" and "Cuba" and got a few more hits.

"What did you find?" Patrick asked, handing her another book from the collection.

"There was a supposed human witch found in Grenada in 1514. He was sentenced to work in Cuba." She frowned. "Apparently, that's where all of them were sent." She sat back, playing with the coins around her wrist absentmindedly.

"Why is that interesting?" Patrick asked.

"Well, see," Cam began, looking at the nox talisman, "these talismans were a gift from my family. When I was a little girl, my abuela told me they were passed down from our ancestors as a protection against demons. She'd said they'd come from the Aztecs themselves, as a gift from God." She tapped her fingers on the journal. "And yet now I'm starting to wonder if maybe someone *else* imported them to my ancestors."

Cam had been toying with this theory for some time. There was a connection between La Colibrí's curse, the talismans, and the upside-down shield people. Cam didn't know for sure how or why, but she knew, in her gut, that something was there. Especially now that a great number of these witches had been sent to Cuba in the late fifteenth century. It coincided almost a little too perfectly with Hernán Cortés, and his invasion of Mexico City with his conquistadores. Could the talismans have been brought from Europe to Mexico, instead of the other way around?

She opened her email and a blank message, staring at it for a long time. She hadn't yet called on her great-aunt María and discussed any of what she was researching. María was responsible for a large subsection of the world, and, unlike Frank, rarely had time for her extended family.

Besides that, María was a firm *dis*believer in the power of the talismans. She'd sigh heavily and accuse her sister (Cam's abuela) of ruining the family name by attaching it to witchcraft. Cam hoped empirical evidence might change her mind, but she had a feeling that, even with all the data in the world, María might still consider it nonsense.

But García family history? That, María had in spades.

Cam cracked her fingers, deciding to go formal with this email.

Dear Tía María,

I hope you're doing well.

I'm working on a theory about the origins of our family talismans. I keep coming across a group of people with an inverted shield symbol. Councilman Grenard tells me it's a sign for the mercenaries who work outside of ICDM. But their tattoo was also found on a group of witches sent to Cuba—witches who might've been the original source for our talismans.

I'm grasping at straws here, I know. But if you could share any insight on the history of our family as it relates to the inverted shield, that would be helpful.

Yours,
Camilla

Cam read over the email a few times, rewording and

reorganizing until it sounded coherent.

Then she pressed send.

CHAPTER TWENTY-FOUR

The battle and hasty escape from Ekur had taken its toll on Anya, and she slept for almost a week. She'd transported them to Chamonix in France, about fifty miles southeast of Geneva in the middle of the picturesque Alps. Jack was able to find a cheap, private hostel. He mostly kept to the room, leaving only to scout the area for possible demon activity, but he saw none.

Although their research had been disrupted, it was clear the next stop in their journey was Charleston, at the US ICDM offices. Jack, of course, had mixed feelings about going back to his hometown, none of which he shared with Anya. For his sake, Jack hoped they would be in and out of the city before the ghosts came for him. And he hoped that Cam had been more successful than they'd been in figuring out this great mystery.

He glanced down at her sleeping form, and the crease between her eyes marring her features. She had been sleeping more soundly, but now, with the reminder that Bael was never far away, it seemed she was back to fitful dreams.

He gently smoothed the crease between her eyebrows with his thumb. She shifted, blinked at him, then went back to sleep, mumbling something unintelligible. Happily, the tense look faded as she fell back to sleep.

The eighth morning in their hostel, Jack awoke to the sound of fingers on computer keys. Anya had a bag of breakfast food and coffee waiting, and gave him the smallest of smiles when he sat up.

"Good morning. Feeling better?" he asked.

"I've got us plane tickets back to the US by way of Milan," she said.

"Never been there before," Jack said, ignoring how she'd ignored his question. "When do we leave?"

"Tonight. It's a red eye." She stretched, exposing her thin stomach under her shirt. "We should get ready to go, it'll take us some time to get to the city." She paused, sniffing the extra shirt in her bag. "Did you do my laundry?"

"Thought I might as well be useful," he said with a shrug. "How are we doing on money?"

She stared at him for a moment before answering. "I think we're okay. Your twenty grand in Amsterdam went a long way."

"Good," Jack said. "Do you think we'll need to do another

job any time soon?"

"Not for a while, I hope. But you never know." She lifted her sword in the air. "Did you sharpen my weapons, too?"

"I told you, I was bored," Jack said, catching the half-smile on her face when she examined the sword closer.

"Thanks," she said, putting it back in the bag. "And…thanks for looking out for me again."

"You know, after a while, Cam and I stopped thanking each other," Jack said, standing and stretching as well. "We just knew we had each other's back."

"Thank you for watching my back," she said purposefully before walking into the bathroom.

"Progress is progress," Jack said with a shake of his head.

They took a bus to Courmaeyeur and then transferred to another bus to Milan. Jack barely noticed the time, for the route took them through the prettiest mountain range he'd ever seen. He promised himself that when everything was over, he'd come back with Cam and they'd go skiing.

Assuming he wasn't looking at fifty years in prison.

They arrived in Milan as the sun was setting, and set off toward the airport, but first, they stopped by a bank, where Anya said her computer hacker had left them new passports and plane tickets.

"Is he in Milan?" Jack asked as she returned with a manila folder in hand.

"I don't know where he is now, but they have a network of

people," she said. "I'm not the only one they work for."

The passport was just as realistic as the one he'd burned before they'd arrived. But when he looked at the plane tickets, his heart sank.

"We're going to Dulles?" Jack said. "Really?"

"It's just a few hours' drive to Charleston," she said.

Eight hours exactly—less if they got out early and missed the traffic. It had become a familiar drive for him, with Sara by his side.

"What's wrong?" Anya asked. "Do you think they'll be waiting for us or something?"

"N-no," Jack said, tucking the plane ticket into his pocket. It just wasn't the sort of thing he wanted to do before heading into Charleston. Like rubbing salt in a wound.

As the plane took off and Anya passed out next to him, Jack tried to remind himself that his emotional issues with D.C. and Charleston were the least of their worries. They had murderous athtars and the whole of the Division hunting them. He couldn't really be picky about which cities they went to.

And yet, he couldn't quite shake the morbidity that surrounded him as they waited for their bags upon arrival.

"We should get out of here quickly," she said, glancing over her shoulder. "There are a few demons in the airport. I'd like to avoid them finding me."

"Mm."

"Are you awake?" Anya asked. "You seem distracted."

"I'm fine," Jack said, and forced himself to smile. "There are our bags."

Pretending to be an Italian tourist, Anya took care of the rental car, telling Jack they'd ditch it somewhere around Richmond and steal another car. Jack, nursing that same numb feeling, simply nodded and did what she said.

He said little as they pulled out on the highway, everything looking so painfully familiar. There was the weird building on the Dulles corridor that he and Sara had always pointed out.

"Who the hell decided that would be an okay design for a building?" he could hear her asking.

"Who, indeed?" Jack muttered as they drove by it.

"What'd you say?" Anya asked.

"Nothing," Jack replied. "Go back to sleep."

Based on the hour, Jack knew the smart thing to do would. be to take Highway 29 down to Charlottesville and then on to Richmond and 95, skipping the horrific traffic on I-66 and I-495. But his body wasn't in his control anymore, and the traffic was surprisingly light all the way into Alexandria.

Numbly, he pulled off on Highway 1. This was routine—his old routine. The Thai place he'd stopped at about once a week. The bank he started their first joint account at. His therapist's office. He'd walked, run, biked this whole area. Being back in this place was like stabbing an old, healed-over wound.

Up the big hill, past the light, first left. His heart was throbbing in his chest as he pulled down his side street and came to a stop in front of the townhouse.

It looked exactly the same. Then again, it had only been four months since he'd sold it. The flowers were blooming. Sara hated how much the house looked "so Northern Virginia" and went to the home and garden store to buy perennials. She and Cam spent an entire weekend digging and planting, and every year, she'd squeal when the first buds would signal the arrival of spring.

She'd be so thrilled to see the bounty of different colors wafting gently in the breeze.

"W…what are we doing here?"

Anya's sleepy, deadpan voice broke the spell, and Jack turned away from the house. "Just wanted to see something."

"This was your house, hm?" Anya said with annoying certainty.

"Yeah," Jack said, putting the car in drive. "It was."

Jack's detour got them caught in traffic, which made him even more agitated than he'd been before. Anya woke up about thirty minutes into the drive, but didn't say anything. Luckily. Every sign, every city, every inch of this road was grating at him, and all he wanted to do was break free from it.

When the traffic lightened, Jack began weaving through slower cars.

"Slow down," Anya said as they flew by another car. "You don't want us to get pulled over."

Jack let up on the gas pedal, but not his mood. "Fine."

"What's your problem?" Anya snapped. "You're acting like a moody teenager."

"Nothing," Jack said, knowing he was being ridiculous but not quite able to shake it. "I just...I don't know. I'm a moody teenager."

"Talk."

He pressed his head into the back of the seat. "It's stupid."

"So is the way you're acting, but here we are. Talk."

"I don't want to go to Charleston. It reminds me of my wife. D.C. reminded me of my wife. It..." He sighed, feeling somewhat better after saying it out loud. "It still hurts."

Anya was quiet for a moment. "I've lost someone before. I know how hard it can be to heal."

"Bael doesn't count," Jack snapped, angry that Sara would even be on the same planet as that monster.

"No, not Bael..." Anya said. "My...my daughter."

Jack nearly swerved off the road. "Your daughter?"

She nodded.

"Was it before you were turned?"

"No." She looked out the window. "When the noxes had their son, Bael wanted a child, too." She looked down at her hands. "Belus can do as they please, you know. So Bael gave me a beautiful daughter. Asherah."

"What happened?"

"The noxes," Anya whispered.

They deserve to die a thousand deaths. The air left Jack's chest. He'd suffered through unimaginable pain, and still he could only imagine what Anya had gone through. To lose a child and to have to carry that pain for thousands of years. No wonder she hated them.

"I'm sorry," Jack said after a moment. "It never gets easier, does it?"

"You forget for a while," Anya said. "I would go a century before I'd stumble on her small pants or her toys. Then it was as if I'd discovered her body all over again. I don't think Bael thought I would kill Mot and his wife, but I did. I remember every moment of taking my revenge on them."

"Why did they do it?" Jack asked.

"Belus wage war," Anya replied dully. "It's what they do. Mot and Xo crossed a line and they paid for it."

"But she's still gone," Jack said.

"She is." She ran her finger along the window. "It's been almost six hundred years. I thought if I took my revenge, it would lessen the pain, but it didn't. Then again, it was more justice than revenge."

"How so?"

"True revenge would've been to take their child from them." She looked at her hands. "Lotan is his name. He's a man now."

"Bael wanted you to kill him, right? When we went to the Underworld?"

She nodded. "Bael wants to be the ruler of the six realms, not just five. Lotan has taken the mantle from his parents and wears it as well as any belu. Some say..." She stared out the window. "Some say he's stronger than his parents."

"Is that why you didn't kill him as a kid?"

She half-smiled. "No, I couldn't kill him then because...

because he was just a babe. A few years older than Asherah. As much as I hurt, I couldn't... He was innocent. My blind rage wasn't that blind."

"Is that why you stayed with Bael? Because of your daughter and what happened to her?"

"It's complicated," she whispered. "We will always have our child, but...it's more than that. I'm forever indebted to him for saving my life. Before I was turned, life was...hard. I was barely thirteen—"

"*Thirteen?*" Jack said. "Bael took you when you were thirteen?"

She nodded. "I was set to be married off to a man my father owed a debt to. I refused, so my father beat me until I ran away. That's where Bael found me, on the banks of the Mediterranean Sea."

"So how are you..." He tilted his head. She looked fully adult to him.

"Bael aged me before he turned me," she said with a small smile. "He wanted someone who looked as old as he did, like Mot and Xo. I don't remember how, or if it was part of the demon transformation. I just woke up an adult, a demon, and ready to take revenge on everyone and everything."

Jack couldn't shake the squick factor of Bael preying on such a young girl.

"I'm just like Ekur, I guess," she said. "Grateful I was given the power to be better than I was. I owe everything to Bael, and he reminds me of that *all* the time."

"And it never occurred to you that you might be stronger than he is?"

She cast him a furtive glance. "I'm not stronger than he is."

Jack laughed. "Maybe not right now, but you were. At your height."

"I will never be more powerful than Bael," she said. "I can't be. He made me."

"He made you into someone stronger than him. After all, why would he send you to do all his dirty work if he could do it himself?"

"Because…" She blinked a few times then shook her head. "I promise you, I'm not stronger than he is."

"You only think that because he's manipulated you. For crying out loud, the man beat you, Anya."

"No, he never… It was never like that. He just got angry. He's a demon lord. He's used to getting his way."

"So what about those bruises I saw?"

She licked her lips. "He just gets angry. He's king of the demons, he can—"

"God, Anya, would you listen to yourself?" Jack asked with a laugh.

"I do listen to myself," she said, casting her eyes downward. "And sometimes he does go too far. But then he turns around and showers me with so much love and attention I might explode. Then I guess… I forget about the rest. When you love someone for that long, it's hard to train yourself to stop. No matter what they've done to you."

"You deserve better. You know that, right?" Jack said.

"Perhaps I do," she said, although she didn't sound convinced.

They continued in silence for a long time after that.

CHAPTER TWENTY-FIVE

Night had fallen by the time they reached Richmond, and Anya told Jack to find a motel on the outskirts of the city. They'd ditch the car in the morning and steal another one, she said, but for now, all the traveling was catching up with her and she needed to sleep.

Except Anya seemed to have an ulterior motive, because as soon as they put down their bags, she announced, "We're not staying here."

"Why?" Jack said, lifting his head from the pillow. "Is there a demon nearby?"

"No," she said with another one of those enigmatic smiles. "But there will be. Get your knives."

"Another vigilante mission? Don't we have plenty of money?"

"Jack, just…let's go," Anya said, handing him his knife holster. "Quit arguing with me."

To be honest, Jack was more intrigued than reticent about leaving the hotel room. Was she taking him to someone like Oce again? Did it have anything to do with their conversation in the car? Or was she just playing with him?

She plopped down in the driver's seat, added the GPS location in her phone, and set it on the dashboard to guide her.

"Where are you taking me?" Jack asked as he sat down in the passenger's seat.

"If I tell you, it'll ruin the surprise," she said with a half-glare. "I promise you won't die."

"Oh, well, that's something."

They drove in silence, except for the GPS voice telling Anya to turn left or right. Her green eyes were bright and alert as she navigated the dark streets, which probably didn't bode well for him. If her surprise was anything like Oce, he would be in for it.

Finally, she stopped on the main street in Carytown, a hip neighborhood with restaurants and shops.

"What's next, boss?" Jack asked.

"Stop calling me that," Anya said, sitting back in the seat. "Go upstairs, and you'll find out."

"Are you trying to get rid of me or something?"

"No, just go. I promise you, it will be worth it."

"What's up there?"

She pursed her lips. "If I tell you, you won't go. Or you'll think too much. So just go up there, get your revenge, and then we can get moving to Charleston."

"Re..." Jack's brows shot up into his hairline. "Anya. Who is up there?"

"Just go—"

"Is it Vicente? The D.C. nox lord?" Jack's pulse skipped as it sped up. "Anya, you're insane if you think—"

"It's not Vicente, but it's the nox that actually...it's the one," she said.

Jack turned in his seat to face the front. The demon's name was Paquito, and he was a newer third demon to Vicente. Cam had tried everything she knew to get the charges to stick to him, but Vicente had too much sway. He'd probably chosen such a low-level thug to kill Sara to prove how powerless the Division really was.

But Jack wasn't in the Division anymore. He'd veered far outside the norm, killing demons extra-judicially and getting involved in things he shouldn't have. But did that mean he was now free to kill Sara's killer? Did that mean he *should*?

"Anya...I can't do this," Jack said. "Paquito killed her, but... it was because of me. I've never wanted revenge on him."

"Then maybe you should start," Anya said. "The demons killed Sara. They're the ones responsible. Not you."

"However true that is—"

"I bet you anything that up there in that house is a young human pissing themselves in fear before Paquito takes them as his spawn."

"And what if he's up there eating Cheerios? I'm not about to kill a demon in cold blood. I don't believe in that eye for an eye stuff." He shook his head. "We're better than that, Anya. I'm better than that."

"I just thought…" she said quietly. "I thought it might help you."

Jack sighed, staring up at the building with one last, forlorn look. "It won't bring Sara back. Let's just get some dinner."

Neither Jack nor Anya were in any mood to chat at the small hipster restaurant Jack took them to. So much so that the waiter asked who'd died.

"Nobody," Anya said with a look at Jack as the waiter walked away. "And that's the problem."

"Anya, I don't understand why you're pressing this," Jack said. "It feels like you're asking me to murder someone."

"Who deserves it."

They'd been having this conversation round and round. "Why is it so important to you?" Jack asked. "Sara died three years ago. What do you care?"

She twirled her wine in her glass. "Because it's the right thing to do."

"Asking me to murder someone is the right thing to do?"

"I'm trying to help you move on," Anya said.

"Did killing Mot and Xo help you?"

"Well, no, but—"

"But what?" Jack said with a sardonic laugh. "So why do you think this is going to help me?"

"Because I don't have anything else to offer you," she finished lamely. "I don't know any other way to be. And I..." She actually flushed. "I wanted to do something nice for you. After all you've done for me."

Jack reached across the table and covered her hand with his. "I appreciate it. But this...this with Sara. It's not something you can fix. It's not something anyone can fix. If it were, Cam would've done it by now."

A borderline pout appeared on Anya's face. "I'm sure."

She couldn't be jealous, but just in case, he squeezed her hand. "I appreciate the thought."

Their food arrived and Anya scarfed hers in silence. Jack still couldn't quite figure why she'd taken such an interest in Sara's death, but chalked it up to one of her quirks.

"It's not as good as fondue," she said, putting her fork on the empty plate.

"Spoiled, are we?" He chuckled and sipped his beer. "This is the best place in Richmond, though."

"Did you come here with Sara?" Anya asked, looking around.

"Yeah, I did," Jack said, but the memory wasn't as fresh or vivid. "She and Cam liked to shop here. Or sometimes just get out of the city."

"I like it," Anya said, leaning back in her chair. "I don't think I've ever been here before."

"Yeah, Richmond's never had a Demon Spring."

She pursed her lips. "I meant, for…fun."

"Do you have fun?"

"I'm having fun right now." She swiped her wine off the table and sat back. "Well, I was until you mentioned it."

"Sorry, sorry," Jack said. "It's just…I'm not used to this version of you."

"Me neither." She chewed on her lip. "But it's like you said in Geneva. Things are good right now. I haven't felt any athtars, and we've been careful. Maybe I can relax…a little."

Jack was surprised she'd remembered something so throwaway, and even more so that she'd taken it to heart. Perhaps asking him to murder his late wife's killer was her definition of relaxing. It was a little sad, actually. She was most at ease barking orders and pushing him away. But when it came to showing honest emotion, she was clueless. She'd lived for thousands of years and yet never really lived at all. He was sure that Bael had given her some good moments, but the bad far outweighed them.

What might Anya's life be like if she weren't constantly on the run? If she were allowed to have friends and fondue, and a real boyfriend who took her out to dinner and doted on her. One that would never raise a hand to hurt her and who loved her despite all her quirks and missteps.

More importantly, if the curse wasn't real, as he suspected, what would she do then? After all, she would eventually die unless she returned to Ath-kur. And even though they'd been taking it easy, Jack was beginning to worry that fate might come quicker than even she believed.

"What?" She gave him a little deer-in-the-headlights look. "Did I say something wrong?"

"Of course not," Jack said. "Since we're relaxing, though, why don't we walk around for a bit?"

"And do what?"

"Just…walk," Jack said with a laugh. "That's how humans relax these days. It's not as bloody as what you're suggesting, but it can be a lot of fun if you're in the right company."

She tapped her fork against her plate, something of a coy smile on her face. "Humans do the strangest things."

But walk they did, down Cary Street in the center of the neighborhood. Anya was visibly uncomfortable, but as they stopped in different stores and Jack showed her things, she began to relax. When they stopped into a toy store, her eyes lit up with glee at all the trinkets, and Jack was surprised to find her the most amused by the not-so-innocent joke section in the back of the store.

"I learn something new about you every day," he said. "Who would've known you have the humor of a twelve-year-old boy?"

She shrugged, but the smile didn't leave her face. "There hasn't been much time for that kind of stuff."

"There hasn't been time for much of anything for you," Jack said, stuffing his hands in his pockets as they continued down the street. Otherwise, they swung oddly against his legs, almost aching to take hers. But that would be too forward, and he didn't want to scare her off when she was in such a good mood.

"I always considered every part of my life transitory, so enjoying the finer things…" She stopped in front of a clothes shop, tilting her head at the dress on the mannequin. "Bael used to shower me with gifts and finery. Every Demon Spring, he'd have the demons in the castle find the humans' latest fashion styles. He'd keep them hidden then surprise me every few weeks."

"Did you ever buy anything for yourself?" Jack asked. He personally thought the dress in question was ugly—a pale pink sweater dress that didn't do much on the plastic figurine.

"I buy things as I need them," she said softly. "The dress in Brussels, for one."

"But that's work. Have you ever bought anything for yourself? Just for shits and giggles." He reached into his pocket and pulled out his wallet. "Here. This is as much yours as mine. Treat yo'self."

"Seriously?" Anya said with a short laugh.

Jack opened the door to the shop and beckoned her inside. She followed him inside, still wearing a look of distrust and disbelief. But the look faded as Jack took a seat on one of the many plushy couches, and she was immediately accosted by the saleswoman. Jack purposely picked up a magazine, another cue to the saleswoman that they were there for the long haul. He caught Anya's disgruntled look as she was ferried off to the changing rooms with an armful of clothes.

"How she doing back there?" he asked when the saleswoman

made an appearance again.

"She's like a damned model," the woman said with a bit of a frown. "I'm actually… She's very thin. Is everything all right?"

"We're working on it," Jack said with a half-smile. "Just help her find something that makes her feel good."

The woman beamed as she juggled several hangers. "You're a wonderful boyfriend."

Jack let that comment slide and went back to the magazine, but didn't read. Instead, he thought about what she'd said about having nothing else to offer him but revenge. He glanced over his shoulder as the saleswoman walked out with Anya and a few extra hangers on her arm. There was a lightness to Anya's face, her ashen skin glowing with youth for once. Even her black hair balled atop her head had come a little loose, sending ringlets down to frame her face. But more than anything, the pleased grin she wore warmed Jack's heart.

Maybe her fate was sealed. But Jack would make sure she enjoyed the finer things before it came to pass.

CHAPTER TWENTY-SIX

After their unplanned stop in Richmond, Jack and Anya arrived in Charleston as the sun was rising across the city, setting a glorious shadow on the ocean. The familiarity squeezed at him, but not as much as it once had. Now, he was feeling the particular closeness of his partner and family without being able to see them. Jack wished he were athtar, just so he could give them a hug and tell them he missed them—even if they never heard it.

When night fell again, Jack maneuvered the car through the city, seeing all his old favorite places like something out of a movie. After all the running, he could scarcely believe he was back home—or the closest thing to home he had.

"The best place to find Cam's notes is going to be on her laptop," Jack said. "She's probably read every one of those books and written a detailed synopsis of anything she found interesting."

"Can you get into the computer?" Anya asked.

"Yeah, just grab the little card she uses to log in," Jack said with a shrug. "I know her password. Sara's birthday."

"Do you think it's still the same?" Anya asked.

"Oh yeah." She'd tried to change it once, after Sara died, but after locking herself out of her computer four times, she decided to stick with it. "If you can get the laptop and the card, we're good."

"There is no *we*," Anya said. "We're out of glamour. I will get inside using magic."

"Do you feel up to using your magic?" Jack asked cautiously.

"Yes."

"Do you?" Jack asked.

"If I can have time to recover, it will be fine," she said, but it lacked her usual bite. "But you'll have to tell me where I'm looking."

"If we're lucky, she's in the basement," Jack said. "That's where the archive is. If she's not there, check the top floor where my grandfather's office is."

"And if she's not in either of those places?"

"Well, we might have to figure something else out."

"Once I get inside, I might be able to sneak around," Anya replied. "I'll dress as a worker, lift a badge from someone. Then I won't have to use magic."

"Good plan," Jack said. "What should I do?"

"Stay here," Anya said. "Without glamour, I don't want to risk you getting caught."

He smiled. "Be careful and don't overdo it."

Anya nodded, and she was gone in a blur.

Jack kept the motor running, watching sailboats cross the water in front of him with detached interest. Summers home from the Academy, he used to run this trail along the water, hoping for a glimpse of some half-naked female runner he could pick up. Or he'd meet Frank and George out here for a box lunch, by order of his mother, who wanted him to do a little less loitering and a little more learning.

Anya's heaving breaths filled the car and she braced herself against the window.

"Find her?" Jack asked.

"No, but I found the books." Anya shook her head. A small drip of blood fell from her nose and she wiped it away. "They're on the side of the car."

Jack sprang out of the car and found them—a stack of them. It must've taken her at least four trips, because that's how many armfuls it took him. Once the books were stashed in the backseat, he hurried to the front seat and put the car in drive.

"Is that enough?" Anya asked, closing her eyes and pinching the bridge of her nose.

"Did you see Cam?" Jack asked. "Or a laptop? A notebook?"

Anya shook her head. "We'll just have to do without."

But Jack wasn't willing to take that for an answer. "Or we go get the laptop."

"Jack, I..."

He reached across the car to take her hand, squeezing it. "Let me handle this. You need to rest."

Both her brows shot up as she stared at his hand and the casual way he held hers. A blush crept up his neck, and he released her.

"I take it you know where the computer is?" she said after an awkward moment.

"Yeah," Jack said. "And luckily for us, I perfected the art of sneaking in and out of my own house a long time ago."

Jack left Anya and their rental car in the back of a restaurant parking lot a mile from the Grenard compound. It was one of his favorites, and he was sure if he walked inside, he'd find a few people he knew. He kept his pace brisk through the evening air of Charleston, his head down just in case he happened on one of his parents' neighbors out for a walk. Most of them were simply rich, old Charleston-bred families, but a few had connections to ICDM and would know about his fugitive status.

The Grenard mansion was surrounded by a six-foot brick wall built by his great-great grandfather. Jack made a beeline for the southwestern corner, where a large shady oak tree grew on the inside. Making sure his parents hadn't installed any new security cameras, he slid up against the wall, feeling for the bricks that jutted out just enough for him to shimmy up the side and reach the top, pulling himself atop the wall. From here, the lights of the house were visible through the oak tree branches. The dining room was lit up, and Jack could practically smell his mother's cooking.

He slid off the roof, landing with a soft *thump* on the mossy ground. He waited, listening for the sound of anyone outside. Then, carefully, he followed the shadows up to the side of the house. If he'd known his window was open, he would've continued to the south side of the house and hoisted himself up into the second-story window. But he was pretty sure that wasn't an option, so he went for Plan B.

Jack crawled up to the back kitchen door and glanced through the open window, searching for his mother. When he didn't see her, he found the spare key under the stone pig statue and quietly unlocked the door. He cracked it open, listening for movement, and when there was none, he opened it enough to slip inside. Half-crouching and half-crawling, he inched across the kitchen toward the back staircase that led to the bedrooms on the second floor.

Unable to stop himself, he paused at the edge of the island, listening to the conversation filtering in from the dining room.

"...symbols, but I haven't been able to find anything substantial." Cam sounded exhausted, but at least she was in good hands with Jack's parents. As much as she'd let them take care of her.

"You know what Dad says about all that nonsense." Jack's father's baritone voice hit harder than Cam's. "It's, well...

nonsense."

"Yes, but, George, why do Cam's talismans work, hm?" Now Jack's mother, all calm and love, spoke. "I don't think we can just dismiss something like this."

"Of course not, dear. I just don't want to see Cam wasting her time on something without merit."

"I'm close," Cam replied. "Whatever I've got, I'm just looking at it wrong." He could almost picture the crease between her brows.

"And there's no word from Jackie?" asked his mother.

"No," Cam replied with more than a little sadness.

The silence echoed from the dining room, tightening the vise around Jack's chest. It would be so easy for him to pop up and say, "Hey, guys, I'm home!" Just one word, and he'd be able to replace the smile on his mother's face and get the tongue lashing he deserved from Cam.

But Anya was fast asleep in the car, trusting that he would return to be her getaway driver, as he'd been this whole adventure. Jack would see this through to the end, even though it tore him apart inside.

"Let me get your plate," Karen said.

Jack jumped and scrambled across the kitchen floor to the back staircase, where he quietly crept up into the darkness. His mother walked into the room with an armful of plates and deposited them in the sink. Seeing his mother drove a knife right into his chest. Her hair was pulled into a smart bun—a sure sign that she didn't have the time or energy to curl it. And no amount of concealer could cover up the sleepless nights she wore under her eyes. She leaned against the counter, closing her eyes. A rare, private moment of weakness.

"Karen?" George called.

"Coming!" she replied, throwing her shoulders back and plastering a smile on her face. She sashayed to the fridge and retrieved one of her famous trifles, then went out into the dining room.

Jack waited on the staircase a moment longer, letting the guilt sink deeper into his chest, then continued up to the second floor.

The hallway was dark, but Jack didn't need to see to know where he was going. Cam always stayed in the bedroom overlooking the gardens, and with a soft click, he opened the door to her bedroom. Her clothes were strewn about the room, very un-Cam-like. But on her bed was her briefcase and lanyard with Division computer card. He plucked it off the bed, but then put it back down.

He went to the desk and found a pen and paper.

Cam,

I'm really, really sorry about this. Don't hate me more than you already do. I'll be home as soon as I can so you can yell at me properly.

Love,

Jackass

He held the note in his hands, debating the merits of leaving it. Cam would know her laptop was missing almost immediately, and send up a signal flare to the Division and ICDM. If his mother thought a demon or someone unsavory had been in her house, she might not be able to sleep at night (if she was at all).

And, if he were being truly honest, he just wanted to let everyone know he was okay.

He placed the note on the center of the bed and took two steps back, still deciding if this was smart, when he heard the telltale signs of someone walking up the stairs. He crept to the window and opened the pane, crawling out onto the ledge and closing it behind him. He pushed himself off the ledge and dropped to the ground, wincing as the pain shot up his legs even with the soft ground. He wasn't as young as he used to be, apparently.

"Son of a bitch!"

Well, Cam had gotten his note. Jack smiled as he dashed through the darkness. He stopped when the window opened, and Cam appeared.

"If you're still out there, you're a bastard, Jack Grenard!" she screamed.

"Love you, too," Jack said, climbing up the oak tree and hurrying back to the car.

Jack drove, and Anya slept—something he was used to by now. It was a good thing, as he wasn't in the mood to discuss what he'd heard. He wanted to sit in his melancholy, framed by the headlights on the interstate with him with quiet music on the radio. Peripherally, he'd known what his absence was doing to his family, but to hear it was a completely different story.

And yet…

His gaze landed on Anya, whose face lit up with every passing headlight.

Once they were out of the city limits, he stopped at a fast-food restaurant to crack her laptop and start transferring data. He felt a zing of familiarity as he stuck her computer card into the slot and typed in Sara's birthday to unlock her computer. Cam's desktop was cluttered with icons—again, very un-Cam-like.

He didn't have time to worry about that. It had been one hour and counting since he'd taken her laptop and soon the Division would activate the security software to kill the machine. Luckily, it was after-hours, so the technology team would take some time to get spun up—assuming Cam called them at all.

Jack plugged in the hard drive and tried to start the transfer, but the Division firewall blocked access to third-party hard drives. His heartbeat drumming in his chest, he quickly created a new account on an online cloud storage solution. The Division was always a few years behind the latest technology and hadn't yet established firewalls against these websites.

One hour, ten minutes.

Jack couldn't upload Cam's entire hard drive—there wasn't enough space for that. Instead, he searched for all documents added in the last month, dragging and dropping to the cloud. She was a fan of a particular note-taking software, so he grabbed everything he could from the local drive. Although he didn't stop to read any of it, there were symbols and headings that looked promising.

He opened her email, seeing a rash of new emails from Kim and Navarro. He was surprised she was still answering them, considering her new locale in Charleston. He grabbed everything sent to and sent from Cam over the past day.

Just as the file transfer completed, the computer screen winked out. The Division IT team had sent out the kill switch.

Jack exhaled, closing the laptop. He wasn't really cut out for this espionage stuff, but he was getting better at it. He just hoped the Division wouldn't be able to trace where he'd stashed the information he'd stolen.

The laptop itself, dead as a doornail, was another question. As much as he hated leaving Cam's machine in the middle of a fast-food restaurant, the Division probably had a lock on his location. At least she might get her machine back after a few weeks.

Looking around the restaurant, he slid the laptop onto the ground under the bench. He made a show of zipping up the empty bag and throwing it around his shoulder. Waving to the teenager at the counter, who was giving him the stink eye for coming in and not buying anything, he briefly considered grabbing a quick burger and fries, but he didn't want to test the time it would take for the police to show up.

Anya woke up with a start when he slammed the car door behind him.

"W-what happened?" she said, blinking in the light.

Jack filled her in as he backed out of the parking lot. "I couldn't get all of it, but I got a lot. I think we'll find some gems of information."

"Well done."

He quirked a brow in her direction. "Really? Praise from you? That's cause for celebration."

She grinned, the playful look coming back into her eyes. "When you perform admirably, you get praised. It's really not complicated."

"I think I've been doing pretty good so far," Jack said, puffing out his chest. "I got the laptop from my parents' house unscathed and I was able to break into it. Not bad for an Academy graduate."

"I…" Her face fell. "There's an athtar nearby."

"*What?*" Jack nearly slammed on the brakes, but pressed the gas instead. "Where?"

She spun in her seat, looking at the restaurant disappearing down the busy street. Jack kept his gaze on the road, ready to react when a demon appeared in the lane. But nothing happened—and that made him even more nervous.

"W-what's he doing there?" Jack asked, his heart hammering in his chest. "And why isn't he coming for us?"

"I don't know," Anya whispered, her face frozen in horror. "But I can't believe it's a coincidence."

"What do we do?"

Anya sat back, wrapping her arms around herself. "Keep

driving. I can't...I can't help them."

CHAPTER TWENTY-SEVEN

"There was one survivor," Cam said. "The cashier. She said Jack was in here a few minutes before it happened."

Cam had been on the phone with the Atlanta security division when she'd received a call from Kim, which she'd ignored. But when the deputy director called again, and Cam answered, she'd wished she'd missed the call entirely.

She'd seen carnage before, but this was something else entirely. Dinnertime at this fast food chain meant the restaurant was packed with families coming from dance lessons and going to soccer practice. This whole scene must've seemed awfully mundane.

Now blood marred the walls, and Cam wondered if any of

them even had a chance to scream. The pair of ICDM forensic experts had determined that most of the deaths were caused by a pair of swords. And, presumably, the laptop that had been stashed under a booth.

Jack's note was folded in her pocket, some sign that he knew what he was doing. It was all she had; for without it, she was starting to really wonder what the hell he was up to.

"Hello? Macarro?" came Kim's voice on the other end of the line.

"Yeah," Cam said, turning away from one small blanket-covered body and staring out the window, where the blue and red flashes lit up the night. "Yeah, sorry, what did you say?"

"I asked if the cashier had seen anything else?"

"No," Cam said. "She said it was…it was instantaneous."

"Well, that settles that. I say we up this investigation into a criminal one and put out a real APB on the two of them. Enough screwing around. Someone out there's bound to see them and bring them in."

Cam released a breath. "I don't think this was them."

"Macarro, you've got to start looking at facts here—"

"I am looking at facts. I'm not jumping to conclusions. There's more than one athtar out there," she said, clutching the paper in her pocket harder.

"You're not going to get a positive confirmation on this. Grenard's been gone for almost a month. It's not completely ridiculous to think he might be under coercion or being moved against his will."

"It is completely ridiculous," Cam said, pulling out the paper and looking at it. His handwriting, his words. His Jackass. "Jack wouldn't let her do this, and he's not… It wasn't them. I know it."

"Your hunches have gotten you exactly nowhere," Kim said. "I've got a recommendation on its way to Navarro and up. I'm willing to go all the way to the US Division headquarters in D.C. to overrule Frank if I have to. After all, it's his grandson. Not a hard case to make that there's nepotism involved."

Cam wished she had some retort, but there was nothing. The rational side of her brain agreed that Kim had a strong case. It had been Division business when La Colibrí's victims had all been demons. But a massacre of twenty humans? That was going to be hard to explain away.

"You do what you feel is right," Cam said after a long pause. "And I'm going to do the same."

Kim grunted in acknowledgment, and the call ended. Cam slid the device into her pocket and walked out of the restaurant, the weight of her thoughts sagging her shoulders. She wished she could erase what she'd seen, and what it might imply. She even wished she could throw her love for Jack out the window, so she could tackle this problem with her steely-eyed rationalism. But none of that was possible. So she stopped by the liquor store to pick up a bottle of cheap white wine to drink in silence in her room.

It hurt to know Jack had been so close and was gone again. It pissed her off that he could hack into her computer using her credentials. And her head hurt thinking about how much farther she had to go to get him home. Well, she just hoped he and La Colibrí would be able to piece together the mystery behind the talismans. Because Cam had come up completely short.

A long drive later, Cam pulled into the Grenard mansion, ready to dive head-first into the five-dollar bottle sitting in her passenger's seat. But there was another car in the driveway, one with diplomatic tags.

Cam groaned and prepared herself for what might be waiting. Perhaps Kim had already submitted her request, perhaps they were there to inform Frank that he was off the Council. Cam counted the number of times Jack had wished his grandfather didn't have the prestigious position he had. She supposed he was going to get his wish.

With a heavy heart, she pushed the front door open. "Hello?"

"Oh, is that Cam?" came Karen's voice. She didn't sound upset, but nothing much bothered Karen. "Come into the living room, sweetheart."

Cam followed the voices and nearly dropped her briefcase. "Myra?"

She hadn't seen the weapons aide since Cam had given the presentation about the talismans before Demon Spring started. Myra had offered Cam a fellowship in Shanghai at the Weapons Institute, and Cam just hoped Myra wasn't there to get an answer.

"Myra was in town for the evening and asked to speak with

you. She came just a few minutes after you left and insisted on staying," George said, standing. "I take it that there was nothing of interest at that restaurant?"

Cam licked her lips, knowing George would find out the truth in the morning, but wanting to spare him and Karen the gruesome details that night. "Jack was there. Briefly. But he's gone."

Karen nodded, her bright brown eyes growing dull. She'd read the note from Jack with a stiff upper lip, but that was probably more for Cam's benefit. Her eyes were rimmed with red, and her cheeks were stained with tears. Cam didn't know how she would take the news in the morning, and it just made her more exhausted to think about it.

"It's been a long night," Myra said after a moment. "I promise it'll only take a moment. Can we step outside?"

Cam nodded and followed the minister out onto the veranda. She hadn't noticed the thick mugginess of the night, but her shirt was sticking to the back of her neck. That cold bottle of wine would be most welcome.

"What's up?" Cam asked, steeling herself for the pain. "Are you rescinding your offer for Shanghai?"

"Oh—oh, no, not at all. You're obviously welcome," Myra said, looking distracted as they stood on the porch. "This…this stays between us, all right?"

Cam's guard was up, but she nodded.

"I saw your partner."

Her eyes nearly bugged out of her head. "W-what? Where?

When? Tonight?"

"No, a few weeks ago. My son got into a small scrape in Amsterdam," Myra said with an unmistakable grimace. "He was…transformed into a lilin."

"Whoa." Cam ran her hands over her face, surprised she could still be surprised by anything. "Is he…?"

"He's fine, but it was thanks to Jack," Myra said. "He found their maker, killed him, and brought my son and his friends back to normal." She stared at the moon. "I can't thank him enough."

Cam wasn't sure which information to pounce on first—that she'd seen Jack, that he'd *helped* her son, or that he'd been in Amsterdam at all. Or that he'd been able to kill a demon. Last time she'd checked, he was pretty awful with those knives of his.

"Did you see La Colibrí?" she asked, finally.

"I'm sorry?"

"Uh… Anat," Cam said. "The demon woman with him?"

"No. He didn't say whether she was there or not. He just wanted the money."

"Money?"

"The other boy's mother paid him handsomely for his trouble," Myra said.

Cam pursed her lips. "Bankrolling his little adventure, I'd guess." That sure explained a lot of his odd behavior, including what he might've been doing in New Orleans. "How did he look?"

"Well, when I saw him, he was…pretty banged up," Myra

said with a small chuckle. "But he was concerned about our kids, and making sure we didn't tell anyone that we'd seen him. He was worried..." She glanced around in the empty night. "He was worried Bael might find us. Especially after I told him Wani had been killed."

"He didn't know?"

"No. At least, he acted like he didn't." She wrung her hands nervously. "He made us swear not to say a word. And I haven't."

"You're telling me, though."

"That was part of the deal," Myra said with a sad smile. "He wanted me to tell you that he was okay, as long as we did it in private. I believe he's very concerned about you."

"I'm sure he is." She clutched the note in her pocket. Damn him for making it so hard to be angry with him.

"Well, that's all I wanted to share. Please don't...don't tell anyone about this conversation. With all these deaths surrounding anyone who talks to them, I'm worried for my son."

"Don't worry," Cam said with a wave of her hand. "Your secret is safe with me."

CHAPTER TWENTY-EIGHT

Jack put the book down and pinched the bridge of his nose. His brain felt like it was leaking through his ears. He'd been reading nonstop for days, when he wasn't driving to another small town, another hotel, another place to stay only briefly. They'd grown accustomed to checking the radio after they left, praying that there wouldn't be another massacre. So far, there hadn't. But they couldn't let their guard down.

Jack hadn't even logged in to check the cloud account he'd set up, afraid it would lead someone to them. Instead, he and Anya pored over the books. She sent an email to her tech guys, to see if they could safely and anonymously get in to his online storage without being tracked. It had been three days since they'd sent the email, and Jack just prayed that no news meant they were still working on it.

In the meantime, he and Anya had been making their way through the books. Unfortunately, all that Jack had read seemed just tangentially related to their research. Cam had a habit of requesting every book in creation as long as it had something to do with what she was studying.

Anya was seated at the small desk, hunched over her laptop. There was a faraway look in her eyes as she stared at the screen, giving Jack the impression she wasn't actually reading at all.

He almost liked it better when she was insulting him; at least then he knew where her head was. She'd barely said a word since they'd left the restaurant, and when news broke of the slaughter, she'd stared at the screen without showing a single emotion. A few weeks ago, Jack might've mistaken that for indifference. But now, he saw beyond her façade to the storm of guilt raging beneath the surface. The woman who'd spent a hundred and thirty years trying to make amends for every soul she'd taken seemed to have added a few more to her tally.

"Hey," Jack said, turning around in his chair. "You okay?"

She nodded.

"Do you want to talk about it?"

"What's there to say?" she replied softly.

Jack sat back, sighing heavily. He was still trying to wrap his head around *why* an athtar had shown up and slaughtered an entire restaurant. It made as little sense as Ekur's late appearance in Geneva. In both cases, Jack and Anya had been on their way out. If they were trying to kill her, and they'd have had no problem in her weakened state, they wouldn't have been dancing around, showing up after they were gone. They would've just done it. So what was their intent?

"Thank goodness," Anya breathed, after an email ping echoed in the silent room.

"What?" Jack said, putting the book down.

Anya chewed on her bottom lip in thought. "I just heard from my hacker. He got into the storage device and downloaded all the information."

"Awesome," Jack said.

"And…and he's moving," Anya finished with an almost grateful smile. "To an undisclosed location, for his own safety. My recommendation."

Jack pushed himself off the bed and joined her at the desk. He chanced a squeeze on her shoulders, and she let him, leaning back in the chair as the data downloaded. Her shoulders radiated tension, so he rubbed them once, testing her reaction.

"What are you doing?" she asked, glancing up at him.

"I don't know," he said, releasing his grip and resting his hands on the chair behind her. "Just trying to make you feel better. Sorry."

"Don't be," she said quietly. She stood, filling the space between them, and half-smiled. "I think your partner would be pretty pissed if she found out I rifled through her emails. Maybe you should take over here."

"Yeah, sure," Jack said, catching her before she got too far.

"Are you all right? For real?"

"Fine," she murmured, sliding by him and grabbing the book he'd left on the bed. She tucked her feet underneath her as she resumed reading, although she didn't seem to be focusing on the words on the page. Jack watched her for a moment, then began sorting through Cam's emails.

The first unread message was from human resources about submitting insurance claims from Demon Spring—how very mundane. There was a reminder to submit her timesheet, too. Cam was always forgetting, often because she was working until one or two in the morning.

After that, an unread email from Frank—this one part of a larger chain. Jack scrolled to the bottom, reliving his journey across the US and Europe through his grandfather's emails. The emails grew less affectionate as the days went on—he was named Jackie in the first email, but in the most recent, just Jack. There would certainly be a long list of apologies he'd have to make when this was all over.

There were gaps in the tracking—they didn't know he'd been in Amsterdam, but they assumed he and Anya had something to do with Adelbert in Brussels. They were also blamed for an incident in Madrid, although Frank wasn't convinced it was him. The break-in at world headquarters was pinned on them, as they'd been spotted on the cameras. The scientist with whom Jack and Anya had spoken had given a deposition, but didn't mention anything about the talismans or vigilantes.

Jack searched the data for the word 'talisman' and a slew of recent emails came up. From what Jack could tell, Cam had been as successful as they'd been in learning more about the talismans. Most of her messages were to the other headquarters in different countries—a few to the New Orleans offices. All had come back with nothing.

But then she'd sent an email to the archivist in Geneva with an image attached—the same inverted shield symbol he'd seen in Brussels.

"Look at this," Jack said, pointing to the image and turning the laptop to show Anya. "I've seen this before."

"It signifies safe meeting places for mercenaries," Anya said.

"Cam's notes say it was also a tattoo that got ten humans burned alive in France," Jack said. "In the sixteenth century."

"Makes sense," she said. "The humans used to be very superstitious."

"That's why Cam requested all these books from Geneva," Jack said, glancing at the old books on the bed. "And look at this: two days ago, she requested more information on each of the original demon emergences. Maybe Wani was onto something."

"I've been around these mercenaries for years," Anya said with a sad shake of her head. "Nobody ever said anything about a talisman, curses, or anything like that. I never saw another coin like the one around my neck or the ones you wear. If I had, I would've told you by now."

But Jack wasn't deterred. There was a thread there, and he

was going to pull it until it unraveled. "This symbol can't be a coincidence. It keeps popping up every time we get another clue about your curse. What do you know about this vigilante thing? The origins of it?"

"There's nothing to tell, Jack. It's a loosely-based system. You do work, you get paid, nobody tells the demon lord or the Division, end of story." She shrugged. "You did a job. You saw how it was."

"Uh-huh." Jack wiped his face. "Does it precede ICDM?"

"Well...yes," Anya said. "It's been around since before I became cursed. Before ICDM, in Europe, especially, anti-demonic defenses were usually based in the churches. They didn't approve of anything that wasn't officially sanctioned and they burned anything that could remotely be considered demonic." She snorted. "Didn't do a damned thing. Fire doesn't kill demons."

But that got Jack thinking, as he scoured through Cam's notes. "'Any human seen practicing demonic witchcraft will be burned as a demon,'" he read. "This is from a diary in Spain in the 1600's, and look—here's that same symbol. Maybe that doesn't mean 'become a demon,' maybe it meant something else. Maybe they associated that upside-down shield with some kind of demonic witchcraft, when, in fact it was *anti*-demonic witchcraft. The churches just made a knee-jerk reaction and banned everything. Wouldn't be the first time."

"It's a weak connection," Anya said. "And what does that have to do with my curse?"

"Maybe the people who cursed you were these vigilantes," Jack said, toying with the talismans. "If they're the ones who had the talismans in the first place, maybe they have more than just these five. Or at the very least, maybe they have an answer as to why you still feel cursed."

Anya chewed her lip. "What do we do, then?"

Jack thought for a moment. "You were cursed in New Orleans. We already know there's a big vigilante community there. I say we go back there and start digging."

"Jack..." She stood and walked to the window. "People are dying because of me. Because of what we're doing. Maybe it's just less trouble to...to go back to Bael."

"First of all, it's not your fault—"

"Isn't it?" she said. "The athtars killed those people because of me. Because of us. If I was stronger, I could have..." She closed her eyes. "Who am I kidding? I couldn't have saved those people. I'm verging on death as it is."

"So you're giving up?" Jack said. "After all we've found?"

"We haven't found *anything*," Anya said. "Eloko lore gave us nothing. Breaking into ICDM headquarters nearly got us both killed. Taking your partner's laptop got a handful of innocents slaughtered. For what? So I can feel better about myself?" She slunk down on the bed. "I can't stand feeling this way, feeling like every time I look at someone, they're marked for death."

"You know he's going to make you go back out there and slaughter humans," Jack said, shaking his head.

"He might not," she muttered.

"Right," Jack said, leaning back in the chair. "And Sara could come back to life."

She dropped her gaze to her hands and whispered, "I just don't know what else to do. I can't keep going like this. I can't keep…I can't keep drowning every time someone dies because of me."

Jack stared at her for a long time. He was tired of this—tired of running. Tired of hiding. Tired of having to watch his back. He marched to the window with purpose, opening the blinds to the dark night outside, daring Bael or another athtar to show up outside the window.

"What are you doing?" Anya asked.

"Calling his bluff." He turned and smiled at her. "We should go to New Orleans, and fuck it, let's just go as ourselves. Let's walk in broad daylight and dare someone to come for us."

She lifted her brows. "You're insane."

"Am I? Or are you, for believing that Bael doesn't know exactly where you are right now?" Jack placed his hands on his hips. "I thought it was strange that Ekur appeared after we left in Geneva. We never would've known he was there, right?"

"Because we just missed him—"

"No," Jack said with a shake of his head. "He wanted us to be gone. If we hadn't returned, he would have killed everyone in that lab. Bael wants the Division to think you're killing people."

"Why would he do that?"

"Because…" Jack paused, the answer coming in a flash of lightning. "Because he wants you to feel like you don't have another option. He wants you completely isolated. The demons aren't your allies, not with Bael's bounty on your head. And if the humans think you're back to your murdering ways, they won't be a safe haven either."

She licked her lips, the indecision clear on her face. "It does sound like something Bael would do."

Jack smiled. "And you're not going to take that bait, are you? Not when we're just about to solve the mystery?"

"Are we, though?"

In two steps, Jack knelt in front of Anya, taking her hands in his. "We're getting close, I can feel it. Let's go back to New Orleans, see what we can find about these vigilantes."

She squeezed his fingers. "You know, Bael's wrong about one thing. I'm not completely isolated." She lifted her gaze to his, and his pulse skipped when a smile reappeared on her face. "You're still here."

CHAPTER TWENTY-NINE

Ten hours later, Jack and Anya drove a stolen car into the main city of New Orleans. Jack couldn't shake the feeling that they were about to find a break—either solving the mystery or stumbling into something worse.

Still leery of attracting unwanted attention, they left the stolen car on the outskirts of town and took a bus to the city center. Anya kept her gaze on the streets, searching for anyone who might give them up. Still, some of the tension had left her face, and it put Jack at ease.

It was late afternoon when they reached the bar—the very first place they'd taken a job. Saving that teenager from the lilins seemed like a lifetime ago.

"Do you think Johnny's okay?" he asked.

"Yeah, he is. I've had one of my computer guys monitoring his posts. He's been living with his aunt, and he's got a new boyfriend. A human one, this time."

In light of what he knew about her—her child, her friendships, her entire persona—Jack just had to smile.

"It's the curse, it makes me soft," she said in response.

"I'm sure it does."

She pursed her lips and pointed to the entryway. "See? There's your symbol." On a stone in the right corner was an inverted shield in a circle.

"At least we're in the right place," Jack said.

She nodded. "Or maybe this is another dead end."

"Maybe," Jack said, sticking his hands into his pants pockets. "But we won't know until we go in. Am I allowed to accompany you, or should I wait my customary ten minutes?"

She tossed him a sly look before walking through the door. Jack chuckled and followed her.

The place was empty, although the lights were already low. Anya made a beeline for the only other soul in the room, the nox bartender that had served Jack the first time he'd been there.

"Hm. Surprised you two are walking around in daylight," he grunted from behind a newspaper. "People been looking for you."

"I'm looking for people," Anya said. "Namely, the people associated with that symbol on your doorframe."

He glanced at Jack. "I don't talk in front of Division

people."

"I'm on semi-permanent hiatus," Jack said.

He shook the paper and grunted. "The symbol was here before I bought the bar. There's a small group of humans that might know something about it. They meet here on occasion, but they got a bunch of different places, or so I understand. 'Round the city."

"Have a name?" Jack asked.

"They're even squirrelier than you are," he said. "Don't give names. Wear hats and hoods. But they got bigger problems than you do."

"I doubt that," Anya said. "Can you tell us anything about them?"

"Depends," he said, putting the paper down. "Can you guarantee I won't meet the same fate as Wani?"

"We don't know who killed him," Anya said after a moment.

"They say he was killed on account of talking to you. Maybe I'll go find me an athtar in the city and tell 'em you're here."

"Go for it," Jack said with a steely look. "They know where we are."

The nox chuckled and put down his paper. "You're ballsy, for a human. Guess you have to be to be flying a middle finger at the King of the Underworld." He glanced at Anya. "And rolling around with the Lady of the Mountain."

"Tell us what you know," Anya demanded. "Or the other athtars won't be the ones you'll need to worry about."

He made a sound, then a smile curled onto his face. "Nah, it was there when I bought it. Maybe you should look up the previous owners. I hear this gig runs in families. Kinda like yours."

Anya stood, sliding a few hundred-dollar bills across the bar. "For your trouble."

"Money won't be worth nothin' if an athtar comes knocking," he said, taking the money anyway.

Like most cities, New Orleans public property records had been moved online, so it was easy to dig up the records. The nox had owned the bar since 1963, and a man named Jacques Broussard had owned it before.

"Look here," Jack said, pointing at the screen. "Here's his obit from 1973, and all his children. Maybe we can find a few of them and ask them some questions. Do you think your hackers could get us some addresses if we give them a name?"

"I don't want to go door-to-door," Anya said, chewing on her lip. "The athtars may not be actively pursuing us, but I don't want to risk them killing any more humans. Especially as we're...well, testing that theory."

Jack couldn't argue that point. "Let me try something else, then."

He took the names of Broussard's children and searched the same city records, finding a few with addresses on file, and a couple with "estate of" addresses. House, house, house, house— all in different parts of the city.

"This one's a lawyer's office," Jack said, looking up at Anya, who was staring at the ceiling. "Over on Magazine Street. We could pop over early, ask him a few questions. Pretend we're clients. That might be safer."

She sat up and pursed her lips. "This feels like another wild goose chase. I say we go back to the bar and beat the answers out of someone."

"You just want to beat something up," Jack said.

"I don't want to expose ourselves needlessly," she said. "And —"

"He's got the symbol."

"What?"

Jack spun the laptop, showing her the website for the law firm. It was small, but over the I in his name was the inverted shield. "Does that convince you this isn't a wild goose chase?"

She crossed her arms. "No."

"Well how about this: Do you trust me?"

She looked taken aback by the question, then became annoyed. "What does that have to do with anything?"

Jack straightened and smiled. "It's a simple question. Do you trust me?"

"I..." She stared at him for a while, her eyes steely and her jaw clenched. "Fine. Yes. I suppose I trust you."

He grinned wider. "Then you need to trust my gut, too. And my gut hasn't steered me wrong once."

"Oh, yeah?" She uncrossed her arms, resting her hands on her hips.

"Well, it was right when it said you wouldn't kill me all

those weeks ago," Jack said, turning back to the computer.

"I didn't kill you because I was cursed," she replied, although there was a note of amusement in her voice.

"Doesn't matter. I was still right. And I know it's right about this. This inverted shield, it's been popping up everywhere. It can't be a coincidence that it showed up in Cam's research, too."

"What if you're wrong?" she said.

"If I'm wrong..." He looked at the computer. "If I'm wrong, you can just go back to Bael."

She blinked once, twice, then her mouth fell open. "W-what?"

"I mean, that's what you want, right?" Jack said with a grin.

"N-no... I mean..." She shook her head, clearly at a loss for words. "Are you serious?"

"As a heart attack," Jack said, sauntering over to her. "If I'm wrong, you should just go back to Bael." He lifted his eyebrows with a smirk. "But I'm not going to be wrong."

A loud breath escaped her lips, and she scowled at him. "You're an ass."

"Finally," Jack said with a laugh. "I was wondering when that part of me would come back."

The law office was located in a building built in 1875, according to the plaque on the front. They'd come early in the morning, checking out the building for entries and exits before waiting in the cafe across the street. Anya, still a bit put off by Jack's earlier joke, was jumpy.

"Relax," Jack said as she spun at the sound of a car driving by. "You're calling more attention to yourself."

"What's with this new, confident person?" she asked.

"Maybe I finally got tired of being a slacker," Jack said, taking a sip of his coffee. "Or maybe it's just fun to poke at you."

"You're poking fun, meanwhile Bael and ICDM are on our tail," Anya said, anxiously tapping her foot against the ground.

"I assume if either show up, we'll make a break for it," Jack said, lowering his shades. "Why are you so nervous?"

"Why are you not?" Anya snapped. "This is…I don't like this broad daylight shit. No glamour. A baseball cap. This just…I don't like it."

Jack had to laugh at that. "You get used to it." He reached under the table and rested his hand on her jiggling leg. "It's okay, Anya. We're safe here."

"Are we?" she asked.

"Yeah. Besides that, look over there."

A gray-haired man had walked up to the lawyer's office, pulling out a set of keys and a handkerchief to wipe his brow. The front door opened and he walked inside, slamming it shut behind him.

After tossing their coffees, they crossed the street, still mostly empty save a few early morning cars, and climbed the stairs. Anya pulled on the door, but it was locked.

"Maybe not open for business yet," she said. "Give me a moment."

She nonchalantly left Jack on the porch, and turned down

the side alley next to the building. A moment later, the door clicked open.

Jack slipped through, glancing at the coffee shop across the street and hoping no one was paying attention this early in the morning. Inside, Jack and Anya listened for their mark, hearing him clear his throat in the back of the shotgun-style house.

"Let's make this quick," Anya whispered.

"We aren't killing him," Jack said with a sigh.

"I know that—"

"Hello?" called the voice. "Margaret? Is that you?"

Anya rolled her eyes and marched toward the back. A moment later, an ear-splitting scream echoed through the house.

"Well shit," Jack said, running.

There he found her holding the old man hostage, a small knife pressed against his neck.

"Anya, for fuck's sake," Jack said.

"I was trying to keep him quiet," she said, pressing her knife tighter against the man's neck. "Are you going to scream? I promise I won't hurt you as long as you don't scream."

"Please don't scream," Jack added. "I also promise we aren't here to hurt you."

Broussard nodded, glancing behind him at Anya. "I w-won't."

Anya released her hold, but kept her sword in her hand. "Good boy."

"You're that demon," he said, rubbing his neck. "The one everyone's looking for. The one who killed all those people. And you're the human who went crazy."

Jack sighed. "I'm not crazy, Anya hasn't killed anyone in a while, and we just have a few questions about the inverted shield symbol and what it means."

Almost immediately, something changed within him. He was no longer frightened. Rather, he grew stoic and resolute. "You might as well kill me. I won't share that information with the likes of you."

"Anya won't tell anyone—"

"Not her," he said, narrowing his eyes at Jack. "You. Scion of that organization."

"What? ICDM?" Jack said with a surprised look at Anya. "I worked for them, but I'm pretty sure I'm fired right now."

"Your family has been a part of that group since its inception," he said. "Therefore, you can't be trusted."

"He can be," Anya said, similarly surprised. "He's been working with the mercenary group, we did a job here—"

"Mercenaries," he snorted. "A group of thugs who've co-opted our message and symbols. Our goals are much loftier. What we do, what we strive for, is in complete opposition with the International Coalition for Demon Management. They've tried to keep us from our work for centuries, and they've mostly succeeded."

"What *is* your goal?" Anya asked.

"To see humanity freed from the slavery of the demons," he said with unwavering seriousness.

"We aren't *slaves*," Jack said with a small laugh. He'd always felt they kissed more demon ass than kicked it, but slaves? ICDM kept a working relationship with demons; they didn't take orders from them.

Did they?

"You believe what you've been told," he said to Jack. "Your family stands to benefit more than most."

"Look," Anya said, pulling the drawing of her talisman from her back pocket. "We're not going to tell ICDM, or anyone else. I just need to know more about this symbol. This curse."

At that, Broussard looked confused. "There's no such thing as curses."

"Obviously, there is," Anya said. "In 1886, I was cursed by someone. They put a talisman around my neck, and it forced me to repent for every soul I took. The talisman is gone, but the curse remains." Anya put her hands on the table. "It's killing me. I have to know why. *Please.*"

Broussard glanced between Jack and Anya. "I have no answers for you."

"Bullshit," Jack said. "We've been following this trail for weeks and it's lead right to you. You've got the symbol. You know what we're talking about. These," he flashed the talismans around his wrist, "have magical properties. I know you know something—"

"Where did you get those?" Broussard gasped.

"They were a gift," Jack said. "From the García family of Mexico. I...well, I lost a few of them."

"If I help you, will you give them to me?" he asked, eyeing

them as if they were more precious than gold.

Jack frowned. Although he'd imbedded three of them in demons, somehow giving them to someone else gave him a queasy feeling. But one look at Anya's big, green wistful eyes, and he knew he couldn't say no. "We'll see what you have to offer. If it's satisfactory, I'll give them to you."

"I'll confer with the others. If they want to meet with you, I'll leave my mailbox flag up at two in the afternoon tomorrow."

CHAPTER THIRTY

Since the bitch had taken Cam's books and her laptop, Cam had returned to the archives to find something else. She knew it was a futile effort; she and Patrick had already scoured the collection. But it was better than sitting at the Grenards', twiddling her thumbs. Or worse—going back to Atlanta.

There were two emails in her inbox from Director Navarro, both requesting a meeting about Cam's future. The Atlanta director's patience must've worn thin a few weeks ago, and Cam was bracing herself for the decision she'd have to make. Return to Atlanta or do…something else.

She knew she was being obstinate. Her investigation of Jack and Anya had run its course. She'd failed to either find them or figure out what they were searching for. No one, not even Jack's parents, would blame her for packing it in and moving on.

Except she couldn't.

She was scared to.

Because at the end of the day, Cam wasn't sure she could cut it without Jack. This thought had come to her late the night before, like clouds revealing the moon. All the chasing, the sleepless nights—even dragging his ass down to Atlanta against his will in the first place— wasn't because she wanted him to feel better and move on. Cam wasn't Cam without Jack.

When the fuck had that happened?

It had been a hard pill to swallow, to see all her behaviors in this new, stark light. Cam had always been independent, strong, brilliant. And now to find out she'd become co-dependent on someone else… the thought made her sick to her stomach.

And yet, there she was, in the library. Instead of, say, calling Myra and telling her to book a flight to Shanghai the next morning.

Or being an adult and calling her manager back.

Or any number of other actual productive activities.

Sighing, Cam leaned against the bookshelf, wiping the small layer of sweat from her brow. The constant war between wanting to do the right thing and not wanting to do anything was reaching a fever pitch in her mind. She fought the urge to bury her head in another book—that would just make it worse.

"Well, Macarro, what do you want to do?" she asked herself. "Jack's not coming back, and if he does, it's not going to be the same. So you'd better nut up and figure out your life without him."

"Agent Macarro?" called a voice across the library. "Are you in here?"

Great, now Patrick probably thought she was crazy, too. "Yeah. I'm in here."

"Oh, good, Councilwoman, yes. Please come in."

Cam wandered out of the stacks, then stopped in her tracks. "Tía!"

María García stood beside the wilting librarian, who excused himself as soon as he could. Frank was with her, too, although he seemed less sure of himself in her presence. María was Cam's idol, and she couldn't have thought of a more perfect time for her great-aunt to appear. She would cut through the nonsense and steer Cam straight.

"You're looking well," María said in Spanish.

"Thank you," Cam replied, glancing at Frank, who either wasn't fluent, or understood that this conversation didn't involve him.

"I'll be on my way," Frank said, with a deferential nod to María. "I suppose I'll see you for dinner tonight, Cam. María, you are welcome to join—"

"I'm leaving tonight," María said, snapping back to perfect English. Then, she softened her gaze. "But please extend my regrets to your lovely daughter-in-law. As well as my thanks, for all they've done for Camilla over the years."

"I will do that," Frank said, before disappearing.

"Are we alone in here?" María asked, flipping back to Spanish.

"I think so," Cam said, clenching her fists to keep them from running through her hair nervously. "It's good to see you."

"I apologize I haven't come sooner. This latest Demon Spring has caused all kinds of issues—as have your partner and his new friend."

"Yeah, so, I've been thinking about—"

"I am here, Camilla, because of what you've been doing and saying to those in the Council," María said. "Namely, what began as an ill-advised presentation here a few weeks ago."

Cam stood a little straighter. "I didn't mean to go over Navarro's head—"

"I don't care about your American boss. What I care about is you pinning my family name to a bunch of witchcraft."

She blinked once, twice, almost sure she'd misheard her aunt. "But they work!"

María sighed, relinquishing some of her intensity. "Camilla, you are a very bright, very motivated woman. Among all my family, you are the one who shows the most promise if you would only get out of your own way."

This wasn't the first time Cam had heard such a thing, but coming from María, it stung.

"I am going to share something with you, something that I need you to keep very quiet. Not even your partner needs to know about it, do you understand?"

Cam's pulse quickened. "I do."

"I cannot stress this enough. You will not speak, you will not insinuate, you will not even hint at a word of this conversation to another living soul—human or demon, is that clear?"

She nodded. "Very."

María took a deep breath and gently took Cam's hand, revealing the talismans around her wrist. "You were not wrong about the power of these talismans. They are a weapon to be used against demons."

"Yeah," Cam nodded. "Jack's been using them all over Europe."

"And that's precisely the problem," María said. "You see, these symbols were imported to our ancestors by the Spanish by way of a man named Juan Garrado. He was descended from the first humans ever to fight against demons, in the Congo."

Cam stilled. "I thought the talismans were from our ancestors?"

"No, love," María said. "We are merely the current defenders of the secret. The talismans are given to our children as a measure of protection, but nothing more. You are not the first in our family to have thought of the offensive angle." She smiled sadly. "And you won't be the last to hear this speech."

Cam shook her head then stood, trying to wrap her head around what she was hearing. She'd thought herself so clever, so brilliant for coming up with such a simple solution to such a large problem. *Of course* someone else would've thought of it.

"You are correct that the upside-down shield is connected to the talismans, although it has been many years since that group has had a talisman to call their own. Our family has taken great strides to stamp out that magic and keep the secret locked away. It's why I was so very against you and Jack receiving talismans, but…Juana overruled me. I should have fought harder against her." She handed Cam a small metal object—a talisman. "I saw him in Brussels. He shot this into an eloko demon."

"This is…" Cam closed her hand around it. "You saw Jack?"

"He was glamoured with lilin magic, I would assume. But there's no mistaking what this is."

"Why were you in Brussels?"

"ICDM has always sniffed around the edges of the truth behind the talismans. I attend every new museum opening, especially those that deal with eloko lore, to make sure they haven't gotten too close."

"I don't understand," Cam asked. "Why is it a secret? If this thing can be used as a viable weapon against demons—"

"But it can't, and that is the problem." María clasped her hands behind her back and turned to the stacks of books. "Camilla, you saw Bael up close. You know what he is capable of."

"Yeah, but I don't know what he has to do with—"

"Bael knows of the talismans. He knows what they do. And he has forbidden us from using them."

"I'm sorry…what?" Cam finally released the grip on her hands and brought them to her face, squeezing her temples. "Bael forbade us from… But who gives a shit what he says?"

Maria's eyes grew sadder. "Did you not witness him killing Nunzia, a powerful demon lord, with a single blow?"

"I did, but—"

"You've seen the images from the bloodbath Anat has left

behind. Bael would be worse."

"So shoot him with a talisman," Cam replied.

"He can stop time, my love. Bael is so powerful he could slaughter an entire continent of humans before we could even mount a rebellion against him." She swallowed. "And he has threatened to do so in the clearest terms."

Cam couldn't believe her ears. "I mean, that's hyperbole."

"Is it?" María asked. "Are you willing to test him?"

With all her might, Cam wished she had the courage to say she was. But…Bael was powerful. Maybe not strong enough to kill an entire continent, maybe not, but he would kill a lot of innocent humans.

Horrified, Cam began to understand her aunt's line of thinking. "I can't believe this. So we're all just…hostages?"

"Bael isn't…the worst," María said, not quite meeting her great-niece's eyes.

"You're shitting me," Cam replied with a slack-jawed gape. "He kills *thousands* of humans every four years. He wreaks havoc on our cities and lets his demon friends do what they want."

"But he lets us live in peace the rest of the time. For us, it's worth it."

"Does the rest of the Council know?" Cam asked.

"No, and they will not be told. They have a tendency to consider themselves above the demons, when it's clear where we lie in the food chain."

"Food chain, huh?" Cam folded her arms across her chest. "You think we're just part of the demonic food chain?"

"Camilla, don't get angry—"

"Too late!" Cam snarled. "This is *bullshit*. You sit there and tell me that all the humans who've died from demons could've been saved. *My sister* could've been saved—"

"This is an unwinnable war," María said, her voice even. "Do you think for a moment that if we started building our defenses Bael wouldn't know? He'd take his revenge before we could even get the money."

"So he was right then. He owns ICDM. He owns all of us."

"I wish it weren't true," she said with a shake of her head. "And as I looked at your sister's face at her funeral, I had to carry the burden."

"What burden is that?" Cam asked. "Knowing you could've stopped it?"

"Knowing that my great-niece had to die so millions more could live," María finished. "Think it over, I think you'll see that I'm right."

The door to the library opened and both Cam and María stiffened, as if Bael himself were going to walk through. Instead, it was Frank, who had a relieved, hopeful smile on his face.

"Cam, they've found them. In New Orleans. Positive identification."

"Really?" Cam said.

"I've got you on a flight that leaves in an hour and a half," Frank said. "Whatever they're doing down there, they don't look like they're going to leave any time soon. This may be our chance."

"Go, Camilla," María said, this time in English. "I know all of us want to see Jackie come home safely."

Cam couldn't force herself to do anything but smile grimly at her aunt. After what she'd just learned, Jack might've been safer if he'd stayed on the run.

CHAPTER THIRTY-ONE

"Are the humans slaves?"

Jack had been chewing on that question all afternoon while they waited for Broussard's signal. They were camped out in the storage room above the coffee shop, surrounded by boxes of paper cups.

"I don't know," Anya said with a yawn. "I mean, we considered them chattel. Bael was king, of course, but I never noticed any...direct contact. He ruled through fear and reputation."

"The more I think about it, the less ridiculous it sounds," he said, sitting up. "I mean, it was always more important to placate the demon versus the human."

"That's because demons can kill you," Anya said with a half-smile and a soft nudge against his side. "Self-preservation doesn't equal slavery."

"I guess not," Jack said. "I don't know. I guess lately, I've come to realize ICDM might not have the humans' best interests at heart."

"Lately?"

Jack chuckled dryly. "I mean, I always knew we catered to them, but to be *slaves*?"

"I think slavery is a bit of an exaggeration. Broussard seems to be a little over the top."

"That's an understatement. It's not as if ICDM is rounding up all the vigilantes and killing them. Well… not any more anyway. I don't remember ever being told anything about them one way or another."

"Why does it bother you so much?"

He shrugged. "I guess I do have something of a stake in ICDM. My family's been involved for centuries, I'm sure my ancestors were responsible for killing some of Broussard's. But I always thought we had the control."

She glanced at him, then back out the window. "You don't sound convinced of that."

Because he wasn't. There had always been so many things that had never sat right with him. Seeing the other side of things, how easy it was to simply do the right thing instead of what was bureaucratically sanctioned, Jack wasn't sure ICDM was as benevolent as he'd always assumed.

"If you ask me, you aren't cut out for ICDM," Anya said with a side glance.

"Oh?"

"Look at your track record. You said your classmates went to cushy jobs in policy, right?" He nodded. "But you went into the trenches with your partner. Field work is hard, I'm sure."

"It is."

"I watched you with those kids back in Amsterdam. And with Johnny. It wasn't about the money for you. It was about helping them."

"Yeah, it was," he said with a sigh. "So what am I supposed to do with myself? I already tried leaving field work, and it just made everything worse. And being a vigilante is a lot easier with an athtar to stop time when I get in over my head."

She tapped the weapons at his hips, brushing her arm against his. "You're different than the person who left Atlanta."

"So are you," Jack said. Movement out the window caught his eye. "Hey, look!"

Broussard came walking out of the house across the street. He patted his forehead with a handkerchief and opened his mailbox, pulling the day's mail and replacing it with one of his own, lifting the flag.

"I guess that's our cue," Anya said. "Stay here."

She was gone and back before he could ask if she should be using her magic. The envelope slipped from her fingers into his and she slid down onto the floor.

"You shouldn't use your magic anymore," Jack said.

She nodded, closing her eyes. "What's it say?"

Jack opened the envelope, pulling out the letter. "Tonight, we're to meet him at this address. He says we'll find what we're looking for there."

"Do you think he's telling the truth?"

"I think he thinks he's telling the truth," Jack replied.

"What does your gut say?"

"W-what?"

"Your gut. You said it's never been wrong. What does it say about this guy?"

"I mean, it doesn't really speak on command," he said with a chuckle. "But it's another lead, and we need to investigate it."

The address turned out to be a cemetery near the interstate, an odd combination of rushing cars and above-ground vaults. Anya had been on edge since they'd left the law office, speaking infrequently and snapping when she did. Jack couldn't blame her. A hundred and thirty years of anguish, and she was about to find out how to get rid of her albatross. When the sun set, she became even more anxious, pacing the hotel room until it was time to head out.

When they arrived at the meeting spot, Anya cased the block, probably more to burn off nervous energy than to secure the area. At nine on the nose, Broussard pulled up in a car with no headlights, rolling down the window and looking more nervous than Anya.

"You are alone," he said, glancing around. "And you

informed no one of our agreement?"

"As agreed," Anya said. "Now tell me what you know."

"Not here," he said, looking around. He handed them another scrap of paper. "Go to this address two streets over."

"I'm getting a little tired of you sending us all over New Orleans," Anya barked. "This had better be worth it."

Broussard met her glare with steely-eyed confidence. "I think you'll find it's worth your time."

"Come on, Anya," Jack said, taking her hand and leading her away from the car. He could practically feel her pulse pounding through her veins, so he squeezed her hand. She glanced to him, her green eyes cloudy, and squeezed his hand back and didn't let go.

Two streets over was residential, with shotgun houses eerily lit by streetlamps. Jack thought they were headed on another wild goose chase when Anya grabbed his arm with her other hand.

"That's it," she said, pointing at a dark building.

Jack squinted in the ambient light; it must've been an old church. "Are you sure?"

"I think I just had one of those gut feelings," she said, walking ahead with their hands still clasped.

Inside, it was just as dark except for a small light at the end of the room. As they crept closer, it was a doorway leading down a staircase.

"This isn't creepy at all," Jack murmured.

"Let's get this over with."

They followed the light down a staircase into a small basement. An older woman was sitting there, seemingly meditating or sleeping. She opened her eyes and offered them the two pillows in front of her.

"Tell me your story," the woman said once they'd settled.

Anya did so, with a wavering voice that betrayed her fear.

"And you believe this curse to be real?" the woman said.

Anya nodded. "This feeling, this guilt. It's killing me."

The woman clasped her hands and took a long breath. "When the first eloko demon appeared, my ancestors were hunters and gatherers. They feared the dwarf demons who took their children and killed the able-bodied men. But they had a weapon against them. The same God who'd expelled the original demons sent a message to the villagers. Symbols." She looked at Jack. "Show me your bracelet."

Jack held his bracelet aloft, but didn't take it off.

"The villagers painted these symbols on shields turned upside-down. It was a miracle, sent from God," she said, carefully running her finger along the metal. "We passed them down from generation to generation until your ancestors stamped out our knowledge. These symbols have been lost to us for generations."

"Why would the humans willingly destroy their only defense against demons?" Jack asked.

"Because the demons have claimed ownership of us," she said. "*They*, not your grandfather and his Council, are the true rulers of this world. They promise death and destruction should the secret of these talismans get out." She turned to Anya. "Surely, you are aware of the power of your King?"

Anya nodded, with a small shiver.

"The Council is merely an extension of his power. They cower before him and implement policies that help his cause. They are no friends to humanity."

Jack couldn't believe that. "My grandfather would never willingly submit to Bael."

"Then perhaps he doesn't do it willingly," she replied with a cold smile. "He is a weak man, choosing to remain a slave rather than become the master."

"Screw the humans," Anya said, taking on a desperate tone. "What of my curse?"

"Show me the symbol."

Anya pulled the paper from her back pocket and handed it to the woman. She furrowed her brow, turning the symbol over, then over again, then rotating it left and right. Then she placed it on the ground.

"This symbol means nothing."

"W-what?" Anya shook her head. "Of course it means something. It hung around my neck for a hundred and thirty years. It *changed* me. I used to not care what happened to humans, and now I *have* to save them. For fuck's sake, *my hair is turning gray!*"

"Even Bael was human once," she said with a coy smile. "What you feel was never put on you. This 'curse' was simply a reminder that a demonic possession does not absolve you of human emotion."

Anya stood, her face a mixture of fury and disbelief. "You're a fucking liar. You… This can't be true. It's not true! I don't believe it."

The woman shrugged. "If you don't like what I say, the exit is there."

Anya took a step back, flexing her hand as if she wanted to wring the old woman's neck. "What if…what if this symbol was different? What if God—"

"The five symbols have been five symbols for thousands of years. There are no others."

"But… but that means…" Anya clutched her stomach. With a cry, she ran from the room.

"You know what I say is true, don't you?" the woman asked Jack, whose eyes were still on the door.

"I had a feeling," Jack said. "But I think she needed to hear it from someone else."

"Sometimes, it takes strength to believe what's right in front of us." She nodded, holding out her hand. "Your talismans, please."

Jack held them in his hands, feeling more than ever that taking them off his person would result in something worse—for him or for this woman and her people.

"Are you sure you want to be messing with this?" Jack asked.

"Are you?" she asked. "A deal is a deal, Mr. Grenard."

Slowly, he unhooked his talismans and placed the bracelet in the woman's hand. "Good luck."

Jack drove their stolen car back to Slidell alone. He wasn't surprised that Anya had disappeared. When he opened the door to their hotel, he also wasn't surprised to see her sitting on the bed.

But the tears on her face, that surprised him.

"Hey, champ," Jack said gently. "How are you feeling?"

She took a shaky breath, holding herself tightly as he closed the door behind him. "Like everything I've ever done was a lie."

"Oh, that's just…" He was going for a joke, but the forlorn look on her face stopped him. "Not everything, I'm sure."

"Everything," she whispered. "I used to be able to blame killing humans on being a demon and saving them on the curse, but…all of that. All of that was my doing. My choice."

"You also chose to save humans—"

"Because I thought I *had* to!" she said, another tear leaking down her face. "I thought I was dying."

"I don't believe that," Jack said after a moment. "I think if you look deep down, you'll realize that you were repenting because you wanted to. Otherwise, you would've gone back to Bael."

"But what does that mean?" She wiped her face. "What does it mean that I didn't want to go back to Bael? What does it mean that when I think about returning, I can't breathe."

"It means you know what he is," Jack said. "But you just don't want to accept it."

"Can you blame me?" She sniffed and more tears fell down

her cheeks. "I've known nothing but that man, that life for three thousand years. And now, now…now there's nothing. I don't want to kill for him anymore. But I want…I want to be with him." She closed her eyes. "Even right now, all I want is to go home. But I don't want to go home."

Jack knew that feeling well. He and Anya weren't all that different. Both grieving souls missing their other halves. Both wanting what they couldn't have—Jack wanting Sara back, and Anya wanting Bael to be better than he was. But just as Jack had come to accept that Sara was gone, Anya needed to let go of the Bael she'd hoped he'd be. If only for her own sanity.

"Anya, look. The last thing I want is to get in the middle of your relationship."

She snorted.

"But I watched him. I saw how he treated you. First, he acted like he was grateful you were safe, but there wasn't any sincerity in it. Then, parading you around like you were some sort of prize he'd won. And just when he knew you were his, he revealed his true self."

"He didn't mean to—"

"If he didn't mean to hurt you, he wouldn't have," Jack said. "What he does to you isn't love."

She licked her lips as another tear slipped down her cheek. "Then maybe I have no idea what love is."

Jack put an arm around her, and she leaned into him. "It's putting someone else's needs above your own. It's about wanting to keep them safe without expecting anything in return. Doing anything to see them happy, even if it means your own suffering."

She nestled her forehead against his chin and he pulled her closer.

"Sara was a lucky woman, to be loved like that," she whispered.

But Jack hadn't been talking about Sara.

CHAPTER THIRTY-TWO

The realization had snuck up on him, knocking the wind from his sails and leaving him stunned.

Somewhere along the line, he'd developed feelings for Anya. They weren't much, just the first shoots of life that could grow into something magnificent. Losing Sara had taken everything from him, and he'd been sure he'd never be able to feel anything like this again. And yet, *something* was there, beautiful, fragile, and new. Alive.

"What?" Anya asked. She was difficult, and came with more than a few tons of baggage. But in that moment, all he wanted was to wipe away her tears and see what her real smile looked like.

Before he could stop himself, he captured her lips with his. A sweet, tentative kiss that was over before he wanted it to be.

Her eyes, still puffy and red, were full of worry. "What are you doing?"

"I have no idea," Jack said honestly. He'd kissed her before—first in loveless passion, then under the influence of lilin magic. This time, kissing her stirred up those feelings he had only just recognized.

Anya put her hands on his chest. "Jack, you don't...you don't care about me. You're just here because you need someone to save. That's what you said."

"Maybe at first. But not anymore." Jack said, cupping her cheek softly and brushing away her tears. He'd been drawn to the sadness in her eyes by his need to reclaim his life. But along the way, somewhere between running from demons and conversations about grief and loss and moving on, he'd started to stay for another reason.

He stayed for the woman who'd helped him battle his personal monsters and learn how to fight again. He stayed for the woman who had such capacity to love that she pushed everyone away for their own protection. He'd seen the woman she truly was beneath all the lies and manipulation. The woman he wanted to protect.

"Jack, I..." She pulled back further. "I don't know if this is the right time. Bael could come back and—"

"Shh," Jack said, kissing her sweetly. "Don't worry about him. Just for one night."

"But he'll hurt you."

"He tried before—"

"No," Anya said with tears falling down her face. "This…this is different."

"How?"

"Because now…" She released a shaky breath as another tear fell. "Now, if this curse was never real, then that means what I feel for you…is. And he won't ever—"

He cupped her cheeks and made her look at him. "Ignore him. How do you feel? What do *you* want?"

She didn't respond right away, her gaze dancing as she stared into his eyes. He could see her response plain on her face, but would she be brave enough to say it? Or would Bael win yet another battle against her?

Slowly, she closed her eyes and leaned in, gently taking his lips with hers. He moved with the same pace, not wanting to scare her off, but also wanting to *show* her how he felt. To make her feel so loved that she'd never entertain the thought of returning to that monster again.

Whatever physical intimacy they'd shared before was all but forgotten. This was emotional, physical, even spiritual closeness —brand new territory. Jack wanted to remember every detail of it, how she felt in his hands, the way her hair cascaded down the pillow as he laid her down—even the tears he kissed away on her cheeks.

She stared up at him with wide green eyes, still red-rimmed from crying, but the smile lit up her whole face. It was a true smile, one that lacked any hesitation or fear. One that gave him permission to keep moving forward.

"I like that smile," he said, brushing his fingertips against her cheeks. "I like seeing you happy."

"You make me happy, Jack," she whispered. "I..."

"What?"

"I have no idea," she said with another thousand-megawatt smile. "I've never really done this before."

"Bull. Shit."

The fragile tension broke, peppered by her light laughing and his deep chuckles. "Jack, I'm serious. This is new."

Jack kissed a trail down her neck. "You already gave me a blow job. I think we're way past being shy around each other."

"That was sex," she said, softly, arching under his touch. "This is...this is different. You, looking at me like this. Saying what you're saying. It's all a bit much."

He cradled her cheek. "It doesn't have to be. If you're not ready for any big, sweeping declarations, we don't have to make any. If you want to stop and go to sleep, we can stop and go to sleep. I'm ready to take this as far as you are."

She lifted her head to kiss him. "I don't want to sleep right now."

He gently led her back to the pillow, finding her hips and the skin of her back with his fingertips. She moaned softly against him, wrapping her legs around his hips. Her warmth seeped into his pants, begging to be touched—to be explored with his fingers and tongue.

He pushed himself onto his elbows, taking a deep breath to calm himself down.

"What's wrong?" she asked.

"It's been a while," he admitted, his cheeks warming with the admission and his growing need. "I don't want this to be over with too soon."

She actually giggled but it was over as soon as it began. "Jack, I don't know if... I mean, I've never actually come with a human before."

"Have you ever really tried?" he asked with a quirked brow.

She licked her lips—answer enough. "And if I can't... You won't be upset?"

"Please don't ever worry about upsetting me. You upset me all the time. And I'm still here." When she smiled, he nuzzled his nose into her neck. "If anything, we'll have a lot of fun while I try. I just want you to feel good, Anya."

This time, she pressed her lips to his fully, passionately, and without reservation. His heart pounding, he bit her lip and sucked on it, sliding his tongue against hers and feeling her out. She tangled her hands in his hair, moaning softly as he found the soft spot on her neck as her warm sex pressed harder against his. He had to take another deep, steadying breath as she bucked her hips against his, sending electricity down his spine.

She smirked and wriggled out from under his embrace, coming to stand in front of the bed. Slowly, she pulled off her shirt and shimmied out of her pants, revealing her white bra and underwear. Jack kept her gaze as she unhooked her bra and let it fall to the floor, then slid off her underwear. As she'd done so many times before, she stood naked in front of him. But now, there was an added vulnerability in her eyes as she watched him.

"God, you're beautiful," he rasped. "I'm so glad I can tell you that now."

"You couldn't before?" she asked.

"I was afraid you'd run away," he said. "And I don't want you to run away. I want you right here."

"Right here?" she said, pointing at the ground with a grin.

"Right here," he said, patting the bed. "Get over here."

She climbed back onto the bed and Jack pinned her back underneath him before she could wriggle away. He roamed her body with his hands, taking his time to note where she jerked and sighed happily—all the while taking his fill from her mouth. His pants were getting very uncomfortable, but he wanted to make this about Anya for now.

She whispered his name as his fingers made their way to the soft, wet folds between her legs, and he about lost it.

"So," he said with a husky whisper, "why did you keep getting naked in front of me? Were you testing me?"

"I…" She shuddered as he drew slow circles with his fingers. "I was trying to convince myself you weren't as nice as you pretended to be. Or there was some other ulterior motive."

That earned an eye roll as he momentarily paused. "Anya, you're a mess."

"Well…?" she said, looking away.

"It's a good thing I never asked for that pity-fuck, huh?" he whispered against her skin and continued his gentle stroking. "Could have ruined a good thing. I don't think I could have kept my hands to myself. Not when you look like this—and feel this good."

She shuddered again, her eyes sliding closed as his circles remained slow and steady. Even as her breath quickened, her face remained tense, as if even now, she wasn't allowed to enjoy these simple pleasures.

"Anya," he said, kissing her lips and removing his hand. "Look at me."

She opened her eyes. He wished he had something breathtaking to say, something that would relieve her of all the fear and thousands of years of abuse. But he was a simple man, and he hadn't lived long enough to know the right words to say.

But she cracked a half smile, guiding his hand back to her sex and kissing him sweetly. Where there had been soft sighs were now louder moans, sending blood right to his groin. The scent of her was filling the room, and he wanted to know what she tasted like, too.

He left a trail down the front of her body, from her breasts to her concave stomach, then the crease of her leg, her thigh, and then, when she looked ready for it, he pressed his mouth to her, sliding his tongue across the same path his fingers had walked. Her legs jerked and she gasped, gripping the pillows between her fingers.

"J-Jack," she whispered.

"Stop?"

"N-no, I'm…" She swallowed, capturing his gaze with that same vulnerable need. "Don't stop."

He grinned, taking her direction with gusto as he held her hips and worked his magic on her. She tasted like a dream, and the way she called his name was intoxicating, making him work faster, wanting to send her over the edge in a blaze of glory. He felt it before he heard it, the waves pulsing out from her core. She clenched around his fingers, crying out in such joy that it almost sent him over, too. But he waited, knowing the rush of being inside her was coming, and he wanted so much more from her before that happened.

But all thoughts went out the window when he saw the look on her face. She turned away from him, her lip trembling.

"What is it?" Jack said, crawling up to join her. "Did I—"

"No, Jack," she said with a watery smile. "You did wonderfully. That was wonderful. I forgot how good this feels."

"You know," he said, as she nestled herself against his shoulder, "you can feel that way any day of the week. Just get a vibrator."

She actually snorted and slapped his chest. "If I'd known you could make me feel like that, I would've pity fucked you weeks ago."

He slid a finger inside her again, savoring how her eyes lit up. More of the lies she'd been holding onto had fallen away, and this one, at least, she was happy about.

"I'm no demon," he said with a kiss to her nose. "But let's see if we can't do that a few more times."

Jack awoke to the strange feeling of a woman in his arms. It took him a few moments to remember it wasn't Sara, but Anya —and a few more minutes to let the sadness of that fact pass. But pass it did, leaving only contentment and this new thing happening between them.

Obviously, they'd taken a step forward, but Jack didn't want to start running yet. After all, the night before had been fraught with emotions and vulnerability. The last thing he wanted was to hurt her, and not because she could snap his neck. What had been something new and fragile had grown overnight into something more substantial, and it frightened him a little.

His fear turned to adoration when she stirred next to him, opening her sleepy green eyes. The brief flash of panic across her face soon melted into a soft smile. She really was quite beautiful.

"Good morning," she said with a coy smile.

Jack chuckled. "So you *can* say it."

"I can, when it's a good morning," she said, tracing her fingers across his chest. "I hope I didn't hurt you last night."

"Not at all," Jack lied, knowing he'd be walking funny for a few hours. "As long as you enjoyed it."

"I..." A curtain descended over her features. "I did."

"It's okay to enjoy things, you know," Jack said.

"He's going to find out about all this," Anya said, sitting up. "And he'll know it wasn't just sex, too. That's the only way I could keep him from being jealous."

"He was still jealous," Jack pointed out.

"You haven't seen him jealous yet," Anya said, crawling from his embrace. "Before, that was about me. But if he gets ahold of you, he'll… Jack, he'll torture you. He'll make you wish you'd never even laid eyes on me. He'll make me kill you—"

"Then let's put a stop to him," Jack said, sliding his hands over her shoulders.

She stared at him.

"Listen, I've been thinking about this for a long time. We aren't… Anya, we can't continue living like this. Bael is obsessed. He'll never let you leave as long as he's alive—"

She jerked, swallowing. "What are you saying?"

"Bael is never going to leave you alone, you know that. I couldn't care less what happens to me. But you…" He brushed a stray hair behind her ear. "All I want is for you to live your own life. Make decisions because it's what you want, not what someone else wants."

"You want me to kill Bael," Anya whispered.

"Unless you can think of another way to get away from him."

"Is that what this was?" Anya said, ripping off the sheets. "You wormed your way into my heart so you could manipulate me?"

"C'mon, Anya, that's not what's happening here and you know it."

"Isn't it?" She clutched at her hair. "This could've been some great charade. You pretending to care so that I will fall out of love with Bael. You with your sweet words—"

"Anya," Jack said, taking her by the shoulders, "that's not what happened."

"Then why would you ask me to do such a thing?" Her anger had melted into panic.

"Because you know that's the only way out of this," Jack said, pulling her into his arms. "He's not going to let you just walk away from him."

"He might," she whispered against his chest.

Jack didn't reply, but tightened his hold on her. "Maybe you and I can colonize the moon."

"I think he could make it there," Anya said, wiping her cheek. She took his hand and kissed it. "I know you're right, but I...I don't think I can do it."

"Because you still love him?" Jack asked.

"Because he's...he's Bael." She shivered. "He's powerful. Even if I could get past my feelings for him, I'm no match."

"You only think that—"

"I don't think that, I *know* that!"

"I—"

A siren wailed nearby, and they stared at each other with the same nervous knowing.

"Jack, we know you're in there. Come out and talk to me. Please don't run."

"Cam?" Jack said, turning to the window. "What the hell is she doing here?"

They hastily dressed in yesterday's clothes, then Anya disappeared and reappeared looking equal parts concerned and perplexed. "Never mind her. Why are there a hundred Division agents standing in the parking lot?"

"I'm sorry, *what?*"

She motioned for him to follow her and crept to the window, moving the curtains only slightly. Indeed, there were at least a hundred black-armor-wearing guards in the hotel parking lot, each of them packing serious firepower.

"What the hell?" Jack said to Anya, sitting back against the wall. "I mean, I know we're both persons of interest, but this seems like overkill."

"Or pointless," Anya said, pointing to herself. "Athtar, remember?"

"Jack, please come out. Don't run. We can talk about it."

"What do you want to do?" Jack asked Anya.

She leaned against the bed. "I don't know. I...I hadn't quite figured out what I was going to do next."

"It's been a bit of a day," Jack agreed.

"Maybe we should turn ourselves in," Anya said, looking at her hands. "Or maybe just run."

"I'm tired of running," Jack said. "Why should we anyway? We haven't done anything wrong."

"The number of guns pointed in our direction begs to differ," Anya said. "Do you think any of them have athtar bullets?"

"Cam might," Jack said, looking out the window again. "But she hasn't drawn it." He stood and crossed the hotel room to the in-room phone, dialing the number from memory.

"What are you doing?" Anya asked.

"Getting some answers," he said.

CHAPTER THIRTY-THREE

Cam put down the bullhorn and chewed her lip. The officer in command had given her five minutes to try to get them to come out, and she'd already wasted three. Of course, when she'd pointed out that Anya and Jack could escape using athtar magic, the officer had retreated.

She'd arrived in New Orleans expecting a small tactical team to provide backup, and instead found a special operations team on loan from Los Angeles. They'd come with guns and shields (though none of them had Cam's anti-demon bullets) and were ready to storm the small, dinky hotel room where their informants had followed Jack and Anya. They were from a unit Cam had never heard of before, and based on the way the commanding officer barked orders, Cam was glad.

"Well, princess?" the officer said, sauntering up. "Are you ready to let me and my team do our jobs?"

"And what, precisely, is your job?" Cam asked, putting the bullhorn on her hip as she faced him. "Because I'm a little confused. On whose orders are you here?"

"You don't have clearance for that," he spat.

"Oh yeah?" Cam said, stepping forward. "Wanna try me? I can get Councilman Frank Grenard on the line. Or how about Councilwoman María García? She's my great-aunt." She poked her finger into the man's chest. "That's my partner in there. You aren't going in with your damned guns blazing."

He chewed on his tongue then sniffed. "We're here on a tip. Been following the Broussard family for a while. These two met with them and we want to know what was said."

"And who the hell are the Broussards?" Cam shook her head, deciding it was better if she didn't get off topic. "I'm not trying to step on your toes. But I have a feeling your bullets aren't going to be much help, especially where she's concerned. Let me try just a few minutes longer."

Just then, Cam's phone rang. She almost didn't answer—not recognizing the number—but did anyway. "Macarro."

"Hey, stranger."

Her heart stopped, and she turned away from the officer so he wouldn't see her shock. "J-Jack? What the fuck?"

"Yeah, that's what I was thinking. Did you really need all this artillery? I mean…athtar? If we wanted to escape, we could have."

"No shit," Cam said. "This wasn't my call, I swear. These guys followed you because you were meeting with some guy named Broussard."

There was some conversation on the other end that Cam couldn't make out, but Jack came back a moment later. *"Listen, can we talk? Without the commandos?"*

Cam glanced behind her. "Let me see." She put her phone to her chest and turned to the commanding officer. "Hey, I'm going in. Try not to shoot me, mmkay?" She put the phone back on her ear. "Okay Jackie, why don't you two come outside. I'll meet you on the first floor of the hotel. Then we can talk."

"And you're sure they aren't going to shoot us?"

"I have no clue," Cam said. "I have a feeling these guys aren't really going to listen to me. But your girlfriend can do her hocus pocus athtar thing, right?"

Jack sighed. *"Yes, if you want to call it that."*

Cam walked toward the hotel. "Are we talking about the hocus pocus thing or the girlfriend thing?"

"Both?"

Whatever catty response she had slipped away when her best friend appeared on the second floor of the hotel, followed by La Colibrí. They wore stony expressions, keeping a wary eye on the army assembled in the parking lot as they headed for the staircase.

"Stand down," Cam called to the commandos. "Let me handle this."

The officer held up his hand, either giving his okay or

another five-minute deadline. Either way, Cam didn't really think he'd start shooting, especially if they were out of the hotel. He couldn't possibly need them dead that badly.

She strode toward the hotel with her shoulders back and chin high. But within five feet of them, she forgot all about pride and decorum and ran toward her partner.

"Jack!"

Cam practically threw herself into his arms, relief rushing through her that finally, *finally* she had him back. To the left, La Colibrí stood awkwardly, watching them embrace, but Cam decided to ignore her for the moment.

"I am going to kick your scrawny ass," Cam said to Jack, punching him in the shoulder. "Dragging me all over the place. Your grandfather is pissed off—thank God he loves you so much. I have a twenty-page manuscript ready to read to you, too."

"Only twenty?" Jack said with a laugh. "That's light for you, Macarro."

"It's gone through several revisions," she said.

"I'm sure it's a masterpiece." He smiled and she nearly burst into tears. It was just so damned hard to be angry with him when he was standing there, looking all healthy and Jack-like.

Colibrí on the other hand, could burn in hell for all Cam cared. "Don't think I'll like you because he does," Cam snarled at the demon. "You have a *long* way to go to earn my approval."

Colibrí frowned, but Jack just laughed. "I think I'd be more worried if you didn't care."

"Your approval is the least of my worries," Colibrí replied. "Why did you bring an entire company of soldiers to the hotel?"

"These guys weren't my call," Cam replied. "Frank told me there'd be a team to meet me. I thought five guys, not…all this."

"Did they tell you why?" Jack asked.

"Only that you were meeting with someone named Broussard. What's that about?"

Anya stiffened, and Jack's cheer evaporated. "Are you serious? All this because of us meeting with Broussard?"

"I don't get it," Cam said. "Who's Broussard?"

"You know the vigilantes you were researching? The upside-down shield?" Jack asked. "They're one of the families who owns it. They told us all about the origins of our talismans. They only *just* agreed to meet with us. Acted like it was some great conspiracy to silence them."

Cam licked her lips. "Yeah, funny story. Turns out, it *is* a giant conspiracy."

Silence met her admission.

"I just found out from my aunt," she continued. "I'm not the first one to think to use them as a weapon. But our family has been actively trying to keep the talismans hidden."

"Why?" Jack asked.

"Apparently, it pisses off *her* boyfriend," Cam said. "Who's threatened to kill all of humanity if we even think about mounting a fight against him."

"And you were explicitly told not to speak of it to anyone," drawled a familiar voice. "María will be so disappointed."

It seemed almost ludicrous to see the King of the Underworld standing in the middle of the parking lot of this rundown, two-story, cheap motel. But there he was, sporting a button-down shirt and khaki pants. Handsome as the devil, wearing a slight smile on his lips and resting his hands in his pockets.

Cam put every ounce of courage into remaining upright and holding Bael's gaze, even as her stomach twisted into anxious, terrified knots. She decided against speaking, however, not trusting her voice.

"Perhaps I should pay another visit to your aunt. It's clear she didn't impress upon you the importance of not sharing your family's secrets." The lack of emotion in his words sent chills down Cam's spine. "And as for the Broussards, I'm afraid they've found their family line has come to its end."

He threw something to the ground—Jack's talisman bracelet, although only two coins remained.

"You son of a bitch," Jack said, stepping forward. "You can't just—"

Bael had a sword at his neck before he could speak another word. "Jackson, I know we've shared Anat, but you should take care when you address the King of the Underworld."

Jack, wisely, did little more than glare.

Bael removed the sword and sheathed it back at his hip, turning back to Cam and sending shoots of fear down her spine. "Because your aunt failed to convince you, let me: If you tell another soul about this talisman weapon you put together, I will kill every member of your family and make your sister's death look a mercy killing." He patted Cam on the cheek. "And trust me, my dear, I will know if you disobey me."

Cam could do nothing but nod. Bael seemed satisfied with her answer, because he spun on his heel toward Anya and Jack, as if he hadn't just threatened mass murder.

"Well, you've led the humans on quite a merry chase, haven't you, Anat?" Bael said. "Only to return here. Did you find what you were looking for?"

She swallowed and nodded.

"And what was it?"

She spoke, but her voice was so quiet it was barely a whisper. "There was no curse."

Bael clapped, as if he were instructing a small child. "If you'd only listened to me. There was no curse, only you and your confusion."

"And you," Anya said, lifting her chin. "There is also you."

"Of course there's me," Bael said with a chuckle. "I am all things. I *made* you, Anat. You are part of me. And now it's time to put aside all this foolishness and come home."

"You... You'd let me come home, just like that?" Anya asked.

"Why wouldn't I? You're my lady, the Bringer of Destruction. The warrior woman. I am incomplete without you by my side." He drew a finger down her cheek. "I promise to let all this go if you promise never to make me miss you again."

For a moment, a flash of something like happiness crossed

her face, but with a glance at Jack, it was gone. "Did you really kill those humans? The Broussards?"

"Of course," Bael said. "You gave them the talismans. I can't have that sort of thing getting out into the population."

"And this," Anya said gesturing to the assembled men. "What is this for?"

"They are here on my orders," Bael said, gesturing to the men who obviously hadn't known that. "You've been so slippery, Anat. I needed to distract you long enough to seek out your presence. Do they bother you?"

"No, I—"

In the blink of an eye, fifty men who'd been at the ready were beheaded. And Bael hadn't even broken a sweat.

"Is that better?" he asked, licking his thumb and wiping a splat of blood from his cheek. "I do hate to have an audience for our conversations."

Cam couldn't breathe—one second they were alive, the next dead. The headless bodies slumped on the ground, blood gushing out of their open necks. Their guns still in their hands. Suddenly, she realized what María had meant about Bael's power, and what he could potentially do to humans.

"Bael..." Anya had grown pale; perhaps the Lady of Destruction didn't like destruction that much any more. "You didn't have to kill them."

"I didn't *not* have to kill them either," he said with a wave of his hand. "It's so unlike you to care. The curse wasn't real. It's time to get over this lunacy. You are a goddess of death. This should be nothing to you."

"But it is," she whispered. "Even though the curse wasn't real, I feel this, Bael. I feel guilt."

"Because you're crazy," Bael said, clasping his hands together. "You're starved of the magic that gives you life, and you're hallucinating. Otherwise, why would you have run from me? You're lucky I love you so much. A lesser man would have let you just disappear." He shook his head. "But I knew if I kept you in my sights, you would eventually see reason."

"What do you mean, keep me in your sights?" Anya asked. "Did you…did you know where I was?"

"I'll admit, I lost you a few times." He chuckled, as if this was some sort of game to him. "But I always found you eventually."

"If you knew where I was…why didn't you come for me?"

"Because you made it clear you needed some space," Bael replied with a shrug. "Was that not what you wanted? If I'd known you were waiting for me—"

"I wasn't," Anya murmured.

"I know," he said, tutting. "Anat, I know everything you feel. Imagine how it hurt me when I felt your heart turning toward another? What is it that this mortal gives you that I can't?"

"Loyalty," Anya said sharing a glance with Jack.

"Am I not loyal?" Bael said. "Have I not spent these past weeks stretching the humans' resources to find you?"

"You killed humans. You killed Wani," Anya said. "All in

the pursuit of making me feel alone. To make the humans hate me."

"You're talking nonsense. The humans already hated you. I did nothing to help."

Jack made a dismissive noise, and even Cam was having a hard time believing that.

Bael shot him a look then turned back to Anya, his cruel smile growing wider as he laid on the charm. "Anat, my love, my beauty. My everything. You've created these falsehoods about me in your mind to justify your disloyal behavior. This human has filled your head with lies. He's manipulated you into thinking that I'm a monster, hasn't he?" Bael's gaze slid to Jack and his smile curled even more. "I'll bet he also told you that you had to kill me so the two of you can be together. I'll bet he confessed his *love*—"

"No, he didn't," Anya said. "He… It's not like that."

"Thank God," Cam muttered.

"Then, pray tell, what is it *like*? Does this human make you feel whole? Does he lift you high on a mountain for the world to see you? Does he make you feel pleasure from the top of your head down to your toes, until you are writhing so much you almost break?"

"He doesn't hurt me," she replied quietly. "He doesn't ask me to do anything I don't want to. He doesn't manipulate me with pretty words to make me do his bidding."

At this, Bael threw his head back and laughed. "What are you talking about? You are the Lady of the Mountain. I've *never* hurt you."

"Bullshit," Jack scoffed.

"Jack," Anya said with an unreadable look. "Bael, you can say what you want, but I...I remember everything. I remember the bruises. I remember every time I ran from you. I know now that this...this curse wasn't the reason I left. It was permission to."

Bael stared at her, looking unimpressed by her monologue. "There was no curse, you said."

"There wasn't," she said. "Which means it was my decision to leave. My decision to make a new life up here. My decision to..." She glanced at Jack.

"Oh," Bael said with a solemn nod. "Oh, I see. I see. So this is your choice, then? Are you going to lift Sharur and strike me down?"

"I could never do that," she said softly. "But Bael...we can't keep doing this. I can't keep living like this." She inhaled and met his gaze. "I want you to let me go. Let me live my life in peace. Find someone else to be your Lady of the Mountain."

"Would you like me to make you human as well?" Bael asked, clearly amused.

"I don't care what you do," Anya said, keeping her steady gaze. "But if you love me, if you ever did, if you loved our child, you'll let me go. I don't...I don't want this anymore."

Bael stepped closer and placed both hands on her cheeks. "My love, I live to make you happy. If this is what you choose, I will do as you please. Maybe someday you'll remember the life we had together—you'll remember Asherah. And you'll come back."

Anya closed her eyes, a tear falling down her face. "Thank you, Bael."

He released her and took a step back, seemingly as ready to cry as she was. "I love you more than my own life, Anat. I will miss you every second we're apart."

And, to the surprise of Cam and probably Jack and Anya, he began to walk away. Anya's tears turned into quiet sobs but she shared a look with Jack and took his hand. Even Cam was pretty impressed that she'd been able to break up with Bael for good.

Bael stopped and turned back with a catty smile on his lips. "But I think I'll take your human as a memento."

Then Bael was gone—and so was Jack.

CHAPTER THIRTY-FOUR

"Not again," Cam whispered.

"N...*No!*" Anya screamed, falling to her knees. The only thing left of him was his knife holster, which she pressed to her body as she wailed.

"What the actual fuck just happened?" Cam said. "Where did he take him?"

Anya's cries had quieted, and she stared at the wall with a numb look that quickly turned into one of fury. "I have to go."

"*Ex*cuse me?" Cam barked, putting her hands on her hips. "Go where?"

"I have to go. I have to go," she muttered, looking down at the knives in her hands. "I have to go."

"Then go!" Cam barked at her. "Can't you bend time or whatever the fuck you athtars do?"

"I don't have the power right now," she said, rising to her feet and pressing the holsters to her chest. "I can't follow them. I need a car."

"A *car*?" Cam blinked at her. "Are you kidding me? *Use your magic*!"

"You stupid human, *I can't*!"

"Going off on your vigilante merry way?" Cam snarled, growing angrier by the moment. "What, Jack's dead so you're just going to move on?"

Her eyes flashed, surprising Cam with their ferocity. "I need a car. Can I have yours?"

"No, you can't have mine. Not until you tell me what the hell you're planning."

"Isn't it obvious? I'm going to get Jack." She looked at the spot where he'd been only moments before. "That's what he wants. He wants me to come to him. Well, I'm gonna do that."

"I'm going with you," Cam said.

It really wasn't a question. She'd traveled to the ends of the earth to find Jack, but in the end, it wasn't even about him anymore.

The words of Tía María rang in Cam's head. Bael had a stranglehold on humanity, and the very people who were in charge of protecting them were passing the buck. On some level, she agreed that the cautious way to go was the right one. After all, she'd seen what Bael was capable of. The only reason why she'd been able to get off a shot at La Colibrí was that she'd had the element of surprise. She doubted she'd be able to do that again, and to an athtar at that.

But the other part of Cam, the part of her that hated the idea of being owned by *anybody,* couldn't sit still. Not when she knew there *was* a way to get Bael out of the picture and fight off the demons. And Cam was going to march that bitch to the front gates of hell if that was what it took.

Anya wearily shook her head. "You can't go with me. You're human. You wouldn't survive the Underworld."

"Jack did."

"Jack survived because Bael allowed it," Anya said, slowly rising to her feet. "But when I return, I will have no such protections."

The sound of Cam's cellphone cut through the hysteria and she answered it with a swift jab of her finger. "*What?*"

"Macarro, it's Navarro," came the voice on the other end. "Good news, the schism just sealed itself up."

The phone slid out of her hand, breaking on the asphalt.

"It closed, didn't it?" Anya said after a few moments.

Cam nodded, surprised at the stabbing pain in her heart. Surprised that she still had a heart at all, in fact, with the amount of damage it had sustained recently. And she hadn't even gotten the chance to read Jack her twenty-page diatribe. He was right; it was a masterpiece.

"That's it," Cam whispered. "He's gone forever. There's no way he'll survive until the next Demon Spring."

"Bael's is not the only entry into the Underworld," Anya replied.

"*What*?" Cam's voice echoed in the parking lot. "Are you telling me there's another schism out there?"

"Y—Maybe." She reached behind her to grip her swords. "I've heard a rumor, but it's unconfirmed. And I don't know if that way will be open to me. It may take some…groveling."

"Can you grovel?" Cam asked. "Aren't you a pride demon?"

"I can grovel if the situation warrants it," she said, looking at the ground. "Jack warrants it."

"Why? Because you two slept together?" Cam asked.

"Because he had no reason to stay by my side," Anya said. "But he did. He saved my life when he could've just run."

"He does that," Cam said. "And I'll never forgive him for it, either."

Anya stopped, offering her a pitying look. "You can come with me as far as Mexico City."

"M-Mexico?" Cam straightened. "Why are we going there?" She gasped, taking a step back. "The nox demons?"

Anya nodded. "Supposedly, the schism created by Mot and Xo remained in place, even after their death." She sighed heavily. "Their son isn't my biggest fan."

"Is anyone?" Cam asked, folding her arms over her chest. "Well, let's get a move on, Athtar. You can bend time and space, right?"

Anya offered her a dry look. "Your partner hasn't been talking to you, has he?"

"No, he hasn't, and fuck you for reminding me of that," Cam snarled.

"It's been over a century since I've spent time in Ath-kur," Anya said.

"I know that," Cam replied.

"All the jumps I made with Jack, it really took a lot out of me," she continued. "I can't go more than a few feet or else I'm out of commission for a while. If we were to go a hundred miles? It would kill me."

Cam slowed her walk. "So you're saying we have to *drive* to Mexico City?"

"We could fly," Anya said. "But I don't have any lilin glamour to hide either of us."

"Lilin…you had lilin glamour?" Jack had some serious explaining to do when he got back.

"The safest route is going to be taking a car through the border," she finished.

"Jack could be dead by then," Cam said.

The demon shook her head with a haunted look in her eye. "No. Death is too merciful. He's going to torture Jack until I come for him."

"Jack's tough," Cam said, ignoring the jolt of panic that surged through her. "He can take pain."

"You don't understand," Anya said weakly. "It's not physical pain. Bael will get inside his head, find his weakness and break him." She put her swords on her back. "Jack is strong, but I fear…I fear what Bael has in store for him is more than even

Jack can handle."

Magic danced along Jack's skin, covered his tongue, burned in his chest as he breathed in and out. His stomach turned, but he clamped his mouth shut, not willing to vomit until he knew exactly where in the Underworld he was.

He cracked an eye open, then the other, when he realized he was alone. It wasn't the same room he'd been trapped in before, but it was similar. Tapestries of Anya's exploits hung from the stone walls, and the window opened to a starry black sky. He lay in a four-poster bed with a blood-red velvet canopy, the sheets beneath him soft and luxurious.

Pushing himself upright, he gripped his head and waited for the magic to settle. The last thing he remembered was Anya telling Bael she didn't want to be with him, and Bael…

Bael taking him.

Something cold wedged in the back of his chest, but he refused to panic. He'd been trapped in the Underworld before, he could figure a way to get back to his realm. As long as he stroked Bael's ego, he could probably play the athtar as well as Anya.

Getting back to the human world would be another story altogether.

As his mind cleared, he began formulating a plan. First, he would get his bearings. Find out where in Bael's gigantic mountain castle he was. Then, he would get a feel for Bael's intentions for him. Obviously, he was bait (and he very much resented that), but was it to draw Anya back into the fold, or draw her to her death?

Finally, he would kiss whoever's ass he needed to find the schism, and get the hell back to the human world.

Straightening, Jack nodded to himself. He would be no one's prisoner, least of all some crazy, narcissistic, asshole demon-king.

Footsteps echoed in the hall outside his door, and he readied himself for whatever it might be. A kappa come to take him to dinner? A lilin, intent on torturing him? Maybe Bael himself, there to gloat about his power.

But nothing prepared Jack for who lay on the other side of the door.

"S-Sara?"

To be concluded in

REDEMPTION
DEMON SPRING TRILOGY
Book Three

ACKNOWLEGMENTS

Thank you to my beta readers Chelsea, MC, and Josh

Thanks to Dani, my incredible line editor, who always takes my book from good to great. The next book, I'll try to remember to glance AT instead of TO.

Thanks to my typo checkers: MC, Lisa, Lilivette, and Mom. Thanks again to Meli for helping me make sure Cam's Spanish was grammatically correct.

ALSO BY S. USHER EVANS

THE MADION WAR TRILOGY

He's a prince, she's a pilot, they're at war. But when they are
marooned on a deserted island hundreds of miles from either
nation, they must set aside their differences and work together if
they want to survive.

The Madion War Trilogy is available in eBook, paperback,
and hardcover. Download the first book, The Island, for free on
all eBookstores.

Empath

Lauren Dailey is in break-up hell, but if you ask her she's
doing just great. She hears a mysterious voice promising an easy
escape from her problems and finds herself in a brand new world
where she has the power to feel what others are feeling. Just one
problem—there's a dragon in the mountains that happens to eat
Empaths. And it might be the source of the mysterious voice
tempting her deeper into her own darkness.

Empath is a stand-alone fantasy that is available now in
eBook, paperback, and hardcover.

ALSO BY S. USHER EVANS

The Razia Series

Lyssa Peate is living a double life as a planet discovering scientist and a space pirate bounty hunter. Unfortunately, neither life is going very well. She's the least wanted pirate in the universe and her brand new scientist intern is spying on her. Things get worse when her intern is mistaken for her hostage by the Universal Police.

The Razia Series is a four-book space opera series and is available now for eBook, paperback, audiobook, and hardcover. Download the first book, Double Life, for free on all eBookstores.

The Lexie Carrigan Chronicles

Lexie Carrigan thought she was weird enough until her family drops a bomb on her—she's magical. Now the girl who's never made waves is blowing up her nightstand and no one seems to want to help her. That is, until a kind gentleman shows up with all the answers. But Lexie finds out being magical is the least weird thing about her.

Spells and Sorcery is the first book in the Lexie Carrigan Chronicles, and is available now in eBook, paperback, audiobook, and hardcover.

ABOUT THE AUTHOR

S. Usher Evans was born and raised in Pensacola, Florida. After a decade of fighting bureaucratic battles as an IT consultant in Washington, D.C., she suffered a massive quarter-life-crisis. She decided fighting dragons was more fun than writing policy, so she moved back to Pensacola to write books full-time. She currently resides with her husband and two dogs, Zoe and Mr. Biscuit, and frequently can be found plotting on the beach.

Find her on the internet:

www.susherevans.com

www.facebook.com/susherevans
www.twitter.com/susherevans
www.instagram.com/susherevans

www.ingramcontent.com/pod-product-compliance
Lightning Source LLC
Chambersburg PA
CBHW030522190726
48283CB00006B/1734